PERIL ON THE PROWL

Other Books by Kris Lockard

Green Ridge

A Matter of Trust

Evil on the Run

PERIL
on the
PROWL

A Novel by
Kris Lockard

Photo credits: Cover: Author
Back cover insert: Keely K. Studios
Book design and layout: Gorham Printing
Printed is 12pt. Garamond

This book is dedicated to the memory of
Jefferson County Sheriff's Deputy Dave Blann
Faithful guardian of all that is Camp Sherman

THIS AUTHOR would like to acknowledge the following persons who helped in the writing of this book. Their knowledge, generosity, and good humor never cease to astound and humble me:

Scott Alt, EMT & Firefighter, Salem Fire Department
Hoa Hoang, M.D.
Susan Regeimbal, Attorney
Sgt. Rob Schulz, Black Butte Ranch Police Dept.
Lori Steinthal, Admin. Mgr, Black Butte Ranch Police Dept.
Jerry Thompson, Cpl., Salem Police Department, retired
Sgt. Steve Vuylsteke, Black Butte Ranch Police Dept.
Duncan Campbell Webb, Attorney

Editors:
Janell Hales
Barbara Lies
David R. Lockard
Susan (Soupy) Thompson

Special thanks to the Black Butte Ranch Police Department who graciously allowed the use of their police canine, Lola, as a character in this book.

—KRIS LOCKARD
Keizer, Oregon

PROLOGUE

A PREDATOR STALKS the forest. It wafts among silent stands of trees and follows the misty air currents of foggy mornings. It lurks in the shadowy edges of sunny meadows. It never rests during the darkest of nights when even the stars disappear. It leaves no opportunity wasted as it strives to satisfy its insatiable hunger. Gazing upon acres of pristine wilderness which may be the last holdout for ancient trees and habitat for fragile animal species, it sees nothing but the potential for exploitation. Being born of a human culture that worships only its own bottom line, it answers to the name of Greed.

CHAPTER 1

BUSY U.S. HIGHWAY 20 runs west to east connecting Oregon's lush Willamette Valley with the Central Oregon high desert. Once out of the valley and into the Cascade Range of mountains, the highway falls like a ribbon from lofty Santiam Pass into the Metolius River Basin. It then stretches out east through old growth Ponderosa pine forests, smack through the middle of the western town of Sisters, and on to the outdoor sports mecca area of Bend. Five miles north of where the highway passes through the Metolius Basin and tucked under the shadow of the craggy Cascade volcano named Three Fingered Jack lies the tiny settlement of Camp Sherman.

Sheltered within U.S. Forest Service land, Camp Sherman consists of a general store, post office, chapel, small school, numerous rustic cabins, and a few camp grounds. Gurgling through the community is the iconic Metolious River, known for some of the best fly fishing anywhere.

Little has changed Camp Sherman in the past one hundred years. The general store has stood in the same building since 1918. Many of the cabins have been handed down for generations since being built by original family members in the 1920's and 1930's. As a result, rarely any of the cabins were ever offered for sale, adding to the closeness of the community members.

One such cabin had finally reached the end of its family's interest and had recently sold to Phyllis and Conrad Wardwell, octogenarians from Portland. Carefully keeping within U.S. Forest Service rules for renovations of historic structures, the Wardwells added space to the downstairs bedroom, installed an additional bathroom, replaced the aging roof, and rebuilt the river rock fireplace. They had decided to leave their big, Tudor-style house in the west hills of Portland with a caretaker and forsake attending Portland Trailblazer basketball games in order to experience living for many months deep in the woods at Camp Sherman.

Now, as an autumn evening softly settled over the forest, the Wardwells were joined in their cabin by their friends and fellow octogenarians Mick and Dave, who had been fixtures in Camp Sherman for years. Mick, a recent widower, was a retired radiologist. Dave, somewhat henpecked by his writer wife, had spent his career in data processing, pioneering in the industry for the State of Oregon's Department of Transportation. Now, the two men, who were also brothers-in-law, would spend most mornings sitting outside the Camp Sherman post office and working on the daily crossword puzzle. Although they claimed it took both of them to get all of the three letter words, the puzzle was really a ruse as the two old duffers chatted with passersby and in so doing, kept a finger on the pulse of the community.

Tonight in Wardwell's cabin, a jigsaw puzzle was the game of choice and both Mick and Dave were bent over their puzzle in rapt concentration. Mick soon noticed the fire was beginning to flutter so he stood up in order to put on more wood. A tall and lean man who had led an athletic life, he now felt his age. He stepped to the fireplace and could feel the ever-present stiffness in his back and legs. He plucked a log from the wood storage bin and tossed it onto an airy pile of embers, scattering sparks in a poufy cloud of ash.

"So when is Deputy Richmond coming?" The question came from Dave. Wiry and remarkably fit for his age, Dave was studying a jigsaw puzzle piece, turning it this way and that.

Dave was answered by Conrad. The retired Navy Commander was comfortably planted in his easy chair beside the fireplace. A longhaired Chihuahua mix, Fido, was curled up in his lap. Conrad said around the edge of his newspaper, "He said he'd come this evening. I surmise it will be sometime after dinner."

"If he ever has time for dinner." Aunt Phil, as her nephew called her,

Conrad's bride of barely two years, emerged from the cabin's diminutive kitchen. She placed a tray of cookies, coffee mugs, and a thermos of freshly made decaf on a side table. She poured mugs of coffee and passed them to Mick and Dave. When she gave one to Conrad, he thanked her with the smile in his eyes.

Conrad was constantly in awe of his good fortune of meeting Phyllis in the office of his attorney and Phyllis's nephew, Adam Carson. Now in the years most people would label as being the twilight of life, Conrad blew labels to the wind and felt his best years were just beginning. Phyllis kept every waking moment special with her refreshing zest for life and unfettered capacity to bestow love on her husband and their circle of friends and family. Every nuance, look, smile, and hug he could share with her was as precious to him as life itself.

Both Aunt Phil and Conrad were built surprising alike, or as she would say, "We're short and thick, like potatoes." Conrad was stout but stood straight as a stake, his military background obvious in his posture. He sported a full head of white hair matched to a bushy mustache. Aunt Phil had vivid blue eyes and short, layered white hair which feathered around her face.

She furrowed her brow and added about Deputy Richmond, "The past few times I've seen Cyril, he seemed really troubled about something." Phyllis was a retired criminal defense attorney and could read nuances as easily as she stepped out of her own shoes. "He never said anything, but there was just that look about him of being preoccupied. He didn't say why he wanted to meet with us tonight, but maybe he'll share whatever is bugging him." She sat down in a chair opposite Conrad and picked up a puzzle book.

"Share with us?" Dave said, "With a bunch of old farts? Nah! We're the invisible generation."

"Not to other old farts," Mick added sagely. "Besides, he's probably still worried about the missing women from Central Oregon. Remember the Portland Police were going to conduct more searches of Forest Park with cadaver dogs?"

Conrad chimed in, "Yes, I do remember. And I agree, I don't think we are invisible to Richmond. We sure surprised the authorities with the work we did on those bones Dave stumbled upon in that abandoned cabin last summer."

"To say nothing about chasing down that evil girlfriend of Adam's in Hawaii," Aunt Phil chuckled. "That had to look like something out of the Keystone Cops." Adam Carson had been deceived by a client's widow into thinking she had a romantic interest in him. She was really trying to persuade him to illegally divert funds for her use from her deceased husband's trust. Once the woman was suspected by the police of murdering her husband, she fled to a remote spot in the State of Hawaii. Phyllis, Conrad, Mick and Dave, Adam, and their friends Beth Welton and Arthur Perkins had done their own investigation parallel to that of the police and located her hiding place. A madcap chase across the expansive and lava strewn Big Island of Hawaii brought the woman to a just but grisly end.

Now, while they waited for the Jefferson County Sheriff's Deputy, the four friends enjoyed their coffee and cookies in front of the gently flaming fire. Mick, still pouring over the jigsaw puzzle, suddenly looked outside into the fading light and announced, "Here comes Richmond."

Phyllis met the deputy at the door. He was still dressed in his uniform. Fifty-one year old Cyril Richmond stepped inside and bent to give Aunt Phil a peck on the cheek.

"Hi, Phyllis. It's good to see you." Prematurely grey with a walrus mustache, Richmond was in his prime but tonight looked worn out. He had steely blue eyes that normally could stop a speeder with one killer glare but tonight his eyes looked like they just wanted to go to sleep. He made the rounds to each of the men, shaking hands and exchanging manly shoulder slaps.

"I hope I didn't hold up your dinner."

"We've had it," Aunt Phil answered. "Have you?"

"Not yet." Richmond's eyes, radar-like, zeroed in on the plate of cookies.

"Well, I'll bet you're hungry then," she smiled and gestured towards the cookies. "Help yourself. Can I get you coffee? It's decaf."

"No, no thanks. I have just a minute. I've been in meetings in Madras all day and I need to get home. My wife will have forgotten what I look like and call the cops when I walk through the door."

"Well, at least take the time to sit down." Aunt Phil pointed to the small couch and Richmond sank into it as though he'd walked forty miles. Without asking a second time, Aunt Phil simply handed him the plate of cookies. He took one with a grateful look at her smiling face.

Cookie in hand, the deputy then leaned forward on the couch. "Sheriff Larkin has been after me, well, has *asked* me to check on a situation." Richmond looked at each oldster in turn. "You know who Andre Sullivan is?'

"Sure," Mick answered. "He's that conceited snob who, with no law enforcement experience whatsoever, ran against Larkin in the last election. It was not too surprising that he lost. Now I understand he's interested in a congressional seat."

Dave said, "You'd think he'd start at a local level like a school board or something where he could learn the process. Oh no, he has to go for some big shot office."

"Right," Conrad added. "I never felt good about him since, on the voter's pamphlet, he listed his only previous government experience as running for office." They all laughed.

"Anyway," Richmond continued, "there is a rumor, and so far, that's all it is, that Sullivan is going to try to put in a large resort in the manner of Sun River up in the burned out area of the B&B fire." Sun River is a vacation and residential resort community fifteen miles south of Bend on the Deschutes River. It has three golf courses, tennis courts, an air strip and luxury vacation rentals as well as a large shopping center.

"How can he do that?" Dave scoffed. "All the land up there is either National Forest or Mt. Jefferson Wilderness! What is he thinking, anyway?"

"Well, you know that the present administration in Washington is doing away with a lot of the environmental protections that have been placed by previous presidents." Richmond took another bite of the cookie.

"Yes, to please his rich, enterprising pals," Mick answered.

"He's also threatened to reduce the size of some national parks as well as opening up national forest land to mining and logging," Conrad added.

"That's right." Richmond popped the last of the cookie into his mouth. "There is talk that the entire Deschutes National Forest on both sides of Green Ridge and including a large part of the Mt. Jefferson Wilderness is on that list."

"No!" Everyone else in the room said simultaneously.

"Well," Richmond added, "if it happens, Sullivan's plan, and again this is just a rumor, is to buy up a huge chunk of it himself and develop this destination resort. He already owns several acres up by the B&B fire as well as another piece over on the east side of Green Ridge, not far from your friends Arthur Perkins and Beth Welton. The trouble is, people close to Sullivan won't talk to me about it, no matter how casually I try to bring it up. That makes me think, more than ever, that there is much more to it than a rumor. Once in office, he will be in a position to sneak reducing the boundaries of national forests in with other legislation and nobody will know enough about it to stop it until it's too late."

"Can you imagine how that would change our lives here at Camp Sherman?" Dave said, looking wide-eyed to Conrad, Mick, and then to Aunt Phil.

Mick added studiously, "Didn't the Oregon Legislature put all of the Metolius Basin into some category called an Area of Critical Statewide Concern?"

"Yes, they did," Richmond answered. "However, the east side of Green Ridge is not part of that designation so it's pretty much up for grabs. That designation for the Metolius Basis passed by such a small margin, Sullivan must think he can get around it or plow it under. Let's face it, the reason it barely squeaked by is that there are enough politicians at the state level who answer only to the special interests with gobs of money."

Conrad added, "If that happens, they could widen the road in here from US 20, completely bowling over Camp Sherman. There will be so much traffic, trucks and stuff whizzing by that our peaceful little community will be no more."

"Goodbye, Camp Sherman. Hello, Golden Arches!" Dave said grimly.

"Okay," Richmond said. "This is where you guys come in. In a couple of weeks, Sullivan is honchoing a huge fundraiser for his campaign. It will be at Black Butte Ranch. Every high mucky-muck in Oregon who is anybody in land development, logging, or mining is invited. It's a silent auction and fancy sit-down dinner type of thing. They are looking for volunteers as servers and what-not."

"I get it!" Aunt Phil said. "We volunteer and dress in servants' outfits and bring them their food and pour champagne, all the time eavesdropping to hear what people are talking about."

"That's what I had in mind," Richmond went on. "Nobody would suspect, er. . ."

Dave finished the statement for him, "Old people!" They all laughed at Richmond's blush of embarrassment.

"Cyril has a point," Mick said. "Our age is our disguise. Who better to go around snooping when no one pays any attention to what old people are doing?"

"Yeah, they probably think, if anything, we're looking for the restroom," added Conrad.

"Right! Our Depends are full." Aunt Phil said and they all howled with laughter.

"Or we're looking for our teeth." Dave had sucked in his lips and said, "Teef."

"No one will ever suspect we're really spies. We'll be The Geezer Underground!" Mick declared.

Conrad shot a fist into the air. "Yes!"

"Long live The Geezers!" Aunt Phil joined in.

Richmond took in the enthusiasm of the group, shook his head while smiling and said, "You guys are terrific! Now, listen, and I've passed this idea by the Sheriff Larkin and he says it's a 'Go' but with caution. The Jefferson County Commissioners are warming to Sullivan's scheme. As you know, Jefferson County is poorly populated and the idea of having this south-western corner where Camp Sherman is located suddenly bringing in tons of tax revenue is appealing. After all, those commissioners are ranchers and other businesspeople who have little or no connection to the Metolius

Basin in general or to Camp Sherman. So, no one else is to know what your mission is. You're just volunteering as servers for the fun of it."

"You can depend on us, Cyril. We will be so incognito *we* won't even know what we're doing," Mick said, smiling.

"When is this gala affair, anyway?" Aunt Phil asked.

"Sometime around the first of next month." Richmond got to his feet. "Go online to Sullivan's web page to sign up."

"We'll do it right now." Conrad nodded at his laptop resting on the small table beside his chair.

"Maybe we should do it individually so it doesn't appear like we're ganging up on them; even though we are. What do you think?" Dave asked Mick.

"Good idea," Mick nodded.

"Okay, I'll let you get to it," Richmond said as he headed for the door. He stood for a moment with the doorknob in his hand, looked back at the little bundle of grey-haired friends and said seriously, "My thanks cannot express how grateful I am to know you." He then opened the door and was gone.

CHAPTER 2

AFTER DEPUTY RICHMOND left, the four friends gathered around the dining table to talk. Fido went with them in the crook of Conrad's arm.

"Okay, we need a plan," Aunt Phil began.

"First thing is to sign up," Mick offered. "It's short notice. I hope they still need volunteers."

Dave said, "They have to be desperate for volunteers. Who would want to help that scumbag, anyway? He has gobs of his daddy's money and shouldn't need to raise any funds."

"Well, that's his MO," Mick added. "He uses other people's money and if he loses it all, he walks away and suffers no loss whatsoever."

"Nice guy," Conrad said. "Okay. I'll sign up tonight for Phyllis and myself. You guys do it first thing tomorrow morning."

Aunt Phil said, "Next, we need clothes to make us look like servers, butlers, whatevers." She then added, "Probably tuxes for you guys."

The men collectively groaned.

"We can start by shopping at thrift stores in Bend," Aunt Phil went on, making plans.

The men groaned louder.

"*I* can start by shopping at thrift stores in Bend," she gave them all a stink eye.

The men laughed.

"Whatever I buy, you guys gotta wear."

"What are you going to wear, my dear? A cute little maid's outfit?"

Conrad wiggled his eyebrows suggestively.

"Well, it may be a maid's outfit but it won't be cute and it won't be little, I can guarantee that!" Aunt Phil paused then said more to herself than anybody, "Let's see, how do you do it, serve the plate from the right and remove it from the left or . . ?"

"What?"

"I'm trying to think how you're supposed to serve a plate at a sit down dinner. Serve from the left, remove from the right?"

"How about reaching over their heads with the plate and dropping it to the table in front of them?" Dave suggested.

"That'll do it!" Conrad agreed.

"And we'll just tell 'em to heap all the plates in the center of the table and then we'll come along and gather the pile in the table cloth and sweep the whole mess away." Mick smiled at his idea.

"What if they're not finished eating?" Dave mused.

"Not our problem," Mick answered.

"Right, and if anybody wants a doggy bag, scrape all the plates into a large black garbage bag and hand it to 'em." Aunt Phil added. "That really happened to a friend of mine. She was so mortified, she just walked out with it."

"Some lucky dog! You'd like that, wouldn't you Fido?" Conrad asked the dog as he tickled the little fawn colored head. "It would take you a week to get through it all." Fido had his chin on the table. His buggy eyes were on the cookie plate.

"Okay, now that that is settled. . ." Aunt Phil began gathering up the remains of the coffee and cookies.

"It is?" Dave asked.

"Yeah, I'm sure there will be some guidelines on how to serve. They're asking for volunteers, for crying out loud. He's too cheap to actually hire professional waiters." She bustled the coffee service back to the kitchen.

"Well, let's find out." Conrad moved back to his chair, placed Fido in his basket beside the fireplace, and picked up his laptop. Bringing up Andre Sullivan's website, Conrad maneuvered through page after page of the candidate's self-declared virtues until he found the sign up section for volunteers.

"Uh-oh," Conrad said quietly but, regardless, got everybody's attention.

"What'd you find?" Dave got up from the table to look over Conrad's shoulder at the web site.

"Well, it says don't bother to volunteer unless you have prior serving experience."

"How's he going to know? Do a background check on everyone who offers to volunteer?"

"Probably."

"Hey, we're spies. We can fake it."

"Besides, we're old people. Who'd question us since we are innocent as lambs and all? If we weren't by now, we'd be in jail."

"Or dead."

"Okay," Conrad said. "Here we go." He tapped in the required information as the rest of them watched, hovering around his chair. As he typed in his birthdate, someone asked, "Hey, isn't that age discrimination to ask for a birthdate?"

Conrad answered, "Probably. However, he doesn't want some old person having a stroke and falling face down in the soup."

"Yeah, that's a nasty thing to do to soup," Mick said wryly.

"You don't have to be old to have that happen. It happens all the time, or it seems to," Dave said.

"That's for sure," Conrad agreed.

"What, falling face down into soup?" Mick asked.

"No, strokes!" Conrad and Dave said simultaneously.

"Oh, those."

"He asks for a birthdate to make sure you are old enough to be bound to a contract and boy, are we ever!" Dave noticed.

"Gee, you're smart." Mick looked at his brother-in-law and laughed.

"You got that right."

"What does it say, if anything, about what to wear?" Aunt Phil interrupted the men's goofiness.

Conrad did some more scrolling. "Here it is! For men, black pants, white long-sleeved dress shirt, black bow tie, black cummerbund."

"Oh boy, I can hardly wait."

"For ladies, long black skirt, white blouse."

"I can do that," Aunt Phil exclaimed. "Except for the skirt. Surely, somewhere in Central Oregon I can find a short black skirt which will be a long black skirt on me. How about you guys?"

"My long black skirt is at the cleaners," Dave deadpanned.

"So's mine but I do have black slacks and a dress shirt, but not the tie or cummerbund," Mick said. "Did it really say cummerbund? I always thought the word was cumberbund."

"I'm surprised you gave it any thought at all," Dave replied.

"Since you guys are such shopping zealots, I'll find that stuff." Aunt Phil said with an eye roll.

Now Conrad entered Phyllis's information onto the website, hit "Enter" and soon they all heard the "ding" of an email confirmation coming from the candidate's website.

"Okay," Conrad said with a sigh of relief as he looked at Dave and Mick. "Now it's up to you guys to do yours."

AS THE FOUR friends worked on their assignment, Deputy Richmond tiredly scuffed through the dust to the Camp Sherman Store parking lot where he had left his truck. He wasn't sure he had done the right thing, getting these old duffers involved. He knew they were tenacious but he also knew that Andre Sullivan was a vindictive asshole. He would react to an opponent first by insulting them, then he would threaten with some idiotic, juvenile bullying. Who knew to what lengths the man would go? If the oldsters' ulterior motives became known, and they became the subject of Sullivan's wrath it would, frankly, break Richmond's heart. Richmond would have to trust the Geezer Underground. They were just zany enough to be able to pull it off. The question was, to what level of mayhem.

As Richmond hauled his weary fanny into his truck, he thought about the meeting he had had earlier in the day with Sheriff Gary Larkin. The sheriff was a reasonable man who, politics of the County Board of Commissioners aside, shared with Richmond his passion for Camp Sherman and the Metolius Basin. When Richmond had revealed to his boss his scheme to engage the Geezer Underground, the Sheriff warned that if it became known that Richmond was behind it, they could both lose their jobs. Regardless, Sheriff Larkin had given the go-ahead to his deputy.

Richmond had lived in Camp Sherman for his entire career with the Jefferson County Sheriff's Office. This was his home. These were his people. He was the guardian. Richmond thought if Sullivan was successful in his quest to destroy what made the Metolius Basin such a naturally pristine place, Richmond wouldn't want to live here anymore. He was acutely aware that the entire future of the Metolius Basin may rely on what happens at that dinner. Oh, would he like to be a fly on the wall!

When Cyril Richmond reached home, his gloomy mood followed him into the house. It lifted, however, when he received a phone call from his boss. Richmond's wish had been granted. Andre Sullivan, keenly aware how controversial he was, insisted there be armed police on duty during the banquet. Even though Black Butte Ranch had its own police force, Sullivan felt he commanded much more attention from local law enforcement. Black Butte Ranch was on the Deschutes County side of US 20, however, the Deschutes County Sheriff asked Jefferson County Sheriff Larkin "For some help with this idiot." Neither sheriff ever expected to collect the fee they would charge for the service from the deadbeat Sullivan, so a bare minimum of men from each county was provided. Sheriff Larkin knew Richmond would jump at the chance to be included.

CHAPTER 3

WITHIN A FEW days of shopping, Aunt Phil was able to come up with black bow ties and black cummerbunds for the men, a white dress shirt for Conrad, plus a long sleeved white blouse and a long black skirt for herself. The blouse had a high neck with lace and buttoned down the back with tiny pearl buttons. She loved it. As for the skirt, she hated long skirts and dresses because she claimed she always looked like someone had thrown a rug over a stump. However, this skirt was neither straight nor full but slightly flared and she thought she could eventually shorten it to wear to Portland Trail Blazer basketball games. Faithful fans of the Blazers, she and Conrad always wore the team's colors, red, black, and white, when they attended the home games.

The morning of the banquet dawned with the lovely amber brightness that only autumn can produce. Before the sun had much of an opportunity to climb very high in the sky, workers at Black Butte Ranch were busy setting up a long banquet table on the expansive lawn. The location of the banquet was stunning with beautiful Lake Phalarope and the Cascade Mountains as a backdrop.

As morning approached noon in Camp Sherman, Aunt Phil fussed with donning her servant clothes and now cursed her lovely new blouse because it buttoned down the back. Hearing her muttering coming from the bedroom, Conrad first went over to Fido's dog bed, the basket beside the fireplace. He scratched the little dog on the head and told him that no, he couldn't go with them but to stay here and guard the homestead. Conrad then turned to go to the bedroom to help his wife fasten the infernal row of tiny buttons.

When Aunt Phil and Conrad adopted Fido from the humane society on the Big Island of Hawaii, little was known of the dog's past. If the truth were to be known, and only Fido and his anonymous past owner knew, the dog used his smallness to often escape and went on elaborate walkabouts, or in Fido's case, scamperabouts. So, as soon as Conrad disappeared into the bedroom, Fido quietly hopped from his basket and up onto the back of the couch. An open window offered a perfect escape route. He poked his nose through a tiny tear in the window screen and quietly ripping the opening wider, he pushed the rest of his small body through. Dropping to the ground, he dashed around to the front of the cabin, his little paws stirring up tiny tufts of dust in the dry forest floor. Trotting to the Wardwell's Volvo SUV, Fido stepped into the shade of a rear tire and waited, his tongue hanging out the side of his mouth. Conrad and Aunt Phil soon came bustling to the truck. Noting Conrad's dusty tennis shoes, Aunt Phil asked, "Did you remember to bring your dress shoes?"

"Oh crap! Forgot," he answered.

As Aunt Phil stood with the truck door open and watched Conrad return to the cabin, Fido stepped from behind the back tire, zipped unseen through the open truck door and in a flash was burrowing under a blanket which was behind the back seat. The blanket was kept there for emergency purposes while traveling the sometimes treacherous mountain passes. Finally, Conrad and Aunt Phil were bumping off down the lane to pick up Mick and Dave with Fido happily ensconced underneath the blanket.

Two miles further east of the intersection with the Camp Sherman Road and State Highway 20 was Black Butte Ranch. A community of vacation properties plus a lodge with a restaurant and two golf courses all thoughtfully etched into the forest, Black Butte Ranch was stunning in its simplicity. If not for the sign on the highway, one would never know the property was there because of its tasteful marriage with the surrounding forest.

By the time Conrad steered the Volvo into the ranch's parking lot, the four friends could see a group of people also dressed as servants gathered around another individual with a clipboard in her hand. The Geezer Underground piled out of the Volvo and fussed around the truck, making sure they had everything they needed. Fido took the opportunity to slip away from the truck and made a mad dash into the woods, hot on the trail to a new adventure.

Aunt Phil, Conrad, Mick and Dave approached the group huddled around Sullivan's crusty volunteer coordinator who doubled as his campaign manager. Brenda Bailey, clipboard clutched in one hand and a pen in the other, shot a well-aimed stink eye through long, mousey brown bangs at the four seniors for being late. She then instructed the entire group on how to set the table and how to serve the main dish; deliver from the left, retrieve from the right.

The ranch's restaurant workers had dressed the long table with white table cloths and stacked next to it racks of glasses, coffee cups, chargers, and flatware. The volunteers were soon hard at work arranging the table settings.

"We should put the spoons on the left and the forks on the right." Conrad sniggered quietly to Aunt Phil. She looked at him and then said, "If we keep pouring enough champagne, no one will notice."

A florist van could be seen making its way along the long, winding drive into the resort. It pulled to a stop and two women popped out and cheerfully began placing massive bouquets all along the center line of the table. Aunt Phil watched the women and thought that having a florist shop would be unique in that your work would always make people happy. She had been a criminal defense attorney in Seattle and although her work made the truly innocent happy, often the most she could do is get the best deal for some unhappily guilty SOB.

"If people don't like what's on the menu, they can always eat the center pieces." Mick said to Dave who smiled as he stepped aside for yet another bouquet.

"Especially handy if they are vegetarians," Dave commented.

Soon Bailey had some of the volunteers working on the blind auction. More tables went up and arrangements from antique dishes, quilts, furniture, paintings, and tours to iconic places around Oregon were displayed.

This indeed was going to be a well-thought out party and she hoped prosperous to the Sullivan campaign's bottom line.

Meanwhile, Fido was having a party of his own. He had scampered largely unnoticed to the lake and was racing along the shoreline chasing Canada geese as well as small shore birds, Wilson's phalarope, which were the lake's namesake. Both breeds of birds spent the summers nesting and raising young in the marshes at the lake's edge. Once their offspring could fly, the birds would be soon migrating but not before Fido had some fun. Since he was so small, the only evidence of his mischief was the squawking and taking to the air of groups of birds which would then settle back to the lake after Fido had dashed by. All this commotion was largely ignored by the busy banquet workers.

Guests were expected to start arriving around 3:00 PM. Champagne glasses were unboxed and the volunteers quickly arranged them on trays to be carried among the guests. Their instructions were to pour enough champagne down their throats to loosen their wallets as they browsed the silent auction offerings.

It wasn't long until the limos started to arrive. One by one they disgorged their load of Oregon's richest: business people, bankers, politicians, the leaders of commerce and industry, many of whom seemed already prepped with bubbly as they staggered to their feet. Conrad, Mick, and Dave stood nearby with their trays of champagne as other volunteers filled new glasses just as fast as they could.

Also there to greet the guests were members of the press; reporters and camera people from The Portland Oregonian, Bend Bulletin, Sisters Nugget, Salem Statesman Journal, and the Eugene Register Guard had their camera lenses at the ready. The patrons, men in tuxes and women in long gowns, luxuriated in the attention as though they were arriving at the Academy Awards. Aunt Phil watched them enjoying their own importance and wanted to hurl.

But hurl she didn't and it's a good thing as she was approached by a fiftyish woman, richly decked out in avalanches of diamonds, who asked her what was being served for dinner.

Aunt Phil didn't blink as she leaned in and whispered, "Spotted owl." The woman paused for just a tic and cooed delicately, "Really? Oh, how lovely!" Her husband, looking around his swollen, alcoholic nose added, "How appropriate!" They giggled as they toddled off, leaning on one another and sipping their champagne.

The Geezer Underground did their best to keep their ears tuned into the chatter that engulfed the group of partygoers. Above the hubbub, they could make out certain comments: "It's about time." "We can make a fortune with this guy in office." "This guy's going to be our ticket." Other than, "He has big plans for that burned out area up towards the mountains," nothing regarding Sullivan's destination resort plans readily came to the surface.

Andre Sullivan made his grand entrance escorted by a bevy of local law enforcement officers. Cyril Richmond was among them, trying very hard to be professional and to not smirk and roll his eyes. Sullivan waded into the crowd of guests, shaking hands and flashing a big grin of expensive dental work. Not a tall man (and his cowboy boots didn't help much), Sullivan disappeared into the crowd and could be followed only by watching the movement of the policemen surrounding him.

An announcement was made that dinner would be served and would everyone please take a seat. Sullivan moved towards the head of the table and the crowd of guests gravitated to the other chairs and were soon seated waiting expectantly for which they had paid one thousand dollars per plate.

The volunteers were made busy serving plates of roasted quail in a caper and butter sauce, fingerling potatoes, and steamed broccolini. Although it wasn't really the rare Spotted owl which has been the subject of intense conflict between conservationists and the logging industry in the Pacific Northwest, Aunt Phil squeezed her nostrils shut and blanched at the thought of these tiny quail being sacrificed to nourish this bunch of blowhards. Recovering her composure, she studiously told Mick, Dave, and Conrad, "Now remember, you serve from the left side of the guest."

"Got it!"

"Aye, aye, Cap'n"

"You bet, Amiga!"

And the little group of spies set off performing their duties, hoping they didn't dump someone's dinner on their lap, or maybe hoping they would.

Meanwhile, Andre Sullivan, with his police escort, stood in front of his seat at the head of the table. The want-to-be senator's thin dark hair was slicked back on his head. His portly stature made him look not unlike a mafia don. He appeared puffed with his importance within this group of important people. Sullivan was stupid enough to think the attendees were here because they adored him. In reality, they were here only because they felt he could do something for them. Mick and Dave exchanged knowing glances. The brothers-in-law were also long-time friends and didn't always need words to talk.

"May I have your attention, please?" Sullivan's voice was amplified by a portable microphone. "Welcome to my party and the beauty of Central Oregon." Everyone clapped and Sullivan smiled expansively as though he were personally responsible for the wondrous beauty of the scene. "I want to thank my fine staff member for the work she did in preparing this lovely banquet for our enjoyment." He waved his arm at his campaign manager. Standing a few feet away, Brenda Bailey grinned inanely and took a small bow as the guests applauded.

"Geez," Dave said to Mick. "What does he think *we* are, penguins?"

Mick said quietly in response, "He treating us just as he thinks of us, as servants."

As the volunteers continued to serve dinners, Sullivan droned on, "As you all know, there are some major changes taking place in Washington, DC." He looked around at the group to make sure he had everyone's attention. "The new federal administration is doggedly reversing environmental sanctions protecting what is scientifically unproven to be endangered species."

"What does he mean, scientifically unproven? The fuck. . ." Aunt Phil admonished.

"Shhh," Conrad put a hand on her arm.

"This is what we had all been waiting for," Sullivan said to clapping and shouted yeahs from the crowd. "Now is *our* time!" More clapping and cheers. "If I am elected to congress, I will see to it that federal lands in Oregon which are now being blatantly wasted will be opened up to enterprising individuals such as yourselves for logging, mining, and real estate development." Wild cheers and a few standing ovations emitted from the crowd. "There is no reason why thousands of acres of this state should be tied up in National Forest and Wilderness designations and left to molder and decay. Let the splendor of the Pacific Northwest be ours and it will be measured in terms of dollars and cents and not in obscure animal and plant species which may be on their way out anyway. How many Spotted owls does one need, anyway?" His question was answered with thunderous applause and cheers.

All the time Sullivan was expounding how he would wreak havoc with current pristine and delicate wilderness areas, Fido was wreaking his own havoc by busily flushing out birds from the edge of the lake, all the time getting closer and closer to Sullivan's party. The Canada geese young, by this time in the fall, were nearly ready to fly. Fido happened across a clutch which were full grown but still without fully developed flight feathers. Their only defense was to run in squawking panic from the barking little dog. The three juvenile geese headed right to the banquet table with Fido in hot pursuit. In turn, the parents of these goose youngsters took off after Fido, honking their fury.

The young geese got just enough air to land on the table top. They thundered down the length of the table, scattering plates, bouquets, and patrons in all directions, their big floppy goose feet making hash out of the spilled food, flowers, and water. Charging through the resulting goose flurry and poo came Fido who had used a particularly substantial patron's lap as a launching pad to gain access to the table top. Happy as a dog can be, he scampered after the geese, closely followed by the young birds' enraged parents whose wide wing span quickly emptied the table of any remaining guests.

At the opposite end of the table, Sullivan's eyes grew large as the three goslings bore down upon him. Swallowing his laughter, Cyril Richmond caught the politician's chair as it nearly tipped over. Sullivan scrambled to his feet with murder in his eyes for Fido but Conrad quickly stepped in, swept the dog into his arms, and scurried off toward the parking lot.

Cyril Richmond, as best he could, tried to read the mood of the scattered patrons. They had come to this affair after some great expense and distance and considered themselves the elite of Oregon. They expected more from their candidate than his dazed mutterings. Disgustedly picking the remains of their dinners from their clothes and grumbling that they were no longer interested in that idiot Sullivan if he couldn't even control a simple banquet, they wandered off towards their awaiting limos.

The table sat forlornly with its table cloths askew, chairs tipped over, dishes, glasses, & flowers strewn everywhere. As Sullivan dumbly gawped at the carnage, Dave quipped to Mick, "Don't you love a good party?"

CHAPTER 4

CONRAD, WITH FIDO happily licking his ear, hustled off to the parking lot with Aunt Phil, Mick and Dave closely following.

"How the heck did Fido get here?" Aunt Phil huffed, trying to keep up with Conrad.

"I don't know but I certainly know it's time for us to leave," Conrad stammered as he handed the dog to Aunt Phil and dug in his pocket for his keys. "Did you see the hate on Sullivan's face? If he could have gotten hold of this dog I think he would have torn him fuzzy limb from fuzzy limb."

"The man has no sense of humor whatsoever," Dave noted dryly, waiting for Conrad to unlock the doors.

They all piled into the Volvo and Conrad drove them off, resisting the urge to floor the accelerator.

By the time they returned to the Wardwell's cabin, they had relaxed and were laughing at what Fido had done to Sullivan's party. Aunt Phil, tightly holding on to the little dog to prevent another escape, led the way inside the cabin and placed Fido in his bed.

"Now, stay there, you little imp!" she said to him and then looked up and said, "Uh-oh."

Conrad came over to see what the uh-oh was about, and then he saw it; the open window and hole in the screen.

"Ah-ha! So that's how he got out!" Conrad exclaimed, noting bits of sunny colored hair caught in the screen.

Dave and Mick also came to observe the dog's escape route.

"Oops!" Dave exclaimed. "Looks like we need a bit of a screen repair there."

Mick leaned on the back of the couch and upon seeing how far it was to the ground said, "Holy smokes! That had to be a determined dog to be willing to drop that far."

Fido remained in his basket during all of this uh-oh-ing, oops-ing, ah-ha-ing and holy smoking. He avoided eye contact and, if anything, seemed to burrow even deeper into his bedding. He knew he had been a bad dog, but for one heck of a fun afternoon, it had been well worth it.

Mick and Dave set to work putting a quick fix on the screen while Aunt Phil and Conrad made sandwiches for everyone. Conrad had made a huge bowl of potato salad the previous day using a now favorite recipe from a family friend, Tony Trelstad. With a platter of ham sandwiches, Conrad's salad, and a bowl of Kettle Chips, the Geezer Underground sat down to enjoy a well-deserved meal.

"I went to a charity auction tea one time," Aunt Phil recalled, munching a potato chip. "They also had volunteer servers and one of them was a local TV newscaster who I thought was really cute."

Conrad rolled his eyes as Mick and Dave chuckled.

"Every time he would come close to my table, I'd guzzle tea so my cup would be empty, anticipating that he'd fill it up. Some other volunteer would come from behind me and fill my cup just as the newscaster guy came along so then he'd ignore me. That happened time after time. The newscaster would get close, I'd swill tea, and some poor shmuck, thinking he was doing the right thing, would reach over my shoulder and fill my cup. I chugged so much tea and had to pee so badly, I finally left and never did get that cute guy to pour for me."

"Another amazing episode in the life. . ." Conrad said as he winked at his wife.

"Do you think Sullivan will find out who Fido belongs to?" Dave asked the question which had been bothering all of them. "The guy is not known for his benevolence toward detractors."

"Well," Conrad answered, "I reached right in front of him to snatch Fido out from under his nose. I don't see how he could miss me."

"Unless there was so much commotion and confusion that who picked up the dog was sort of lost in a blur," Mick added hopefully.

"Blur is right!" Aunt Phil beamed at her husband. "Conrad, I didn't know you could move so fast."

"Motivation is the key," Conrad replied proudly.

"I can be motivated too, but only by the prospect of pie or cookies," Dave said.

"I'm surprised you didn't say donuts," Mick laughed, having known Dave for decades.

"The whole disruption was an accident," Aunt Phil declared. "It was unfortunate for Sullivan but, at the same time, fortunate for Oregon in that it took the edge off any advantage he may have in front of all those influential people. As for his total lack of diplomacy in dealing with those who pull his chain, on purpose or not, I say, bring him on!"

"Hear-hear!" They all agreed.

About the time the last of the salad had been scraped from the bottom of the bowl, there was a soft rapping at the door. Conrad opened the door to find Deputy Cyril Richmond leaning casually on the door jam, one arm behind his back.

"Come in, Cyril," Conrad said cheerfully, stepping out of the way. "I'm afraid we don't have a whole lot to tell you."

"Hi, Cyril!" Aunt Phil gathered up plates and with the help of Mick and Dave cleared the table.

"Conrad's right," Dave told Richmond as the deputy entered the cabin. "Most of what we heard confirmed the rumors that Sullivan appeared to be planning to decimate a lot of national forest land in the name of progress. Which, as we all know, would be a disaster for Camp Sherman."

"I did overhear someone say that Sullivan had big plans for some burned out area," Mick added. "I'm assuming they were talking about the scars left by the B&B fire a few years back. Oddly enough, no one seemed to know, or at least mentioned, that Sullivan owned property adjacent to it."

"Yes, I suspect he's keeping the existence of his property really quiet,"

Richmond answered, one hand still behind his back.

"Anyway," the deputy continued, "I just want to thank you four for your help. I appreciate that you took the time and effort even though we didn't learn much which was new. However. . ." Richmond pulled his arm around to the front of his body to reveal he was carrying a box of dog biscuits. "I especially want to show our gratitude to this little guy." Richmond got down on his haunches and held out the box to Fido. "He certainly made hash out of Sullivan's party."

Fido came to immediate attention when he sensed what Richmond had in his hand. He hopped out of his bed to the laughter and applause of everybody in the room. Tail wagging furiously, Fido bounced over to Richmond who was opening the box, and the dog daintily took one proffered biscuit from the deputy, then happily trotted back to his bed to devour his gift.

Conrad looked at Aunt Phil and said, "I guess we need to acknowledge we have one more member of the Geezer Underground."

Mick said, "Fido is an undercover Undergrounder."

Cyril Richmond handed the box of dog biscuits to Conrad and cautioned, "Well, don't disband anytime soon. We haven't heard the last from Andre Sullivan. One thing for certain, he's come up against a speed bump. How much it slows him down remains to be seen. He may not get much funding as a result of his disastrous party, but he'll get it somehow. If he is as determined as I think he is, he will resort to using his own money."

"We'll be ready, Cyril!" Aunt Phil said. "Just give us the word, although I don't think he'll have any more parties anytime soon."

THE REPORTERS HAD a field day with Sullivan's dinner. A photo of the guests scattering amidst gobs of glop being kicked up by three geese and a dog made it to front pages all over Oregon. The headlines didn't help:

SULLIVAN DUCKS MUCK FLUNG BY GEESE.

FLYING GOOSE GOO RUFFLES FEATHERS.

POLITICIAN CRIES FOUL AS FOWL UPSET FUND RAISER

GOOSE POO FLIES AS POLITICIAN DUCKS.

ANDRE SULLIVAN HAD stomped furiously around the ruined banquet table as the restaurant employees tried to clean up the mess. Brenda Bailey, who had adoring eyes only for her boss, followed him about wringing her hands but couldn't ease his angst. No one else, not even the reporters, dared approach him while he impotently kicked at the grass and ranted his fury to the trees, the lake, and the mountains.

Sullivan had indeed noticed the old codger who snatched the fucking little dog off the table and powdered off with it. Sullivan also noticed the troop of ancients who followed him to the parking lot. It didn't matter whether the incident was a conspiracy or an unfortunate happenstance, the dog had made Sullivan look like an idiot in front of the very people who could get him elected. Nobody does that to Andre Sullivan and walks away from it. Nobody! He'd find that bunch of old farts with their dog and make them pay, even if he had to burn down the forest to do it.

CHAPTER 5

NESTLED DEEP IN in the forest on the opposite side of Green Ridge from Camp Sherman is a sturdy, A-frame log cabin built by retired banker Arthur Perkins. Having been a widower for many decades, Arthur had built his cabin with the idea that this was where he would spend the rest of his life. In his early seventies, Arthur was tall and lean for his age. A white rim of hair circled around the back of his head and was matched with a neatly trimmed mustache. His constant companion was a big, black mixed-breed dog he had named Max. Arthur was well aware that as he aged, his enthusiasm for life seemed to ebb more than it flowed. About the time he felt he didn't have much reason to get up in the morning other than to pee, Beth Welton walked out of the woods and right into his heart.

Beth was a diminutive Portland philanthropist and author of a widely popular series of children's books. After her husband's death from ALS, she fled to a cave on Green Ridge to escape from a homicidal, money grubbing daughter. Beth felt she was better off hiding in the mountains she loved than fearing for her life in her home in Portland. Little did she know that the morning she chose to steal corn from Arthur's garden was to be the beginning of a relationship with a man whose unconditional love became the most precious thing she had ever possessed.

Arthur plopped into his chair next to the huge river rock fireplace in the cabin's great room. He slapped his glasses onto his face and shook open the front page of the Sister's newspaper, *The Nugget*. "Well, would you look at this?" Smeared across the top half of the page was a picture of candidate

Andre Sullivan, grimacing as he ducked away from a young goose galloping down a table top, splattering goop in all directions. A long-haired Chihuahua dashed in rapt pursuit of the goose. Just a bit out of focus were the unmistakable head and shoulders of Conrad Wardwell reaching into the picture to grapple up the happy little dog.

"What's that, dear?" Beth was reading a novel around the furry body of a Maine-Coon cat named Booger. Arthur held the paper in front of Beth's lovely face and watched her big blue eyes widen in surprise. Her mop of grey curls bounced like springs as she first looked at the picture and then at Arthur and then back at the picture.

"That's Conrad, isn't it? And...and Fido?" she stammered. "Really? What on earth have they been up to?" She looked quizzically at Arthur's face.

"It looks like they were involved somehow in that big bash Andre Sullivan put on at Black Butte Ranch yesterday."

"Sullivan, he's a bit of a scamp, isn't he?" It was a statement, not a question and as close as Beth Welton ever came to calling someone a crapwad.

"You can say that again. That guy has cold lips from kissing the mirror," Arthur said with distain as he quickly read the article. "Looks as though Fido and the geese interrupted a campaign fund raiser Sullivan was putting on at the Ranch. I know Conrad doesn't support that bastard. We just might have to make a trip over to Camp Sherman to find out what he was doing there."

"I'm in," Beth declared as she laid her book on the end table and removed all twenty pounds of Booger from her lap. "Oof! Sorry Boogs. You gotta move." She brushed the cat hair from her pants and headed to the closet for a jacket.

Booger parked on his haunches with his ears flattened out to both sides of his head. He was not happy with Beth deserting him and taking her lap with her. The consolation that he was able to settle down into the chair she had warmed was somewhat sufficient until she returned.

"Come, Max!" Arthur said to his dog. Max scrambled to his feet from where he had been sprawled on the living room floor. "Let's go visit Conrad and Phyllis." Max, not wanting to be left out of an adventure, happily hurried to the kitchen door, his long tail slapping the furniture and walls as he passed.

IRONICALLY, AT THIS same time, Mick and Dave were on their bench outside the Camp Sherman post office working on their crossword puzzle. However, their attention was distracted by the same article in *The Nugget* that Beth and Arthur had read.

"Well, so much for being incognito," Dave said to Mick.

"Hey, you two!" The squeaky voice of Old Bowels pierced the morning air. "What the heck is Conrad doing on the front page of the paper?" Old Bowels was a grizzled firefighter who had needed so many hernia operations that someone on his crew gave him that nick-name. He had been called Old Bowels or O.B. for so long that it was doubtful if anybody remembered his real name. His doctors had told him he couldn't work as a firefighter any more so he retired and volunteered at the fire station in Camp Sherman keeping the equipment in top shape.

"What do you think, O.B.?" Mick hedged.

"I dunno, but I'll bet it's a heck of a story! I wish I would have been there." Chuckling, Old Bowels continued on to the store for his morning coffee.

Mick looked at Dave and said, "People are going to be recognizing Conrad in the paper and asking us what is going on. I think we need a strategic planning meeting with Conrad and Phyllis. Now!"

"Let's go," Dave answered. The two legged it across the store's parking lot and headed down the dirt lane which led to the cabins built along the river's edge.

ONE HUNDRED AND FIFTY miles away, attorney Adam Carson picked up the Oregonian from his small Victorian's porch in NW Portland. He gazed at the front page and upon recognizing his Aunt's husband on the cover said, "Holy shit!" He also knew Aunt Phil would be involved in some way. "What the heck have those two been up to?"

Adam, in his early sixties with a stocky build and swarthy good looks, went into his office to call his aunt. The room used to be the parlor of a one-story cottage which had served as servants' quarters for a huge Queen-Anne Victorian house located across the street. The mansion had since been demolished and Adam had turned the little cottage into his home and office for his estate planning legal practice. Two bulldogs were curled together in front of the fire. He sat at his desk and dialed his aunt's new land line phone number in her cabin. He knew her cell phone couldn't receive calls in Camp Sherman unless she drove out to a bend in the forest service road the locals called "the phone booth." That was the only place to receive a cell phone signal unless they drove the five miles out to US 20.

As Adam listened to the Wardwell's phone ring, Dave and Mick were knocking at the cabin's door. Still in their bathrobes and settled in front of the fireplace, both Conrad and Aunt Phil flew out of their chairs. Conrad went to the door and Phyllis snatched up the phone and scurried into the bedroom to dress. Fido, his buggy eyes wide, watched it all from the safety of his basket next to Conrad's chair.

Conrad opened the door to Mick and Dave standing side by side with the newspaper held in front of them, the picture of Conrad facing towards the door.

Aunt Phil answered the phone. Adam asked if she had seen the newspaper yet that morning. "No, honey, we get the Oregonian on-line but haven't brought it up yet. We were sitting here drinking our coffee. Dave and Mick just came to the door."

As she entered the bedroom, she looked over her shoulder to get a glimpse of the newspaper Mick was carrying and knew at once they were in trouble. "You're calling about the picture in the paper, aren't you? We were volunteering at that fundraiser. Yes, well, it's a long story and we thought it would be a fun thing to do. Mick and Dave did too. We don't know how Fido got there. We think he stowed away in the car somehow. He chased up some geese. Yeah, right onto the table. Just destroyed the dinner, the party, everything. It was terribly funny, actually. Did Sullivan say anything to us? Oh no, we left before things got sorted out. Yes, we're fine. We know he's a jerk. Don't worry about us, okay?"

But Adam did worry about them, especially being on their own out there in the woods. It was a good thing he didn't have kids to worry about because his Aunt and her husband were enough to cause his hair to gray. You'd think old people would have the sense to just sit around and molder, but these two gave a whole new meaning to the word "retired."

It was the weekend and for the first few days of the following week, Adam didn't have much going on in his office. Maybe he'd pack up the dogs and drive over to Camp Sherman. Even take his golf clubs. Scare Arthur Perkins up for a round or two. Yup, that's a good idea!

"Duncan, Noodles, come on, let's go see Aunty Phil and Uncle Conrad, okay? You like to play with Fido. Besides, we might have to bail the whole goofy group out of jail!"

Noodles, the younger of the two dogs, bounced to her feet and scampered around Adam's shoes, pulling on the shoestrings and making excited snuffling noises. Duncan, being true to Duncan, opened one eye and glued it to Adam's face, wanting to make sure his boss was serious before he expended any energy getting out of bed.

Adam, with Noodles running after him and Duncan unfolding his arthritic old body to follow, headed down the hall to his bedroom to pack.

⁂

OUTSIDE A STARBUCKS coffee shop in downtown Portland, three Portland homicide detectives were taking a rare coffee break together. The early fall morning was bright, clear and warm. All three men had taken off their jackets as they sat in the sun.

Tall and lanky, red-haired Corporal Jerry Banning said, "Hey!" His Adam's apple took a quick tour up and down his skinny throat. "Isn't this Cyril Richmond?" Banning held up the front page of the Portland Oregonian so the other two men could see the picture of Deputy Richmond grabbing the chair of Andre Sullivan. Sullivan was diving to the ground in the face of three young Canada geese racing towards him on the top of a banquet table.

The other policemen, Sergeant Trevor Kowalski and Lieutenant Shawn Avery, peered at the picture.

"That's Cyril, all right!" Avery declared, smiling. The rumpled lieutenant and his homicide team got to know Cyril Richmond last summer while they worked on a murder case together.

"Looks like he's trying not to laugh." Kowalski, large enough in the shoulders to make two policemen, took a huge bite of yet another donut, the calories of which were lost on his six-foot, five-inch frame.

"Wouldn't you?" Avery chuckled.

"Heck, I'd just let the birds run him down, then I'd laugh. What's going on there, anyway?" Kowalski asked.

Banning was reading the article and then told the others of the campaign fund raiser and the disruption by the birds and a small dog.

"Couldn't happen to a nicer guy," Kowalski mumbled around the last morsel of his donut.

"You can say that again!" Lieutenant Shawn Avery, in his mid-forties and who had spent half his life with the Portland Police Bureau, took the paper from Banning and carefully studied the picture.

"What do you see there, Shawn?" Kowalski asked, wiping powdered sugar from his fingers.

"Well, I'm not sure, but doesn't that look like Adam Carson's uncle-in-law, I guess you'd call him? There, reaching for the dog?" Avery held the paper so the other two men could see the picture.

Kowalski answered, "Yeah. I think you're right. Wardwell... Conrad Wardwell, right? If he was there, I'll bet Adam's aunt was not too far behind."

"Most likely, she was leading the way." Avery said to the other men's laughter. Avery then said, "Sullivan...Sullivan. . . isn't he the guy. . ." Then he creased his forehead and got a far-away look in his faded blue eyes.

Kowalski looked at Banning and said, "Uh-oh, that brain of his is doing that effing computer thing again, digging up something about a case from years ago." The lieutenant had a reputation for never forgetting a case, no matter how old.

Banning quipped, "Hey, don't complain. It means job security for us."

Avery stood up, tossed a few bills onto the table and said, "Come on, guys, we need to do a little research on this Andre Sullivan."

CHAPTER 6

MICK AND DAVE had settled onto the couch in Wardwell's cabin and were sipping hot mugs of coffee. Mick said seriously, "We think we need a planning session."

Dave added, "So we get our stories straight when people ask what we were doing at Sullivan's fund raiser."

"We were volunteering," Aunt Phil said simply. "No more to it than that, really. There is no reason to mention what Cyril asked us to do."

"Okay," Dave replied. "So what if he asks us again to do something."

"We disguise ourselves better," Conrad answered with a smile.

"You mean like a real disguise; face paint, wigs and stuff?" Mick asked with an apprehensive sideways look to Dave.

"Sure! That will be a blast!" Aunt Phil liked the idea. "I'll wear a long white wig and go as the ghost of Christmas past, although I really wouldn't need the wig," she then laughed enormously.

"I'll shave my beard and Dave can grow one," Mick suggested

"I can't grow a beard," Dave exclaimed. "I tried once by not shaving for a week. Nobody could tell the difference."

"Not even one of those itty bitty soul patches the guys grow under their bottom lip?" Conrad asked.

"Nope."

"Come on, Dave, even *I* can do that," Aunt Phil laughed.

"How about if I wear a lampshade on my head instead," Dave offered.

"Anybody who has been to a party with you would know it's you," Mick declared.

"Oh. Darn."

"Using walkers would be good," Conrad suggested. "We could toddle along, all hunched over. . . just like we do on a regular basis. And then we'll keep the walkers because one of us might really need one someday."

"Let's hope not," the other three said in unison.

Conrad appeared thoughtful for a moment, then said, "Listen. We all know Sullivan is batshit crazy. If he doesn't get his funding one way, he'll do it another. The Metolius Basin and Deschutes National Forest are too precious to let him go off running amok. We need to keep an eye on him and we don't need direction from Richmond to do it."

"We don't?" Dave, Mick, and Aunt Phil asked collectively.

"Heck no! It's better if Richmond doesn't know what we're doing until we discover something worth telling him. Otherwise, he may feel he needs to pull us off our mission, he being a lawman and all. Serving at a banquet is one thing; chasing Sullivan all over hell and gone wearing costumes is entirely something else."

"Good idea."

"And if we are properly disguised, Sullivan will never know he's on our radar," Dave said.

"Yeah," Aunt Phil added. "As long as we don't disguise ourselves as rich people, he'll never pay us any attention."

"OK, so how do we follow him or know where he's going?" Dave asked.

"We take turns staking him out, then follow him?" Mick suggested.

"Well, we can't use your pickup, Mick," Dave answered. "There is no way of being clandestine when you're orange."

"We could use our Volvo," Aunt Phil suggested.

"Too big," Mick replied. "That would be like trying to sneak up on someone while riding an elephant."

"Point made."

"How about Dave's truck?" Conrad asked.

"I don't have a truck, I have a Prius," Dave said. "It's not your normal, everyday pursuit car."

"But's that's even better. No one would suspect it," Mick said, warming to the idea.

"How many geezers can we get in a Prius?" Aunt Phil asked.

"As many teenagers as we used to get into Volkswagens when we were in high school," Mick answered.

"That's more geezers than you'd ever want in a Prius," Conrad remarked. "That's for sure."

"Regardless, I like the Prius idea, mainly because it's the best of our options," Conrad continued.

"Okay, the Prius it is," Dave declared.

While this discussion was going on inside the Wardwell's cabin, Beth and Arthur pulled up outside in Arthur's pickup. Max was safely tied in the pickup bed. Upon sliding out from behind the driver's seat, Arthur told his dog to stay in the truck. He and Beth then made their way to the cabin's front porch and knocked.

"Come on in!" Conrad said warmly as he flung open the door. Peeking around Arthur and Beth, Conrad noted Max was still in the truck bed, great puppy dog eyes doing the whammy thing to Conrad's heart. "It's okay to bring Max in too. The more the merrier!"

Arthur returned to his truck to let out Max. As he, Max, and Beth crowded into the Wardwell's tiny living room, Arthur took one look at the individuals assembled there and said, "Okay, we want in on it."

Beth followed up with, "Whatever it is!"

Everyone laughed.

"We know you had to be spying on Sullivan," Beth said as she walked into the kitchen carrying a pan of huckleberry muffins. Aunt Phil followed her and took small plates out of a cupboard.

"Damn, and here we thought we were so good at being sneaky," Mick said.

"So, you were *all* in on it?" Beth asked from the kitchen, looking around the living room at the gathering. No one said anything so she knew she had guessed right. "How fun is that!" she added, smiling.

"Well, Conrad, we knew you didn't support the bastard, so why else would you have been there?" Arthur said, pulling up a stool from the eating bar in the kitchen.

Without mentioning Richmond, Conrad said, "We had heard he is planning on putting in a destination resort right here in the Metolius Basin."

"Or maybe even in Camp Sherman," Mick added.

"Oh, my!" Beth said. "But this is all National Forest Land."

Dave added, "He's threatening, if he gets in office, to do away with environmental restrictions, minimize the size of national forest lands, and allow development, logging, and mining."

"He talked about starting with the elimination of the entire Deschutes National Forest," Mick added.

"No kidding?" Arthur asked, incredulous. He and Beth exchanged looks.

"What can we do to stop him?" Beth asked.

"Funny you should ask," Mick said. "We were just discussing keeping track of him; who he sees, what they talk about."

"Yeah, we were talking about disguises and following him where ever he goes. We'll need all the help we can get." Dave added.

"Okay, we'll do what we can!" Beth said with a smile. She and Aunt Phil started passing out the plates of muffins.

"One thing for sure," Dave said as he eyed his muffin and then grinned at Beth and Aunt Phil. "With you two around, we won't starve."

Aunt Phil looked at Beth and said, "You know who could help us with costuming and makeup?"

"Sophie Summers!" Beth and Aunt Phil said simultaneously.

"Who's that?" Conrad asked.

"Sophie is a friend who heads up the performing arts theater in Sisters," Beth explained.

"She also owns a hair salon in Sisters. That's how I met her. She lives in her family's cabin just a bit downstream from here," Aunt Phil added.

"I've known her for a long time," Beth continued. "She's trustworthy. We wouldn't have to worry about her spilling any beans."

The men looked at one another, nodded simultaneously, and Conrad said, "Sure. Go get her."

SOPHIE SUMMERS LIVED in a flower surrounded cabin three lots downstream from Aunt Phil and Conrad. When she answered the door to Beth's knock, she was wearing a long dress with flowing sleeves. In her hand was a small pitcher which billowed with sweet peas, pink roses, and purple clematis blossoms. Sophie Summers was a lithe woman of medium height in her late fifties. She wore her mane of kinky rust colored hair tied softly behind her neck. Her brown eyes were surrounded with smile lines and her freckled face beamed with the joy of seeing Beth.

"Oh, hi, Beth! Come on in!"

Beth stayed on the porch and holding open the screen door said, "Actually, Sophie, I came to see if you have a minute to come help us. Phyllis and Conrad and a host of our friends would like to know if you could help us with costuming and makeup for a project we're working on. We're meeting in the Wardwell's cabin as we speak. We're not ready for anything yet, we just are talking about it."

"Count me in, Beth! You know I love doing that kind of thing. I was just going to walk these flowers up to Phyllis, so let's go!"

The two women made their way to Wardwell's cabin by following the dusty path which ran along the Metolius River. Their happy chattering flowed in harmony with the murmuring of the water.

Beth and Sophie entered Wardwell's cabin, bringing in with them the sunshine and the smell of sweet peas. Upon spying Sophie with the flowers, Aunt Phil first covered her mouth with both hands in surprise and then reached for the flowers. "Oh, Sophie! How lovely of you! Sweet peas! My favorite! Come on in here and meet our crew."

The group welcomed Sophie and filled her in on what they knew about Sullivan and his plans. They outlined how they were going to try to keep track of the man and remain one-up on his schemes. Sophie, in good humor, fell in love with the idea of these oldsters sneaking around behind the politician's back and doing what they could to thwart his plans. Loving Camp Sherman and the Deschutes National Forest as much as anybody, she climbed completely on board.

AS THE GEEZER Underground discussed strategy, Adam Carson was making his way up the Mt. Hood freeway from Portland. US 26 was a beautiful drive with the bright colors of vine maple dotting the forested hills. He soon reached the heavily wooded area around the tiny communities of Zigzag and Rhododendron. The forest of huge old growth Douglas firs always made Adam marvel at the beauty of a forest left to its own devices. Here in the Mt. Hood National Forest, like in Camp Sherman, humans tastefully tucked cabins here and there among the trees and allowed the forest to move on, in its own slow pace, providing life and shelter to the animals, birds, plants, and insects which have been on this planet long before humans evolved.

The Oregonian newspaper had quoted Sullivan's comments about opening up national forest land for development, starting with the Deschutes National Forest. If eliminating national forest lands was in Sullivan's sights, the Mt. Hood National Forest had to also be on that list.

Why, oh why, Adam thought as he passed through the heart of this wilderness at the base of 11,240 foot Mt. Hood, cannot people co-exist with nature? The Andre Sullivans of the world and their money grubbing followers had no place here. There were other ways to make money without exploiting the very earth that provides life. These people needed to be stopped and Adam had concluded this was why his Aunt and her friends had made their way into Sullivan's fund raiser. Well, if that was what those old codgers are up to, Adam surmised, they could count him in too.

Once over the summit, the highway swung to the south-east and traveled through the Warm Springs Indian reservation. This was the home of three indigenous tribes who have known for thousands of years how to live without raping the land. Instead of learning from them, the white Europeans who were sweeping this country two hundred years ago suppressed the Indians, confined them to unforgiving, barren land, and decimated their numbers with white man's diseases. A fine way to treat those who got here first.

Adam's journey through the high desert communities of Madras and Redmond went smoothly. The sight of the Central Oregon Cascade Mountains as he approached Sisters always took his breath away. Nearly three hours after he left his cottage in NW Portland, Adam was pulling into the tiny lane that led to his aunt's cabin at Camp Sherman. The small dusty parking area outside the Wardwell's cabin was all but filled with Wardwell's Volvo SUV and Arthur's pickup. Adam found a way to squeeze his Explorer alongside.

"Alright, you hounds," Adam said to his dogs. "You wait here for a sec. I have to make sure it's okay to take you inside. The two of you and Fido are good at creating pandemonium." Adam noticed that the bed of Arthur's pickup was empty, meaning Max had also been invited inside the cabin. "Make that double pandemonium."

When they heard the knock on the door, Aunt Phil said, "If this keeps up, Conrad, we're going to need to add more room onto this cabin."

Dave took a gander around the crowded little room and said, "Yup, it's balls to the walls!"

Aunt Phil opened the door to her smiling nephew and gathered him into her arms. She drank in the smell of him, loved the sturdy feel of him, everything about him. "What a wonderful surprise, Adam! Come on in here! Did you bring the dogs? You're staying, aren't you? Where's your suitcase? Do you want something to eat? Oh, it's good to see you!"

Mick smiled and said to Dave, "Everybody needs an aunt like that."

Dave answered, "Do you suppose she'd adopt us?"

Adam shared hugs and handshakes all around until he noticed an unfamiliar woman sitting quietly on a stool by the kitchen bar. He took in her lovely smiling face and his heart suddenly leapt around wildly in his chest. He quickly looked away and felt somewhat horror struck that he was experiencing the same feeling he did a year ago when he stumbled into a relationship with a gorgeous woman, a relationship which went terribly wrong. He scolded himself, *Goddamn it, Adam, you doofus! Don't let your heart run off with your hormones now, Old Chum. Be cool! Be cool!*

Beth, noticing the anything but cool expression on his face, stepped forward with a smile and said, "Adam, I'd like you to meet Sophie Summers. Sophie, this is our friend Adam Carson from Portland. He's been my attorney for years and is Phyllis's nephew."

Sophie gracefully slipped from the stool and held her hand out to Adam. "Nice to meet you, Mr. Carson."

Adam took her hand in his as though it was a baby bird and tongue tied, stammered, "Nice to meet you too, So.. Sophie." He couldn't take his eyes from her warm brown ones which smiled at him with tiny flecks of sunshine.

"Sophie is my hairdresser and is also the director of a community performing arts center in Sisters," Beth continued, amused at Adam's reaction. "She has a cabin just down river from here and we asked her if she could come by and give us some ideas for makeup and costuming for the project we're working on." Beth looked to Adam and then to Sophie, and back to Adam.

"Adam," Conrad tactfully approached Adam who was still dumbly holding onto Sophie's hand. "Come and sit down and let us tell you what has been going on."

Sophie Summers let her hand slip from Adam's and glancing at Beth with a slight upturn of her mouth, climbed back onto her stool.

Adam suddenly acted like he'd just come to and said, "Oh, let me get the dogs out of the car first, Conrad. They surely have to pee by now."

"Then bring them inside, Adam," Aunt Phil said cheerily, looking at Max, who stood exuberantly wagging his tail and also at Fido who was trying to stay out of the tail's way. "A party is not a party without at least four dogs!"

MEANWHILE, IN A BEND hotel, Andre Sullivan was admiring himself in a mirror. Sullivan pictured himself addressing the U.S. Congress. His only wish was that the U.S. wasn't a democracy so that he could become a dictator. He knew he'd love being a dictator. Wearing nothing more than a watch and socks, he was too self-absorbed to know he looked ridiculous. His self-adoring mood was interrupted by his phone. He answered and listened intently to his campaign manager, Brenda Bailey, his expression going from serene to furious in less than 30 seconds.

"What do you mean, the Metolius Basin is protected by some sort of legislative action? It's called a what? An 'Area of Critical Statewide Concern?' What kind of crap is that? You mean someone has already anticipated someone trying to stick a resort up there? Damn it, damn it, damn it! Now we have to figure out how to get around that or think of something else."

Sullivan paced the floor of his room as he talked, passing back and forth in front of the window, as unconscious as the king in the children's fable that he had no clothes on.

Still barking into the phone he said, "Brenda! You know that old guy with that rundown cabin next to my property? No, on the east side of Green Ridge. Yeah, that one. Remember what we did in Portland? With all those old people? Yeah. See to it."

Sullivan shut up just long enough for Bailey to get a word in edgewise. It didn't take Sullivan long to interrupt. "Damn it, Brenda! You know who will do it. Just get it done!"

CHAPTER 7

AT THE PORTLAND Justice Center, the three homicide detectives convened in Lieutenant Avery's office. Avery told Corporal Banning and Sergeant Kowalski that while they had been at Starbucks and had seen Andre Sullivan's picture on the front page of The Oregonian, he had a vague memory that somewhere in the past, there was a case of a suspicious death involving a home fire and for some reason, the name Sullivan was connected with that case. Avery couldn't put his finger on the name of the deceased as it wasn't his case and the investigating officer was long since retired and had died. Avery sent Jerry Banning to his computer, searching for Andre Sullivan's name in association with any case ever.

The most prominent case Banning found was years ago in Seattle when Sullivan, under the guise of a corporation, acquired grants from the federal government to renovate an old hotel used to house low income people. The first thing he did was evict the tenants with the promise they would be moved back in when the project was finished. His corporation then hired a contractor to do the work. When it was finished, the previous tenants were never moved back in because the hotel was immediately sold for a fortune. The contractor didn't get paid so sued Sullivan's corporation, but the money had disappeared into a vast mish-mash of obscure corporations which did business with offshore banks. The corporation subsequently went bankrupt. Through a bankruptcy judge the contractor and his sub-contractors got paid a vastly reduced amount; whatever, if any, was left from the federal grants.

Trevor Kowalski was tasked with researching past owners of a considerable number of properties in the greater Portland area which Sullivan now owned. Kowalski's project deepened when he researched properties adjacent to the ones owned by Sullivan Properties, LLC. He found that current owners were corporations in which Andre Sullivan was listed in State of Oregon Corporations Division records as a party of interest. Subsequently, Kowalski uncovered entire neighborhoods where the current owners of record were various corporations which all had a connection to Andre Sullivan.

Sullivan had made a bit of a name for himself in the Portland area for acquiring run-down properties from the estates of deceased individuals, fixing up the dwellings to minimal living standards and then either renting out the house or selling it on a contract. What he was known for was not that he acquired the homes from estates of dead people, but that he would, at the first missed payment of the new buyer or renter, quickly evict the tenant in accordance with the stipulations designated in the contract or rental agreement, and turn over the property on a new contract or rental agreement, making a bundle on fees in the process.

Late in the afternoon, the policemen started having some luck with their search. Sergeant Kowalski had made a chart of the properties Sullivan owned from tax records he researched. Going back on each individual property using State of Oregon death records, he could see a trend: all owners were deceased immediately prior to Sullivan or a corporation owned by Sullivan acquiring the property. With Jerry Banning's help, they checked into the Oregon State archives of death certificates. All these previous property owners had three things in common: they had died shortly before title was transferred, the individuals were elderly when they died, and the listed cause of death was vague; either "probable" heart attack or the "results of old age." In some cases, the exact cause was complicated by the bodies being severely burned. Ah-ha! Avery didn't believe in coincidences and now he was able to remember why Sullivan's name rang a bell. Sullivan was so eager to buy those properties, he would often pester the police as to when the investigation was to be completed so he could make a move on purchasing the

48

property from the decedent's estate before anybody else did. Since neither the police nor the medical examiner determined that the deaths were due to criminal activity, nobody connected the dots. Avery suspected that the decedent was considered just another old person who would have died soon anyway, so the death was never considered beyond anyone's expectations.

Another peculiarity was that the pathologist who performed the autopsies on these old people was the same person. A call to this pathologist, the current medical examiner, Dr. Herman Diggs, confirmed Avery's suspicions. When he asked what "probable" means in an autopsy, Dr. Diggs sighed impatiently and said that if the ME had sufficient indicators that pointed to heart disease including the use of blood pressure medication, evidence of alcoholism, smoking, obesity, ear lobe creases and since no crime could be determined, a complete autopsy was not performed. In the instance of "probable" heart attack being the manner of demise of most previous owners of Sullivan's properties, the autopsy reports showed the hearts themselves were not even examined. In the instance where the person died as a "result of old age" it was because he or she died from an existing ailment often associated with old age, such as cancer or organ failure or a compromised immune system. Avery knew of lots of people with cancer, organ failure, or immune system abnormalities who had survived long enough to die of something else, like murder. In many cases, no autopsies were called for because no one in the deceased family felt there was a good reason.

Dr. Diggs, haughty superiority in his voice, said he was very busy and if the Lieutenant had no other questions, he needed to go. Avery thanked him for his time and Dr. Diggs, without saying goodbye, hung up.

Avery hung up the phone in disgust both at the doctor's tone as well the attitude revealed toward the elderly. Avery said to no one in particular, "Yup. It's just another old person. No need for an autopsy. Gonna die anyway. Just gimme my inheritance and let's move on. Shit!"

Thoroughly pissed, he launched himself out of his chair and stomped his way through the squad room to where Corporal Banning's and Sergeant Kowalski's cubicles sat side by side. He entered Banning's cubicle and leaned against the desk. Kowalski stood and hung his long arms over the wall separating the two cubicles. Avery shared with the other two men what he learned upon talking to the medical examiner.

"So, what do we do now?" Jerry Banning looked at Avery and then at Kowalski.

"We can suspicion murder all we want in Sullivan's acquisition of those properties," Avery answered, "but it's too late to prove it on the bodies which were cremated. We won't get authorization to exhume any buried bodies until we have more concrete evidence of foul play. The only thing we can do is keep an eye on Sullivan and get the word out. If every lawman in the state keeps a close eye on this guy's business dealings, he'll trip up sometime and we'll get him. I'm going to go call Cyril Richmond and see what he knows about this guy. Sullivan seems to be currently concentrating on Central Oregon. Right now, Jefferson County is the best one to watch what he's currently up to."

DEPUTY CYRIL RICHMOND was in his truck when Avery's call came to his cell phone.

"Deputy Richmond, this is Shawn Avery, Portland Police."

"Lieutenant! Are you finally ready to come over here and do a little fly fishing? They're rising to May flies as we speak and the store just got in a shipment of brand new ones."

"I wish I was, Cyril. But I have a situation I'd like to discuss with you."

"Shoot!"

"Andre Sullivan," Avery said.

"Crap in a bucket! What the heck has he been doing over there in Portland-land?"

"Well, we did some snooping and found that years ago up in Seattle he defrauded the government on a low income housing renovation. He was never charged because his involvement was buried in a vast network of phony corporations. More recently here in Portland he started buying up properties from the estates of old dead people. Now he's renting the houses out or selling them on contracts and evicting the tenant upon first offense.

He has made a bundle in fees and late charges every time he turns one over."

"He's been a busy boy over there."

"In retrospect," Avery continued, "reviewing the autopsies and death certificates of the previous owners of those lots, we're not positive there were no crimes committed. The causes of death were all too similar and equally vague; the word probable kept popping up."

"Ah. I know. It means no one bothered to be positive as to the cause of death because they were old people. 'Old' equates to dying and soon."

"You've got it! So, what I'm saying, I understand he's in your jurisdiction right now. I thought I'd give you a heads up to what we suspect is his MO."

"I appreciate that, Shawn."

"Another thing: the properties he acquired were close to other properties he already owned. So, bit by bit, he builds a little empire of properties that are all together."

"So, at some point in time, he can sell it off as a whole."

"You took the words outta my mouth."

Cyril Richmond thought for a moment and said, "He has purchased a couple of pieces of land, one on each side of Green Ridge, from the lumber companies that sold off some acres years ago. There are some privately owned pieces around here, more than you'd think, especially on the eastern side of the ridge. Do you know who Arthur Perkins is?"

"Yes, as well as Beth Welton," Avery answered.

"Years ago, a lumber company bailed on a whole bunch of property on the east side of the ridge. Perkins purchased his lot then and so did Sullivan. I'd have to look at a plot map to be sure, but I think Arthur shares a boundary with Sullivan."

"Yikes!"

"You're thinking what I am, Shawn?"

"Sullivan buys up a bunch of adjoining properties and does something with it, like a resort or something."

"Exactly! He's been thwarted from using land west of the ridge because several individuals from Camp Sherman persuaded the State Legislature to protect the Metolius Basin. Sullivan may try to usurp that declaration, we don't know. However, east of the ridge is still pretty much free game."

"Well, keep an eye on him, Cyril."

"Will do and thanks for the heads up."

THE MEETING AT the Wardwell's cabin began to wind down. Sophie Summers slid from her stool. She announced to the group that she would go to her cabin and bring back some make-up supplies for whenever they would be ready to pursue finding Sullivan. Adam offered to walk with her.

"Okay!" she said as she looked into Adam's friendly hazel eyes. "Have you ever walked the river trail to the Allingham Bridge and back? It's a loop, down one side of the river and back up the other side. It's only about a two mile round trip and it's really pretty.

"Nope, never have," Adam said frankly and returned her smile.

"Okay! From here, we can go back upstream to the store and cross the river there, then follow the trail downstream to the Allingham Bridge, cross again and come back up this side of the river. I'll get my stuff at my cabin before we come back here."

"Lead the way!"

"Oh," Sophie added as she spied Adam's two bulldogs looking forlornly as though Adam was going to abandon them forever. "Do you want to take your dogs?"

"Sure, if you don't mind."

"No, of course not."

Conrad said, "Do you have leashes, Adam?"

Aunt Phil smiled happily at her husband as he assumed a parental role although he was never fated to be one.

"Yes, Conrad, in the Explorer."

Conrad said, "OK, off you go then." His eyes smiled as he watched Adam and Sophie leave, the dogs scampering beside them.

The Allingham trail was as Sophie had said, a loop, down one side of the river and back up the other side. Adam and Sophie back tracked to the store, crossed the river, and then followed the trail downstream, often stopping to let the dogs sniff and rustle around in the brush. Adam thought that perhaps his newly adopted female Bulldog, Noodles, had never been on a hike before. The spunky little dog wagged what bit of a tail she had and ran this way and that, dragging a laughing Sophie with her.

They walked alongside the clear blue Metolius River. The water gurgled and rushed along a rocky river bed that had harbored the eggs and smolt of native fish for millions of years. Humans had lent a hand by enhancing the stream with fallen logs to help provide quiet pools where migrating fish could rest and their babies could find safe hiding places.

Sophie often stopped and looked into the water with practiced eyes hoping to spy the bright red backs of Kokanee salmon who were due to start arriving at their spawning grounds. She pointed out to Adam the yellow leaves of the tamarack trees; one of the few confers which loses its needles in the fall, and marks the pine forest with bright splashes of color. She found herself compelled to show this sweet, quiet man all the unique bits of charm which made the Metolius River Basin so very special to her.

"So what brought you to Camp Sherman, Sophie?" Adam asked, brushing the tall strands of bunch grass away from his face.

"My parents spent many summers here, Adam," she answered over her shoulder as they made their way down the trail. "The beauty of this place left such a deep impression on me that I feel as though I grew up here."

How similar was this story to Beth Welton's childhood and why, when Beth's world fell apart in Portland, she was also drawn to the sanctuary of the mountains and forests of her memory.

When they arrived at Sophie's cabin, Sophie quickly popped inside to grab her makeup kit. When she came back out the door, Adam, who had been holding the dogs, asked her about the cabin's history.

"In 1930 my grandparents built this cabin. When they both passed in the 1970's, my parents kept the cabin in the family. About ten years ago when my marriage was over, I moved to Sisters and opened a small hair styling salon. I maintain a small apartment over my salon and spend the winters there. I volunteer with the community theater in Sisters but spend the summers here at the cabin. Both the Sisters and Camp Sherman communities have embraced me and treated me like a long, lost daughter even though I really am a bit of an outsider."

"So does the land your cabin is on belong to the Forest Service like Aunt Phil's?"

"Yes. We all have long term leases for the land along the river but the cabins belong to us. Now, where your friends Beth and Arthur live on the east side or opposite side of Green Ridge from us, that land is privately owned. Some of it still belongs to the Forest Service but some pieces are privately owned like Beth and Arthur's. A lumber company also owns a lot of it. So, theoretically, that could all be bought up for private development. Now, on this side of Green Ridge, as long as the Forest Service owns this land, we don't have to worry about someone coming along and buying it. Having said that, if some pirate like Andre Sullivan can get in a federal office, all of that could change."

"Well, if Aunt Phil and her friends have anything to do about it, that won't happen."

"I admire their spunk!" Sophie replied. "They are good examples of what to become as we get older, don't you think?"

"Yes. You bet I do. Sometimes I get exhausted just trying to keep up."

Sophie's laughter brightened an already sunny day. The two talked non-stop, finding comfort in each other's company as though they had known each other for years. The uncanny coincidence was not lost on either of them. By the time they neared Wardwell's cabin, each bore a glow of perspiration, and a comfortable bond had formed.

Also after the meeting, Dave and Mick returned to the post office to resume their work on the crossword puzzle. Old Bowels clattered up in his ragged 1947 Ford pickup and, upon spying Mick and Dave, pulled over and slid out from behind the driver's seat. When he closed the truck's door, the entire vehicle shook as though to fall to pieces. Approaching the post office, he asked worriedly if either Mick or Dave had seen Wilbur Martin.

"Nope," Dave answered.

Mick added, "Other than Dave, Wilbur is the craziest old coot still allowed to run loose around here. Maybe he finally got locked up."

"Nah, I don't think so. Yesterday he was supposed to meet me to go fishin' and he never showed up. I went by his cabin and knocked but he wasn't there. This mornin' I drove over to his cabin again and he still wasn't there. I don't know what's goin' on. Since his daughter moved back East, he doesn't have anywhere to go, 'cept the store or fishin' or climbing yet another mountain. If he was planning on going climbing, he wouldn't have agreed to fish yesterday."

"Is his truck there?" Dave asked.

"Yup."

"Did you go inside his cabin?" Mick asked.

"Nope, but maybe I ought to do that, huh?"

Both Mick and Dave stood as Dave said, "We'll go with you."

The three duffers piled into Old Bowel's pickup and rattled off. It didn't take long to reach the dusty track into Wilbur Martin's twenty-five acres on the east side of Green Ridge. Martin's cabin was a single-story log structure that had squatted in a small clearing since 1928. Pine needles occupied the majority of the aged shake roof and the cabin's small mullioned windows were hazy with grime. The front door hinges loudly protested the opening of the unlocked door. All three men suddenly stepped back as the pungent odor of death wafted out the door and washed over them.

Stepping back another step, Old Bowels said, "Mick, yer the doc. You go in first. I don't think I can do this."

"Thanks a lot."

"We'll do it together," Dave said as he stepped around Old Bowels and into the doorway.

After some minor shuffling at the door, the three entered the cabin's main living space. A dilapidated couch and upholstered chair sat in front of a lava rock fireplace. The fireplace separated the living area from an old fashioned kitchen with a small but very cold wood stove. Through an opening onto a screened-in sun porch, they spied a boot lying on the floor. Attached to the boot sprawled the very dead body of Wilbur Martin.

"Aw, shit, Wilbur! Nooooo!" said Old Bowels as he started for the body of his friend.

Mick grabbed Old Bowel's arm and said, "There's nothing we can do for him and this may be a crime scene. We need to get out of here."

Dave pulled out his cell phone and said, "Let's get Cyril Richmond up here."

CHAPTER 8

DEPUTY CYRIL RICHMOND stood in the ragged front yard of Wilbur Martin's cabin. Inside the log structure, a crime scene team was going over everything, and by the direction of Richmond, doing it a second time. Richmond and the crime scene team had just come from a cabin fire and resulting forest fire that occurred overnight near Summit Spring, not far from Wilbur's cabin. The forest fire had been quickly squelched by the Sisters-Camp Sherman Fire Department which was still at the scene mopping up after the fire. The cabin that burned had belonged to an elderly recluse by the name of Emil Emerson. He lived alone with his dog. The old man's badly burned body was found in the cabin debris. The dog appeared to be missing.

Richmond had crossed his arms over his chest and was chewing on his mustache as he thought about his discussion with Lieutenant Shawn Avery of the Portland Police Bureau. A quick check of property tax records had revealed that Wilbur Martin's twenty-five acres and Emil Emerson's fifteen acres bordered on Andre Sullivan's thirty acres. Were these two deaths of solitary old men due to the same MO that Sullivan was suspected of in the Portland area?

Richmond soon resorted to pacing in front of Wilbur's cabin while he waited. He stewed over his fear that Jefferson County had possibly become a target for Andre Sullivan's greed. Not only due to the resources in the mountains and forests, but the county was large and grossly underfunded because of a low population. This condition left the county prime for exploitation by those who chose to step outside the law. If so, the only thing standing in Sullivan's way was one small Sheriff's office. The pressure of this threat came crashing down on the deputy's shoulders like a falling old growth Ponderosa pine. What Richmond didn't know was that he had at his back a gang of very determined old people.

Two of which were patiently waiting out by the road. Old Bowels had left Dave and Mick to wait for the police while he went home to phone Wilbur's daughter with the bad news that her father had passed away. As the two oldsters watched Richmond pace, Mick said, "He looks worried."

"More than usual?"

"Yes, to the mustache chewing level."

"Do you suppose he thinks this has something to do with Andre Sullivan?"

Mick looked at Dave and replied, "Maybe. What do you think?"

"It does seem strange that Wilbur was going fishing one day and is dead the next, even at his age. If this was the work of Sullivan or his minions, we need to move fast and not let any of them out of our sight."

"Right. Oh, here comes Richmond." The two clammed up and turned to face the deputy.

"Boys," Cyril Richmond said, "I'll give you a lift to the Camp Sherman store. The crime scene team is just about finished here and the coroner is on his way to pick up Wilbur's body as well as what is left of Emerson's. They have to go to Portland for the autopsies 'cause they don't do 'em at the State Police lab in Bend anymore." Richmond then did a double take at Mick and Dave and reading their faces said, "What are you guys up to?"

The two looked at one another and said in unison, "Us?"

"Yeah, you. Do I need to tell you, and this includes the rest of the Geezer Underground, to stay out of the investigation of Wilbur's death?"

"Huh? Us?"

"I thought so. Listen," Richmond put his hands on his hips which wasn't easy because of his duty belt which bristled with all sorts of fearsome apparatus, "this Sullivan thing may or may not be getting dicey. Absolutely no way are you guys to try to do anything about it. Do you hear what I'm saying?"

"Huh? Us?"

Richmond rolled his eyes and opening the door to his pickup ordered, "Get in the back seat."

The back seat of Deputy Richmond's truck was essentially a jail cell without the toilet. The windows were barred and would not open. The doors locked from the outside and there were no door handles on the inside. A bullet proof window separated the front seat from the back. There was a small sliding door within this window but it was closed and remained so as Richmond fired up his truck and they headed off, spewing gravel in all directions.

Dave turned to Mick and asked dryly, "Do you think we pissed him off?"

"Yeah, the guy can fucking read minds."

"That makes him a good cop but he still needs us. He doesn't know it, but he needs us."

"Yeah."

THE TRIP BACK to Camp Sherman didn't take long and during the ride, Cyril Richmond made several calls from the cab of his truck. Neither Dave nor Mick could overhear due to the thickness of the window. When they arrived at the Camp Sherman store parking lot, Richmond drove right past and headed down the lane to Wardwell's cabin. Pulling to a stop in front of the little dwelling, Richmond got out of the truck and opened the back door so Mick and Dave could slide out.

"Come with me, please," Richmond said as he strode to the cabin's front door.

Conrad answered the knock. "Conrad," Richmond began, "if Phyllis is here, I'd like to have a word with all of you," motioning to where Mick and Dave stood behind him, "may we come in?"

"Why, of course!" Conrad stood back while the men entered. Conrad looked questioningly at Mick and Dave who just shrugged.

Aunt Phil came out of the kitchen wiping her hands on a towel. Richmond acknowledged her with a smile and a nod but remained standing as the others settled around the small living space.

"I thought I'd give you an update into our investigation into Andre Sullivan," Richmond began. "I can't tell you much because it's still an ongoing investigation. You know that. What I can tell you is that we think he's slimier than we had ever imagined and is possibly also very dangerous."

Richmond scanned the faces of everybody in the room. Four sets of intelligent eyes looked back at him and he knew that try as he might, there was no way he was going to fool any of these oldsters. They had seen just about everything during their long lives, done most of it, invented a lot of it and therefore little could surprise them. He also knew that any one of them would throw caution into the wind in a heartbeat if they felt it would do some common good.

"I want to make sure I'm clear with each and every one of you. Do not interfere with this investigation in any way! Please! If we discover anything I can share with you, I will do that. I promise. In the meantime, just lay low. However, if you do hear on the grapevine anything about this man, no matter how seemingly remote, please share with me. At this point, the Sheriff's Office is flying blind and we are not entirely sure what we are up against. We'll need all the info we can get."

As Richmond returned to his truck, he hoped he had given them enough information to keep them out of trouble, but, at the same time, given them something to do by keeping their eyes and ears open and to report any gossip they ran across. By so doing, he hoped he could keep them safe. He settled behind the wheel, feeling that he possibly had diverted the worry he felt for involving the Geezer Underground in the first place. However, he found himself still fuming. Muttering to himself, he said, "If Sullivan disturbs as much as a hair on any of those old people, I'll pound that son of a bitch into the ground so far even Google won't be able to find him!"

THE DUST FROM Richmond's truck hung in the warm, still air. Inside the Wardwell's cabin, Dave, Mick, Conrad and Aunt Phil looked around the room at each other. Aunt Phil, already having been informed about Emil Emerson's death and his burned out cabin said quietly, "Something else must have gone terribly wrong."

Mick and Dave explained about the death of Wilbur Martin and how the sheriff's men also treated his cabin like a crime scene. "Cyril paced and fussed and I was afraid he was going to have a mental hernia worrying about what the crime scene team was finding."

"He told us to lay low," Conrad said. "But, heck, we'll have plenty of time to do that after we're dead! We have to get this show on the road and keep track of that mudder fudder Sullivan."

"My thoughts exactly." Aunt Phil was often amazed how Conrad's and her own thoughts often ran parallel. She looked out the window and said, "Oh, good, here comes Adam... and our darling costume and makeup consultant, Sophie!"

Conrad got up from his chair and said, "I'll call Beth and Arthur and get them back over here."

BETH AND ARTHUR, having been summoned, were at the Wardwell's cabin in just a few minutes. Mick and Dave filled everyone in on the death of Wilbur Martin and the information Deputy Richmond had told them, plus all they had gleaned from what Richmond was tactfully vague about. They all agreed that they needed to make a move to track Sullivan and those individuals closest to him. In order to do that, they needed to acquire tracking equipment and get it installed on any vehicles being used by the Sullivan crew. Just where to get it and how to make it work remained a puzzle until Aunt Phil and Conrad locked eyes and said in unison, "Tommy Jax!"

Tommy Jax was a reformed thug who had made Aunt Phil's acquaintance while he was being hauled in on a murder charge in Washington State's King County. Aunt Phil had been a criminal defense attorney in Seattle and was able to exonerate Jax on a technicality. She shrewdly sniffed out a mix up in the crime scene investigation which made Tommy Jax a free man and the Sheriff and County Prosecutor impotently furious. Jax never forgot the favor Aunt Phil had done for him and resolved to turn his life around. He and his partner, a very peculiar man by the name of Oliver, lived in opulent luxury in an abandoned brewery in the scummiest of scummy places in the warehouse district of Seattle. Just what they did for a living no one wanted to ask. However, Aunt Phil and Conrad knew that Jax was just the guy to set them up with an illegal tracking system.

Conrad and Aunt Phil informed everyone on who and what Tommy Jax was. Aunt Phil went to the kitchen to use the cabin's land line to phone Jax in Seattle. Meanwhile, Conrad fired up his laptop. He went into Jefferson County's tax records to see who else besides Wilbur Martin and Emil Emerson owned property on Green Ridge in the same vicinity as Andre Sullivan. What he found chilled him to the bone: on the south side of Sullivan's land lay twenty acres in the names of Arthur Perkins and Beth Welton.

CHAPTER 9

ANDRE SULLIVAN WAS lounging in his Oxford Hotel room in Bend with one cowboy booted foot resting on a small coffee table. There was a glass of bourbon in his hand and a half-empty bottle on the table. He answered his cell phone on the first ring.

"Andre, we gotta talk." The voice on the other end was rushed, panicked.

"I'm busy, Doc."

"No! We gotta talk now! A cop called me!"

Andre was silent for a moment.

"What kind of cop?"

"Portland police; a Lieutenant Avery. He's with homicide, Andre, ho-micide!"

"What did he want?"

"What do you think he wants? He asked all sorts of questions about autopsies and death certificates for old people. Although he wasn't specific, I think he's questioning what we did with all those elderly property owners, Andre."

"You're imagining that, Hermie. It couldn't be connected."

"Andre! Are you kidding? Of course it is!"

"Just a minute, Cousin, just a minute. I'm thinking."

"You gotta do more than think, man. This will open up the whole can of worms; the prostitute ring with those missing women, and your 16 year-old sweetie. You remember her? What was her name? Did you even know her name? Andre?"

"It's not my fault those prostitutes died! You're the one who botched the abortions. And the girl's name was Candy."

"Candy. Sure it was, you pervert. Wouldn't your constituents love that story?"

"Don't threaten me, you bastard! I know enough to send you to death row. I know what you did to your sister."

There was tense silence on both ends of the connection.

"Damn you, Andre!" another moment of silence. Then the voice continued, "Another thing, 'Senator', today I get this message Jefferson County is sending me two more old dead guys. One is severely burned. They died alone in their homes, cabins up on Green Ridge. You have property on Green Ridge, don't you, Andre?' Are these guys more of yours? Are you operating over there too?"

"Just do them like you did the others."

"This cop is on to something! I can hear it in his voice. You gotta put a stop to this. You've gone to the well too many times! I'm sick of doing this shit."

"Shut up and stop worrying! I'll have him taken care of."

"Who? Avery? Are you nuts? They don't operate alone, you know. You can't eliminate the entire Portland Police Bureau!"

"I think you need to leave Portland. Now!"

"Maybe, but there's no place I can hide, Andre. You can't either. They'll be all over us like flies!"

"Don't get hysterical, on me, Herman! I gotta talk to some people. I'll get back to you."

Andre Sullivan hung up without saying another word and refilled his glass of bourbon, this time to the top. This kind of crap drove him nuts! He sat for a moment, looking at the opposite wall but not seeing it. He sipped the bourbon. It burned all the way down his throat.

WHEN CONRAD TOLD the group whose cabin shared a border with Sullivan's, all eyes turned to Beth and Arthur. Beth said, "You don't suppose Sullivan is planning ahead in case he loses the election and can't abolish any National Forest land for his resort? Now he's looking at the east side of Green Ridge?"

"Well, there is a lot of land over there which is privately owned." Arthur added, "Years ago that big lumber company sold off a bunch of stuff. I suppose Sullivan thinks he can buy it up piece by piece if he can do away with the owners and eventually have enough to sell to a developer or develop it himself." Beth and Arthur's eyes grew large as they turned to each other and needed no words to convey that they should return to their cabin. "You guys will have to excuse us. I think," and here Arthur looked at Beth and received her nod of approval, "we need to both stay with the cabin until this whole Sullivan thing gets sorted out." He then said to Beth, "Let's also look into security systems. Damn! Who'd think we'd need that here, of all places?"

Adam offered, if their guest room was available, to spend the nights with them until they had a security system installed. "With Max as a fourth sentry, we should be able to detect if any of Sullivan's dirty minions come around."

"Good! Thanks, Adam!" Beth commented, "Certainly Booger will be no help."

"He'll hide in the rafters." Arthur stood up and said, "Well, we better leave. We hate to jump ship, but hopefully it won't be for long. Maybe just until we find out how Wilbur Martin and Emil Emerson died."

"In the meantime," Conrad addressed the crowd. "We have to find Sullivan and his henchmen. If he's still in Bend, he's probably at the Oxford. He'd turn his nose up at anyplace else."

Mick suggested, "Dave, let's you and I dress like homeless guys. We can shuffle and stagger around like drunks and, at the same time, place tracking devices on their cars."

"Sounds good to me," Dave replied. "But how does that make us any different than we are now?"

"Oh, I dunno. Maybe not shave or bathe for a while. We'll need to get some crummy clothes."

"Your closet will do."

Mick rolled his eyes and said, "Actually, I was thinking about a thrift store."

"Oh, okay," Dave stood up. "Let's roll. Since we have to go to Bend, we can prowl around and see if we can spot Sullivan. Go into a few bars and ask if anybody's seen him."

Sophie stood and offered to go along to help select convincing apparel.

"I'll drive," Adam announced. He dug his keys out of his pocket and said to Phyllis, "Aunt Phil, would you dog sit while we're gone?"

"Sure, honey. Good luck and be careful! You won't know who will overhear you asking questions about Sullivan."

"We'll pose as reporters or something." Adam gave her a kiss on the cheek. He noticed how soft and fragrant she was. "Don't worry."

She said, "In the place of my sister, your dear departed mother, it's my job as your aunt to worry. You can't stop me."

THE LITTLE SQUAD of Adam, Sophie, Mick and Dave pulled to the curb in front of a shabby thrift shop on the outskirts of Bend. Sophie bounded eagerly out of the Explorer and trotted through the front door of the store. This was going to be fun for her and she was pumped. Mick and Dave were not so enthused and slid out of the back seat somewhat reluctantly. Adam was amused by it all and followed the gang into the store.

Sophie walked to a rack of men's coats, shuffled them about, and pulled out one. She looked to Mick and back at the coat and then to Mick again. "Here," she said, handing it to Mick. "Try this on."

Mick shrugged into the coat and stood with the coat's shoulders half way down his upper arms, his hands not even visible at the bottom of the sleeves. The hem of the coat hung to his knees. Sophie beamed at him and said, "Perfect!"

"Yeah?" Mick said as he looked into the hollow end of a sleeve for the end of his arm.

"Sure. You're homeless, remember? You'll wear whatever you can find. We'll get it back to the cabin, rip a shoulder halfway off, drag it in the dirt and you'll be all set."

"Gee," Mick said, still looking for the end of his arm.

Sophie then surveyed a rack of pants, picked a pair with a 48 inch waist, scurried over to a shoe rack, looked at Mick again, and fished out a pair of shoes which had to be three sizes too big. "Here," she announced triumphantly. "Toss these pants and shoes into a pile with the coat and drive over the whole mess a time or two with your truck. We'll hold the pants up with these," she said as she jerked a pair of suspenders out of a pile.

"Gee," Mick repeated.

"Now, for you, Dave. How about if we make you an old, feeble guy?"

"Okay," Dave answered. "That should be easy."

"Adam," Sophie said with a smile to Adam who had been leaning up against a rack of shirts, enjoying watching Sophie at work.

"Yes, Ma'am!"

"Go ask the clerk if they have any walkers or those crutches with the arm band thingies."

"Okay!"

As Adam consulted with the clerk, Sophie cast an assessing eye at Dave and again dove into the rack of pants. Less than three minutes later, she had pants, shirt, jacket, and shoes which she guaranteed Dave wouldn't fit.

The clerk happily rang up the bill, including a walker which looked as though it had been thrown over the edge of the Grand Canyon. The crew took off again. This time it was for downtown.

Andre Sullivan was not hard to find. Adam pulled his Ford Explorer to the curb just down the street from the Oxford Hotel in downtown Bend. As soon as he stepped out of the car, he could hear angry voices coming from an open window high on the side of the hotel. Adam stepped back into the car and lowered all four windows so that Mick, Dave, and Sophie could also hear the argument. Although most of the words were hard to make out, it was clear that the unmistakably whiny voice of Andre Sullivan was admonishing some poor shmuck who was inside the room with him.

"When I say 'burn it' I mean burn it! Either do a complete job or hit the road! Your ilk are a dime a dozen, Brenda!"

The answer was not audible, but it wasn't long before Sullivan's campaign manager, Brenda Bailey, stormed out the front door of the hotel and got into a Mercedes SUV parked along the curb. Slamming the door and starting the engine with a roar, Bailey blasted off down the street and turned the corner, the Mercedes tires screeching their protest.

"Let's go!" Mick commanded and Adam wheeled the Explorer into an illegal U-turn and shot down the street in pursuit of the Mercedes. Bailey led them out Franklin Avenue, under the Parkway, and out to 3rd Street or US Highway 97. There she turned right against the light and charged off to the south, weaving in and out of traffic. Adam lost ground at the light but when he turned the corner, all eyes inside the Explorer were riveted on the highway ahead trying to spot the Mercedes.

"There she is!" Sophie, Dave, and Mick said in unison as they spied the Mercedes abruptly turn into the parking lot of a sleazy motel showing little upkeep since being built in the late 1940's.

The Explorer cruised past the motel, with all eyes searching the parking lot for the Mercedes which had pulled in front of a unit numbered, 12.

"How lucky can we get?" Adam said triumphantly. "With just one trip, we know where Sullivan is and also where either Bailey is staying or where she is visiting persons possibly associated with Sullivan's dirty deeds."

"Did someone with better eyes than mine get her license number?" Dave asked hopefully.

"I did!" Sophie said from the front seat. I'm writing it down as we speak.

"Good!" Mick added. "Let's head for the barn."

SEVERAL HOURS LATER, in rays of the late afternoon sun, a huge Bentley Mulsanne ghosted past the Camp Sherman store's parking lot and squeezed down the dusty track to Wardwell's cabin. The car was so quiet it seemed as though it didn't even raise dust. It floated to a stop in Wardwell's parking space.

"Good job, Oliver!" came a deep voice from the back seat. "I never could have found this place on my own."

A fleeting smile graced the thin face of the man named Oliver. He knew Tommy Jax was well aware of the superb guidance system on the car, but appreciated the good intentions of the compliment.

The driver's door opened and Oliver placed one booted foot onto the soft dirt of the forest floor. The rest of his body, an odd contraption of long, reedy limbs, unfolded itself from the car as though made from a Gilbert Erector Set. Gaunt was hardly the word to describe Oliver. Skeletal was more accurate. He then opened the back door for Jax.

In direct contrast to Oliver, Tommy Jax was a man whose body was anything but subtle. Jax extracted all of his nearly four hundred pounds from the back seat. The suspension system of the Bentley audibly sighed in relief. Jax took in all of the Ponderosa pine forest surrounding the little cabin, the murmuring of the Metolius River as it gurgled past, the cries of woodpeckers, and the scolding chatter of a pine squirrel.

"Wow!" was all he could say. He looked at Oliver who, quite Oliver-like, replied only with a smile in his eyes; this was truly a wondrous place.

They heard a screen door bang shut and looked up to see Conrad approaching them from across the small yard.

"T.J! Oliver! How good to see you!" Conrad greeted the two men with handshakes and the manly slapping of shoulders. He couldn't help but compare Oliver's cold and boney hand to the huge, warm and soft paw of Tommy Jax. "You have no idea how much we appreciate you helping us out," Conrad continued. "We think we may be up against a real psycho."

"Psychos are right up our alley, Conrad," Tommy Jax laughed, eagerly pumping Conrad's hand.

Aunt Phil emerged from the cabin and was immediately engulfed in an enormous hug from Jax. Oliver shyly extended his hand for a shake which Aunt Phil gently accepted, afraid he'd dissolve into dust if she hugged him.

Aunt Phil invited the men to come inside the cabin. Jax took one look at the diminutive size of the doorway and then noticed there was a picnic table on a grassy spot overlooking the river.

"Let's go over there!" Jax indicated toward the table. "Oliver, would you please get the equipment out of the trunk?"

As Oliver moved towards the back of the car, Jax explained to Conrad and Aunt Phil, "We brought some tracking equipment and if we can get it installed, we'll be able to follow your creepy candidate and any of his henchmen. The trick will be to get it installed."

Dave, Mick, Adam and Sophie had spilled out of the cabin by now and introductions were made all around. Dave looked at the group and said, "Well, we're just the bunch to do it!"

CHAPTER 10

AS EVERYONE GATHERED around the picnic table, Tommy Jax explained the system he and Oliver were going to use to track Sullivan and his minions.

"Vehicle tracking relies on two things," Jax began, "global positioning satellites and a cellular system. The coordinates are transmitted to the tracking computer which will then send that information to Oliver's phone. The phone has a GPS screen much like what's in a car. Each car we place a bug on will show up on the screen in a color unique to that bug. That way, we'll know which car is which but, of course, we can't tell which person is driving which car.

"Now Phyllis has explained that there is scant cell service here in Camp Sherman so Oliver and I have rented a house at Black Butte Ranch to use as our headquarters, so to speak. We have already set up the tracking computer in the house, and as soon as we get the bugs placed on the cars, we'll be all set. The computer will sound an alarm whenever one of the bugged cars starts moving, so we'll be able to keep track 24 hours per day."

"Wow! How cool is that?" Dave said, being the computer guy.

"Now, our challenge is to find and bug all the cars," Mick announced. "We have done some preliminary surveillance and found where Sullivan is staying, which is at the Oxford in Bend. We also identified one vehicle his campaign manager was driving. She led us to a scummy motel out on US 97. Other than that, we don't know how many people he has with him or how many vehicles are going to be involved."

"Well, that's a start," Jax replied. "I understand you have developed some disguises?"

"Yes," Aunt Phil explained. "Sophie here. . ." Sophie Summers blushed at the attention and Adam felt his heart do its leaping thing. "Sophie," Aunt Phil went on, "is a volunteer at the community theater in Sisters and is a makeup specialist. She has outfitted Mick and Dave with stuff to make them look like homeless guys."

"With all due respect to Sophie," Dave said, "she didn't have to go very far to make us look like that."

Everyone laughed, including Mick.

"Okay," Jax continued, "do you know how many vehicles we should prepare for?"

Conrad answered, "one for sure, a Mercedes SUV. Sullivan must have one for himself at the hotel, and for henchmen, we don't know."

"Well, what do you think, Oliver," Jax went on. "We can be assured that Sullivan doesn't do his own dirty work, so do you think at least two more?"

Oliver gave Tommy Jax an almost invisible nod.

"So we should be prepared for three and, to be safe, four vehicles. We have that many sets of bugs, don't we?"

Again the subtle nod. Then Oliver retrieved from a briefcase, four sets of two sensors each in plastic zip bags. He tossed these onto the table. All the sensors were black but the bags were marked with the color the sensors would register on Oliver's phone: red, black, blue, and yellow.

"Each set has two sensors. We'll place them in different places on each car. In case one falls off, we'll have a backup," Jax explained.

"Cool! Now all we have to do is find the cars and plant the bugs,"
Conrad said.

"Well, we have located one car, so we can start with that," Dave suggested. "Let's start at the Oxford Hotel. If we can't find the Mercedes there, we can head on out to that sleazy motel."

"Okay! Let's roll," Mick said, standing.

"Wait a sec," Dave said. "Where on the car do we plant these sensors and how do they stick on?"

"Easy," Jax answered. "There is a sticky substance on the back of each sensor. You just peel off the tape which covers the stuff and stick the bug on. We've found this more effective than magnets because not all car parts are steel. If you don't have much time, stick them where ever they won't be readily seen. We always try to put one under a fender and, if you have time to place the other one, put it inside the back or front bumper."

Always? There seemed to be so much to learn about this man Tommy Jax that Conrad wasn't sure he really wanted to know.

"Who all is going on this mission?" Aunt Phil asked.

Both Mick and Dave pointed to each other and said, "Him."

"Oliver should also go in case you have a problem with the equipment," Jax said. "And, in addition to the driver, one more for a spotter. That probably should be it for now. If you get ID'd by Sullivan or his minions, the fewer of us they know about the better."

"I'll be the spotter," Adam offered.

"Good thinking, T.J." Conrad said and smiled to himself when Jax referred to himself and Oliver as members of the team. He speculated neither Oliver nor Tommy Jax knew Sullivan from Bozo the Clown, but as soon as Phyllis explained what the man was trying to do, both Jax and Oliver came on board and appeared as intent to foil Sullivan's plans as anybody.

"One more thing," Jax said as he pulled another plastic bag out of the box. All four of you get a small radio and a wireless earpiece. The radio," here Jax held up a device about the size of a pack of cigarettes, "goes in your pocket and the earpiece fits into your ear canal so that it doesn't show. These are on all the time so that you can all talk to each other without using cell phones which would be pretty obvious to anyone watching. While Mick and Dave are doing the bugging, the driver and spotter can hear everything that is going on and sound an alarm if suspicious persons or police come around."

Adam asked, "What car should we use? I'd offer the Explorer but we don't know if Sullivan saw us leave the hotel hot on his assistant's heels."

"You're right, Adam," Jax said. "And the Bentley is hardly a subtle pursuit vehicle."

"We can use my Prius," Dave suggested. "Nobody would suspect a Prius

73

driver to be anything but totally wholesome."

"Yes, but you have one," Mick said, chortling.

"Right, but it's really my wife's buggy. She lets me use it only on the rare occasion when she doesn't want to bother hauling me around, like today."

"Okay!" Mick exclaimed. "Come on, Dave, let's get garbed up."

The two charged off to Wardwell's cabin to put on their costumes. When they emerged twenty minutes later, not even Roger or Kathy White, owners of the Camp Sherman Store, would have known them. Dave leaned heavily on the walker. His shirt was unbuttoned and untucked, leaving a dirty and tattered undershirt showing, the outfit was finished off with scuffed shoes and saggy, unmatched socks. Sophie had smeared his face with real dirt and also rubbed it into his hair. She told him to grab handfuls of dirt and rub it around his knuckles and fingernails. Mick was outfitted nearly the same, with the exception of the jacket which was miles too large. Sophie had torn out the hem in the back, leaving the lining hanging and shredded. At the last minute, she handed him an empty wine bottle in a dirty paper bag.

Oliver was already behind the wheel of the Prius and Adam was riding shotgun when Mick climbed in the back seat and Dave piled in after him, walker and all. Then they were off!

As the dust from the Prius hung in the still afternoon air, Conrad turned to Aunt Phil and said, "Oh, to be a fly on the wall!"

"Well, if one of you doesn't mind driving my car," Tommy Jax suggested, "we can follow, but at a discrete distance, of course. We can also keep our eyes open for anybody watching Dave and Mick place the bugs."

"Mind?" Aunt Phil said. Then she eagerly turned to Conrad and said, "Hey, do you wanna arm wrestle to see who gets to drive a Bentley?"

"Nah, you go ahead," Conrad said with a wink at Jax. "You always beat me at arm wrestling."

"Aw, you're so sweet, honey. How 'bout I drive in to Bend and you can drive back. Is that okay with you, T.J.? I mean I don't get honked at very often. I used to get honked at because I was sexy, now I get honked at because I'm in the way."

"Sure. Just don't forget me. The Bentley is the only car I can fit into outside of the bed of a dump truck." Tommy Jax laughed, appropriate to his size, enormously.

With Sophie offering to watch the dogs, Aunt Phil eagerly got behind the steering wheel of the big car. She adjusted the seat so she could reach the pedals and see out. She fired up the engine and although she could see from the tachometer that the engine was running, she turned to Conrad and whispered, "You can't even hear it!" As they silently emerged out of the dusty lane into the area around the Camp Sherman Store, many heads turned to watch the Bentley drift over the bridge and disappear down the woodsy Forest Service road towards the highway.

IF OLIVER NOTICED any obvious difference between driving a portly six thousand pound Bentley and the diminutive Prius, he made no comment. However, he seemed to be enjoying himself as they zipped right along and soon found themselves approaching the Oxford Hotel in downtown Bend. They didn't spy the Mercedes SUV Brenda Bailey had been driving so they passed the hotel and turned at the next corner. Oliver pulled to a stop at the curb and Mick and Dave, wrestling with the walker, managed to stumble out of the back seat. The plan was for the two of them to wander back to the Oxford and make their way around to the parking lot in the back of the building in order to look for the Mercedes. Adam would walk with a book under his arm to a small coffee shop at the corner across from the hotel and watch from a table on the sidewalk. Oliver would stay with the Prius. They could communicate, if need be, with their radios.

Tommy Jax had called them from the Bentley to tell them that he and Aunt Phil and Conrad would park a couple of blocks away and keep watch on the goings and comings to the hotel and be ready to pick up Mick and Dave if an emergency occurred.

Mick and Dave walked with Adam to the corner. Adam continued around the corner and took a table on the sidewalk. As Mick rummaged through a trash bin outside the coffee shop, Dave started across the street, slowly pushing the walker ahead of him. The light had turned to (wait) long before he made it across. He never looked up at the cars which had stopped for him. He tried to make it look as though he was greatly concentrating on putting one foot ahead of the other. Mick waited until the next walk sign, crossed the street, and rummaged in another trash bin while Dave slowly made his way toward the end of the hotel. Mick followed, several minutes behind.

Once in the parking lot, the two men stayed together talking. However, each guy concentrated on looking over the other's shoulder to scan the lot for the Mercedes.

Mick said, "I think I see one the right color back about four rows. We'll have to get closer to see the license plate."

"Okay," Dave said. "I'll head over that way and if it's the right car, I'll fake a fall and plant the bug wherever I land."

"Go for it!" Mick replied. "When you fall I'll come to help and plant the other bug."

"Here I go," Dave said, shoving the walker a few inches ahead of him and then shuffling his feet to catch up. Meanwhile Mick checked a gutter alongside the parking lot for cigarette butts, hoping he wouldn't find any.

The back door of the hotel opened and a bell man stepped out and lit a cigarette. He spied both Mick and Dave in the lot and said in a booming, authoritative voice, "Hey, you two bums! Get outta here or I'll call the cops." He started to walk toward where Dave was heading with his walker.

Mick tried to head off the bell man by asking if he could spare a cigarette. Coming up to the Mercedes, Dave fell, sending enough swear words into the air to color it blue. As he rolled around on the ground, he reached under the rear of the car and quickly placed a tracking sensor on the inside of the bumper.

Mick hurried over to help Dave to his feet as the bell man followed. Leaning over to grab Dave by the arm, Mick placed a sensor in the left rear wheel well of the Mercedes. Struggling to his feet, Dave waved at the approaching bell man and said, "I'm all right. Thanks!"

The bell man stopped and said, "Well then get outta here, you two."

"Okay, okay," Mick and Dave muttered. Mick then helped Dave maneuver the walker back to the entrance of the parking lot. Mick planted a parting shot at the bell man asking him again if he couldn't spare a cigarette. The bell man just shook his head in disgust and returned to the building.

"Geez, you've got guts!" Dave quietly said to Mick as they shuffled back out to the street.

"I had no idea you knew so many swear words!" Mick replied, trying not to laugh. "Where'd you learn all those?"

"Remember, I've been around you for fifty years."

The two loitered on the street corner for a few moments before Dave headed across the street, with Mick following a few seconds behind. They went around the corner where the Prius was parked.

As soon as Mick and Dave disappeared around the corner, Adam took another discrete look up and down the street, folded his book and casually left the coffee shop in the direction of the Prius. Mick and Dave had loaded the walker and had piled into the back seat by the time Adam reached the car. As soon as Adam plopped into the passenger seat and closed the door, Oliver had the car in gear and they were melting into the traffic in downtown Bend.

CHAPTER 11

CONRAD, AUNT PHIL, AND Tommy Jax watched all of this from the Bentley. Conrad was about to suggest to Aunt Phil that they switch drivers so he could drive the big car back to Camp Sherman when Tommy Jax leaned forward from the back seat, pointed between the seats with his big ham of a hand and said, "Hey, is that Andre Sullivan?"

"Where?" Conrad and Aunt Phil asked simultaneously. Then they spied Sullivan coming out of the hotel.

All three watched as Sullivan climbed into a Lexus SUV parked at the curb in front of the hotel.

"Aha!" Aunt Phil said. "Another vehicle! We need to follow it."

As Conrad called Adam to tell of their discovery, Aunt Phil threw the Bentley into gear and stepped on the accelerator. The Bentley's huge engine flung six thousand pounds of automobile into action with the quickness of a gazelle.

"Holy shit!" Aunt Phil exclaimed as she briefly felt like a mere passenger rather than the driver and gave the steering wheel a death grip as they barreled after the Lexus.

"Don't lose 'em!" Conrad exclaimed as the Lexus wheeled around a corner. He then turned to Jax and said, "I love car chases in the movies but I never thought I'd be in one."

"Hold on!" Aunt Phil warned when the Lexus disappeared around another corner.

Conrad replied, grabbing the door handle, "That's what I told my heart during the last c-o-o-o-r-ner!" Aunt Phil dove after the Lexus, the Bentley's tires squealing in protest.

"This car is a hoot!" she declared.

"Don't follow too close," Jax cautioned. "As soon as Oliver and the gang catch up, we can switch positions with them. They'll spot this car following them really easily."

"Where is the Prius?" Aunt Phil asked. "Can anybody see them?"

Both Conrad and Jax looked forward and backwards as well as up and down the cross streets.

"Nope," Conrad said.

"I'll call 'em," Jax said.

After making the call, Jax then relayed to Conrad and Aunt Phil what Adam had told him; that shortly after the Bentley had taken off after the Lexus, they could see on Oliver's phone that the Mercedes SUV left the hotel's parking lot and followed in the same direction the Lexus had taken. Once they had all turned South on US 97, Adam could see far ahead that the Bentley was in front of the Mercedes. He suggested to Jax that the Bentley should pull off somewhere so no one will figure out they are following Sullivan. The gang in the Prius would then take over to see where Sullivan and the pursuing Mercedes were headed.

"Sounds good to me," Aunt Phil stated and immediately swung into a Walmart parking lot. However, so did the Mercedes. The gang in the Bentley pulled over and watched from a distance while the Mercedes continued on close to the store and parked. Brenda Bailey exited the Mercedes and proceeded into the store. Jax called Adam back to tell him what had happened.

"Well, keep watch on her," Adam suggested. "The Lexus just turned into that same slimy motel and pulled in front of unit number twelve. Dave and Mick want to see if they can place a bug on the car."

"Okay," Jax answered. "Tell 'em to be careful!"

Oliver had pulled into the lot next to the motel. The lot used to be a service station, now defunct, with broken windows and trash scattered about. It was separated from the motel by a drought ravaged hedge of arborvitae. Dave and Mick got out of the car. They talked softly to each other for a moment to verify that their radios still worked. Mick then started toddling past the motel on the sidewalk carrying the empty wine bottle in its sack. He shuffled and faked a limp. He paused his shuffle long enough to take a long phony draw on the bottle. Once he cleared the motel office, it appeared that he had attracted no attention. Via the radio in his pocket which picked up his voice, he told Dave that all was clear.

Dave, having left the walker in the car and armed only with two sensors, ventured into the motel's parking lot. He staggered a bit and paused once in a while to look around as though confused. He bent to pick up a scrap of paper and as he approached the Lexus, continued to look at the paper. Once behind the Lexus, he dropped the paper, bent over to retrieve it and placed both sensors underneath the back bumper.

Suddenly the door to the motel unit swung open and a gruff looking fellow emerged sporting a three day beard and tattooed biceps bulging from the short sleeves of a red polo shirt. He yelled, "Hey, you! Get away from that car! What are you doing?"

Dave straighten up and deadpanned, "Sonny?"

"Go on, you old fart. Get outta here!"

Agreeing that was a very good idea, Dave said, "Okay," and staggered off but the guy with the biceps started after him.

"Dad!" came a voice from around another car. "There you are!" Adam stepped forward and grabbed Dave by the arm. "We've been looking all over for you, Pops."

Then Adam addressed Biceps, "I'm sorry, but he does wander off. I hope he didn't bother you."

Dave grabbed Adam by the shoulders. "You look familiar. Do I know you?" He then took Adam's face in both his hands and planted three sloppy smooches on his nose. He then turned to Biceps and, reaching for him declared, "Kissy, kiss, kiss!"

"Get away from me, you demented old fool!" Biceps fended him off and quickly retreated into Unit #12.

Dave then said quietly to Adam, "Thanks! Now, let's get the hell outta here!"

By the time they cleared the motel parking lot, Oliver had picked up Mick.

"Hurry and get in," Mick said, opening the door. "Conrad called and Oliver's phone confirms that the Mercedes is coming this way."

WHEN BRENDA BAILEY had exited her Mercedes and made her way into the Walmart store, she had no idea the large man who followed her through the door was no other than Tommy Jax, notorious Seattle underworld crime figure cum philanthropist and pro bono private investigator for The Geezer Underground.

Although it was difficult for such a large man to be discreet, Tommy Jax was able to keep Bailey in sight. He managed to follow her path to the sporting goods section of the store. Here he watched as she gathered up several cans of tennis balls. On her way to the barbecue section, she walked right past Jax who had suddenly found a pup tent very interesting. It never registered to her that the man never could have fit inside.

Bailey weaved between rows of outdoor barbecues and picked up two containers of charcoal briquette lighter fluid. She then made her way to pet supplies where she picked out a device for throwing balls for a dog. When Bailey finally left the Walmart parking lot, Aunt Phil and Conrad ducked their heads for fear she would recognize them from the disastrous dinner party at Black Butte Ranch. As soon as Tommy Jax returned to the Bentley, he reported what the woman had purchased and they were all somewhat bewildered as to why she bought what she did. Upon communicating with the crew in the Prius, they decided to rendezvous at Drake Park to discuss what they knew.

Drake Park was on the portion of the Deschutes River that widened and drifted through downtown Bend like a quietly moving mirror. Although appropriately dotted with ducks, the park was named in the 1920's for developer Alexander M. Drake. The park served as a lovely and restful haven for both humans and beasts.

Having parked their cars on different streets, the two teams met at a picnic table beside the water. The grassy river bank was alive with dog walkers, baby strollers, and families feeding the local water fowl. First Tommy Jax told everyone what Brenda Bailey had purchased at the Walmart store. Then Mick and Dave told of their encounter with Biceps and how Adam, hearing in his earpiece Biceps confronting Dave, saved Dave's skin by pretending Dave was his demented father. The entire crew felt some achievement in getting two known vehicles bugged, but besides that, they still had not a clue what they were going to do now.

"We sit and wait," Mick said. "We keep an eye on their movements and see what they do."

"So now the best thing to do is check in with Beth and Arthur and bring them up to date," Adam added. "They'll need to know we have accomplished something, anyway."

The group decided to head back to Camp Sherman and Oliver and Jax would go to their rented house at Black Butte but first, the entire crew would stop at Beth and Arthur's cabin.

CHAPTER 12

WHILE THE REST of the Geezer Underground was chasing Andre Sullivan and his minions all over the town of Bend, Beth and Arthur had an unexpected visitor at their cabin, Deputy Cyril Richmond. When Richmond's pickup pulled into the driveway, Max the dog and Booger the cat, in the way of dogs and cats, rushed to their habitual places upon the appearance of a guest: Max, tail wagging as though he was trying to shake it off, raced Arthur to the door. Booger headed for the rafters where, as a large furry lump, he could lurk in the darkness and watch the goings on in the great room.

Deputy Richmond doffed his cap as he entered the cabin. He quickly ruffled Max's ears then shook hands with Arthur and greeted Beth as she ushered him into the great room. They all took seats, Richmond sat on the edge of the couch, his elbows on his thighs and his hands clasped between his knees. For a moment he stared at the floor. How was he going to tell these kind and generous people, without scaring them to death, that a murderer may be lurking in their neighborhood? Little did he know that they already knew or even how they had been informed.

"We have a situation," he began, "that you need to be aware of. There were two individuals found dead in their cabins on acreages not far from here. We are not sure yet how they died, but the deaths are suspicious. They mirror similar deaths that have occurred in the Portland area. Jefferson County has been contacted by members of the Portland Police Bureau to be on the lookout for a certain individual or individuals that we know now to be operating in this area."

Beth exchanged looks with Arthur.

"Now, I don't want to cause any panic here, but until we can sort all of this out, I'd like to suggest that you keep your doors locked. If one of you needs to go somewhere, don't leave the other one alone in your cabin and, at any time, don't answer the door to anyone you don't know."

Arthur said, "Although Max here is a pretty good alarm system, we were just talking about getting an electronic alarm installed and were in the process of searching companies when you arrived." Max, upon hearing his name, thumped his tail where he had sprawled in front of the fireplace.

"Well that's good," Richmond replied. "There was a time when one wouldn't think locking doors and alarm systems were needed in Camp Sherman, and it burns me up when one of these sleazebags happens to show up."

"Cyril," Beth asked, "can you tell us a little more about what was going on in Portland? I'm from there, you know, and in the few years before I left, I lost several dear friends, it seemed, one right after the other. They were all older, and age brings ailments, of course, but as far as I knew, nothing that would cause any of them to drop dead so soon."

"Interesting you should say that, Beth. The deaths Portland homicide detectives were talking to us about all concerned older people. Their houses, some of them burned, were all in the same general area. In a short period of time, the properties were then bought up by obscure corporations nobody ever heard of. The police researched through Oregon business filings and found the ownership of those corporations could be traced back to the same individual. One chunk of adjoining properties has since been razed and, because the zoning was appropriate, was sold to a California outfit which put in a shopping center."

"So the overall objective then," Arthur concluded, "was to make a mint developing those lots. It began with getting rid of the owners of the individual properties." By this time, Max had maneuvered himself over to where Arthur was sitting. The big dog then flopped onto his back and was enjoying a massive belly rub.

"At this point they have no proof, but that is the suspected scenario,"

86

Richmond responded. "I may have told you more than the Portland investigators would have preferred. Good detectives will keep the particulars close to their vests but the folks here at Camp Sherman are..." here Richmond paused and, for a moment, gazed at the fireplace but not seeing it, as though concerned that yet again he was getting too personal for a lawman. "...special to me so I feel that the more you know about the 'whys', the better prepared you are to protect yourselves."

"Cyril," Beth asked. "What about the west side of Green Ridge where most of the historic cabins are? Do you think those people are also in danger?"

"At this time, we don't think so. As long as that area is National Forest land, we are not currently as concerned as we are for people who own their land." Richmond got to his feet and then knelt down next to Max and joined Arthur in the belly rub. Max thought he'd died and gone to heaven. "Make sure that on your phones, 911 is on speed dial as well as my personal cell phone. The same for your land line. 911 can contact me on my truck's radio if I'm out of cell phone service, which, as you know, is sketchy."

Richmond straighten up and made his way to the front door followed by Beth, Arthur, and the deputy's new found best friend, Max. He opened the door, turned around and said, "I'll let you know if I learn anything new or that it appears the coast is clear."

"Okay, Cyril. Thanks for stopping by. Good luck in catching this bastard," Arthur replied.

The deputy slapped his cap back on his head and said, "Right-o," and off he went.

Arthur closed the front door and snapping the dead bolt locked, looked at Beth's worried face and said, "Well, doesn't that beat all?"

NOT ONE HOUR later, the Prius and Tommy Jax's Bentley pulled into Beth's and Arthur's dusty driveway. Upon hearing the cars pull up and stop, Arthur looked out the front window.

"Cyril didn't mention any particular vehicle to look for, did he?"

"No, why?" Beth answered as she peeked around Arthur's shoulder. "Oh, isn't that Dave's Prius? I haven't a clue what that other thing is though. Have you seen anything like that before?"

"Not on this planet," was Arthur's reply. He then added incredulously, "Is that Conrad behind the wheel?"

"That guy with the big grin on his face?" Beth chuckled. "You bet it is! But, who are those two?"

Who Beth was referring to were Mick and Dave. Both men climbed out of the car and shook the dirt out of their hair and took their jackets off but still looked like bums. It wasn't until both stood together and beamed through the window at Beth and Arthur that the latter recognized them with roars of laughter.

Beth and Arthur opened the door to no less than five harmless fellow Geezers plus Tommy Jax and Oliver. Introductions of Jax and Oliver were made and the group was ushered into the cabin's great room which, after being filled with nine humans, didn't seem so great.

Arthur pulled in chairs from the dining room and Tommy Jax graciously offered to stand, as did Oliver. Beth took orders for ice tea or coffee but before she left for the kitchen with Aunt Phil in tow, cocked her head at Oliver and said, "Oliver, I do believe you have an admirer."

Everyone, including Oliver, who was leaning against the fireplace, looked to the floor. There they found Booger, who had chosen to descend from the safety of the rafters to plop his furry fanny at Oliver's feet, look up at the thin man and purr, sounding somewhat like a tractor at idle.

Oliver, like an oil field pump jack, stiffly bent from the hip to scratch the cat between his ears and under his chin as a person well versed in cats would know to do. Booger's purr increased in volume.

"Nice cat," said Oliver as a mere hint of a smile escaped his lips.

BETH AND ARTHUR relayed what Deputy Richmond had told them about how Portland homicide detectives were investigating old cases regarding elderly people dying in their homes. The deaths were all eerily similar and from vague causes. Some of the homes had been burned. Then the properties were bought up by an individual who sold the whole lot to a developer. The Geezers looked around at each other and Conrad said what they all were thinking, "We were on the right track after all."

Adam then told Beth and Arthur about their caper in Bend with Sullivan's cars and what Tommy Jax observed Brenda Bailey purchasing at the Walmart store. The group was quiet while they contemplated of what use tennis balls and BBQ lighter fluid would be to killers.

Aunt Phil narrowed her eyes and asked, "Remember, those of you who were there, my cousin's condo on the Big Island of Hawaii?"

Arthur, Adam, and Beth all nodded their heads.

"Well, she told me of a pyromaniac who was setting rangeland fires on the island. The Big Island has a lot of cattle ranches. Most people would never think of cattle ranches being in Hawaii, but there are. As far as I know, they never caught who was doing it but the fire guys found at the source of ignition charred round things, like balls. They determined they were tennis balls."

"You don't suppose," Beth speculated, "they soaked tennis balls in some kind of flammable stuff like gasoline or lighter fluid and tossed the balls out into the dry grass?"

"They may not have been able to handle a flaming ball with their bare hands," Conrad concluded, "but I'll bet if they used one of those things that you can throw a ball for a dog..."

"Like this?" Arthur stepped out onto the porch and retrieved from a large basket a throwing device to use when playing fetch with a dog. Max immediately was on his feet and had his nose deep in the basket where he dug out a well-used tennis ball.

"Sorry, Max," Arthur told his dog when, carrying the device, he re-entered the cabin. "We'll play later, okay?" This Arthur said knowing full well that with Max, it wasn't okay. Ball in mouth, the big dog collapsed onto the floor with a sigh to await his turn.

"I guess we can't do much with this info right now," Mick concluded. "However, we can continue to watch where Sullivan and/or his minions go. You're getting an alarm system installed?" This question was to Beth and Arthur.

"Yes," Arthur answered. "We hope to get some bids back soon."

"In the meantime, I can stay with you, if that's okay?" Adam asked.

"Of course, Adam. You know you are always welcome." Beth answered with a smile.

"Uh," Tommy Jax spoke for the first time. "We, I mean Oliver, can install one right now."

"Huh?" Beth and Arthur said in unison.

"Yes, Oliver and I have developed an alarm system that's easy for anybody to install and we always carry one in the trunk of the car just in case we get a chance to demonstrate."

Arthur looked at Beth smiling her approval and said, "Gee, demonstrate away!"

Within a couple of hours, Oliver had installed the most sophisticated alarm and fire alert system Arthur had ever seen. Oliver placed many tiny cameras, looking no more like cameras than fly specks, at strategic points throughout the inside and outside of the cabin as well as in the surrounding trees, rocks, and shrubs. Booger followed closely on his heels and didn't let the thin man out of his sight.

"This is all wireless technology," Jax explained. "Each camera not only sees what is out there but even detects rapid changes in temperature. That could mean a fire or even the body heat from a prowler. It then transmits a wireless signal to this computer..." Here Jax pulled from a carton what looked like an ordinary lap top. "A high resolution color image will appear along with which camera detected it. We'll program your house computer and all your lap tops, IPads, and phones to relay the same information so you can see what is going on anywhere inside or outside the house, even if you are in Sisters or wherever. With one click, you can summon the police and fire department. You can also, by choice, activate an ear-splitting alarm along with flashing flood lights, all of which are guaranteed to wet the pants of any crook within a mile."

"Wow! Kind of like a prison system," Conrad said.

"Don't ask us how we know these things," Jax said with a grin.

Again Conrad had put his foot in where he didn't really want to go concerning Tommy Jax.

Mick asked, "Since wireless cell phone service is so iffy in the Metolius Basin, how can we rely on transmission getting through?"

"Satellite," Jax replied.

"Oh, ho!" Mick said, as though he understood how that worked.

After the system was completely installed and tested and retested, the members of the Geezer Underground prepared to go their separate ways. Adam could tell that Beth was still nervous so he said he'd stay with them for a few nights just to have another set of eyes and ears in the cabin. He promised to return shortly with his luggage. Conrad and Aunt Phil, with Adam in the middle of the back seat, went with Dave and Mick in the Prius back to their respective cabins. Tommy Jax and Oliver made their way to their rented home at Black Butte Ranch.

Tommy Jax rode in the back seat of the Bentley through the fading light of evening. He said, "I'm glad we could install that system for Beth and Arthur. In fact, we could do it for all of the Geezers. I really like those people."

Oliver answered, "Yes, T.J. I do too."

CHAPTER 13

THE MEETING IN unit #12 of the shabby motel on US 97 lasted far into the night. Crammed into the small, stuffy space were Andre Sullivan, who had turned the one small chair backwards and straddled it; Brenda Bailey, who was hot and tired and stood stiffly as she wouldn't even lean against a wall because the place was so filthy; and sprawled on the stained and sunken bed was Biceps, who, at birth, was named Percy Lumpsucker. If there is anything to the theory that criminals develop low self-esteem because of having weird names, it was never evident with Percy. Having the intellect of a gnat, it was doubtful he had even a gnawing hint that his name was anything unusual. If he did, he covered it up with massive quantities of tattoos and never again gave it a thought. The handle "Biceps" was given to him by Sullivan who just couldn't bring himself to call a thug Percy.

"Okay," Sullivan droned on, "we have to give up on the west side of Green Ridge because it's too steep to put houses on and there is that fucking group of locals who protect the ridge like they gave birth to the damn thing. They are way too fierce. Once we get in office and can wipe out national forest designations, we'll deal with those people. So, in the meantime, this is what we're going to do."

Bailey rolled her eyes. She was used to her boss flitting from one objective to another because he never bothered to do enough research on anything before taking a plunge. Even though she wrote all of his campaign speeches, he adlibbed enough that she was always having to appease the press to get him out of the noose he'd verbally wrap around his neck. People wondered why she followed him around like a lost puppy. There was nothing compelling about this man. He was rude, crude, and cruel. However, he promised to all who were his minions unlimited riches and power if they could help him get into public office. Bailey had always abnormally found power attractive. Another factor for her loyalty to Sullivan was that she didn't have much choice. Now that she had associated herself with Sullivan, nobody else in the political community would have anything to do with her.

"There is a wealth of opportunity on the east side of Green Ridge. We are going to own all the available land from Green Ridge road to the top of the ridge. Once we are able to, er, displace the current owners, we'll go in there and subdivide, cut in some roads and utilities, and the lots at the top will sell for a fortune! They'll have 360 degree views of the Cascades as well as Black Butte and Smith Rock. There are a few more properties which need, er, adjustments to force them to be put up for sale. First off, Biceps, is you need to go back and finish what you started. Why didn't you burn that other cabin, you fathead?"

When Sullivan got no response other than snoring sounds coming from the bed, he hollered, "ARE YOU LISTENING TO ME LUMPSUCKER?"

"Huh?" Percy said as he yawned.

"Listen to me, dammit!"

"Geez, it's late, Andre!" Biceps whined.

Brenda, knowing so well how her boss expected his minions to share his enthusiasm for his passions, added as she headed for the door, "It is 1:30 in the morning, Andre. Enough is enough. Come on, we can finish this tomorrow. Let's go back to the hotel."

Before the door was closed behind Sullivan and Bailey, Biceps, still fully clothed, had snuggled into the grimy bedspread and was snoring again.

AN ALARM SOUNDED from the computer in a bedroom of the rented house at Black Butte Ranch. Oliver scrambled out of bed and said loudly, "T.J! Come 'ere."

Tommy Jax made his ponderous way into the room. Oliver sat in a desk

94

chair. Jax lowered himself to the edge of the bed which sagged and groaned in protest. The computer screen showed a red blip which represented the Mercedes SUV registered to Sullivan Properties, LLC. The blue light from the screen was the only light in the room and lit the men's faces like an otherworldly aura.

"Should I notify the others?" Oliver said quietly.

"Not yet," Jax answered. "Let's see where it goes first."

Their eyes followed the blip from the motel on US 97 to downtown Bend until it turned into the parking lot of the Oxford Hotel.

Oliver asked, "Do you think they'll stay there?"

"I would say so," Jax said with a yawn. "It's late and they are probably turning in. If they leave, we'll hear another alarm."

THE EIDERDOWN COMFORTER under which Beth and Arthur cuddled was soft and warm. However, it brought little comfort to Beth who lay wide awake in Arthur's arms. Every tiny noise she heard put her senses on edge. When the wind would sigh and make a tree branch caress the cabin roof, her eyes would widen even more. But it was the ice maker in the refrigerator downstairs when it dumped a load of cubes into its hopper which made Beth jump so much she was afraid she had awakened Arthur. She didn't need to worry as he was already awake.

"Relax, Beth," Arthur said into her hair and nuzzled her neck. "That was just the icemaker."

"I'm sorry," she said. "After what Cyril Richmond told us today, I'm nervous. Even with Adam and the dogs downstairs, I'm on edge."

"You could go to Portland and spend a few days with Tony, Nancy and the kids until this all blows over," Arthur suggested, even though he knew any day here without Beth would be misery for him.

"I can't leave you, Arthur," Beth answered simply. "It's funny, but all those months I hid out in that cave on Green Ridge, I slept soundly, even though I was a lone human in an animal's world. A cougar or even a small bear could have easily gotten into that cave but I never lay awake waiting for it to happen. I figured I'd deal with it if and when it occurred. However, dangerous humans are far scarier to me than dangerous animals. Maybe it's because dangerous humans operate with the added element of hate that doesn't exist in the natural world."

"Hate is a powerful motivator," Arthur replied. "So is greed, and it's greed that is the motivating factor of whomever is trying to obtain these properties in a devious manner. That is what we need to be wary of."

"Arthur, how can that alarm system that Oliver and Tommy Jax installed tell the difference between a human walking on our property and, say, a deer or another critter which happens to be passing through?"

"I don't know, except they tested it numerous times with Max playing the part of a critter and he never set it off." Arthur answered then added with a chuckle, "Maybe it counts legs."

"Oh, Arthur, you're so funny. I don't see how I can be worried when I'm with you."

"I'll remember that the next time we're hiking and come to a loose, rocky scree slope that we have to cross."

"Just make sure you go first, darling, and I'll follow you anywhere."

The two cuddled closer and both were soon fast asleep.

THE NIGHT LAY softly around the cabin as Adam Carson, with the bulldog Noodles curled up at his feet, stayed awake but not because of fear. He was awake because he was luxuriating in the comfort of this big bed in Beth and Arthur's guest room and in the quietness of the forest around him. He didn't want to miss a minute of it. He loved being here in these mountains and with people who were dear to him. He would retire here someday, he hoped. Then he could soak up to his heart's content the peace and gentleness that was Camp Sherman and the people who lived there.

Was Sophie Summers going to play a part in his future here? He didn't know but she seemed like a lovely woman, secure within herself, and full of fun and adventure. If she was willing to share a bit of her life with him, that would certainly go a long way to making his dream complete.

First he had a job to do; rid these woods of the threat that exists for all forested lands of not only Oregon, but the rest of the nation as well. That threat is exploitation by persons who never saw themselves as stewards of anything other than their own interests. When the forest is gone, the water too polluted to drink, the air not fit to breathe, what are people going to eat, money? The world has become too crowded to think that resources are going to last forever. If Andre Sullivan proved to be one of those people, Adam vowed to the darkness in the room that he would expose the man for the fraud that he was.

Hearing his other bulldog Duncan gently snoring while curled up with Max in the great room, Adam quietly got out of bed and stepped through the doorway of the guest room. Max raised his head at Adam's entrance and thumped his tail from the throw rug in front of the fireplace.

"You guys doing okay in here?" Adam quietly asked as he looked around the room. He walked through the shadows of the dining room and into the kitchen, listening as much as looking. Everything seemed abnormally quiet but he couldn't find anything out of order. Shrugging, he returned to bed. He turned onto his side and closed his eyes. He had to put his faith in Tommy Jax and Oliver's security system and anything else they could bring to the fight, legal or not. Being an attorney, he found a bit of humor in combining forces with these interesting individuals who lived a bit on the suspicious side. Whatever it took, Adam was confident the peculiar combination of Jax and Oliver with their knowledge of technology plus the fearless and crafty Geezers would see their mission to fruition. With this revelation secure in his consciousness, Adam drifted off to sleep.

THE ONLY OTHER person in the forest who was still awake was Jefferson County Sheriff's Deputy Cyril Richmond. He was in his home office examining the screen prints he had taken of the fourteen autopsy reports Lieutenant Shawn Avery had sent him from the Portland Police

Bureau and was comparing them with the one he had received that day for the autopsy of Wilbur Martin. They had remarkable similarities: the deceased were all elderly, died alone, causes of death were vaguely either probable heart disease or complications due to old age, plus the autopsies were mostly incomplete. No blood tests were done nor were any organs removed and examined. However, the similarity which stood out the most to Richmond was that the pathologist, Herman Diggs, MD, was the same person on all reports. It seemed peculiar to the deputy that in an office the size of the Multnomah County Medical Examiner, the chances would be slim that the same doctor would perform all of these autopsies.

First thing in the morning, Richmond would share this information with his sheriff and then place a call to Lieutenant Avery for more information on just who this doctor was.

CHAPTER 14

JEFFERSON COUNTY SHERIFF Gary Larkin looked over the top of his reading glasses at Deputy Richmond. Larkin, a big man in his fifties with close cropped grey hair, had just spent several minutes examining the autopsy reports from Portland that Richmond had brought to the sheriff's office that morning.

"Cyril, I agree there seems to be something very fishy going on here. You talked to this Lieutenant Avery in Portland. Have you talked to him since you got this autopsy report on our guys, Wilbur Martin and Emil Emerson?"

"No. I wanted to see what you thought. We cannot determine from the examination of the scene of Martin's death that positively a crime was committed. However, there was a footprint that we cannot identify, so we're using that as our reason to declare a crime scene."

"What about the other cabin, the one that was burned?"

"Owned by a recluse. No one else on the title. Body badly burned. We also sent it to Portland but the medical examiner won't do a complete autopsy unless we suspect a crime had been committed, which, at the time we were called to the scene of the fire, we didn't. It appeared the guy had some sort of medical emergency, fell, and took a kerosene lamp with him."

"And, at that time, you didn't know about Wilbur Martin."

"No, not until two days later, in the morning."

"What did you think of the crime scene in Martin's cabin?"

"Wilbur was face down on the floor. In my experience, that seems consistent with someone who has had a massive heart attack and just keels over. The autopsy describes contusions on his face, which makes sense if he fell face down. However, I have this nagging feeling, after seeing how many of those Portland autopsies describe the same facial contusions, those injuries could have been caused by someone striking the victim in the face with something really hard like a pipe. The killer makes certain the victim falls face down. They are old, somewhat fragile, it's not hard to conceive that the cause of death was a sudden failure of a critical organ like the heart. Hence you have perhaps the perfect murder. Wilbur's floors were dusty and over the years he had worn paths in the dirt. There were enough unidentifiable footprints to represent a small army."

"Have you talked to Martin's family?"

"Not yet. He has just one daughter. She lives in New York. She is supposed to fly in this morning to the Redmond airport. Martin's body has been sent to a funeral home in Bend. Wilbur apparently had made arrangements for his burial years ago. They'll keep him on ice until they receive her signature before they bury or cremate him. Emerson's body is in our own morgue, for the time being."

"Make sure they don't do anything with either body until we're satisfied there was no crime committed. Okay, more about those footprints. Who discovered the body? They would have left prints as well as the crime scene team."

"I took pictures of the bottoms of the shoes that were being worn by Wilbur's three friends, the ones who found his body. I was able to match those to photos taken of the floor around where the body was found. However, there was a print near the back door of the cabin which didn't match any of Wilbur's shoes that we could find or those of his buddies. That print must have been fairly fresh as it hadn't been stepped on. Also there are a couple of partials around the body which may be the same shoe but were pretty much scuffed out, probably by Wilbur's friends."

"Hmm," Sheriff Larkin scratched his chin then looked at Richmond. "First, we need to talk to the daughter and get her permission, but I'm thinking we need to order another autopsy on Martin as well as the Emerson corpse. In light of what you suspect is happening at the State Medical Examiner's office, we'll get one done here by the State Police. They used to do them at their facility in Bend and maybe they know of a pathologist now working for a county which doesn't send autopsies to Portland."

Richmond smiled at his boss, "You took the words right out of my mouth. They may conclude old Wilbur and Emil did indeed have heart disease. If they don't, we have murders on our hands."

WHEN EMILY MARTIN stepped from the Alaska Airlines jet at the Redmond Airport, there was a contingency of folks there to greet her. Old Bowels was there as well as Mick and Dave. They wanted to make sure Emily knew there were people here to support her. In addition, Deputy Cyril Richmond stood apart with his arms folded over his chest. The other men knew he wanted to talk to Emily before they took her to the mortuary to see her dad.

Emily Martin was an attractive woman in her late fifties. She was a bit overweight, but elegant and fashionable. A closer view revealed her face as pale and shell shocked. She looked around the lobby and was somewhat confused until Old Bowels stepped up to her and, upon recognizing him, she fell into his arms, sobbing. Once she was able to pull herself together, she thanked O.B. for coming to meet her plane. He then introduced Mick and Dave as her father's friends. She gave each one a weak smile and a strong hug.

Old Bowels then told Emily that a Jefferson County Sheriff's Deputy was also here to see her. Richmond stepped forward and extended his hand. Emily took it as Richmond placed his other hand over hers and told her how sorry he was for her loss. He then told her that he needed to talk with her before she gave the mortuary instructions for the disposition of her father's body.

"Sure, Deputy Richmond," she said, looking into his kind blue eyes. "Why don't we do it right now? This airport should have some place where we can talk, don't you think?"

They found a remote corner of the lobby where they could sit and quietly talk. Deputy Richmond filled Emily in on their investigation and why, without revealing any suspects' names, the police felt a subsequent autopsy was necessary. She agreed wholeheartedly and said, "Dad would understand and would want you to catch the bastard."

Old Bowels and Mick and Dave picked up Emily's luggage and carried it for her to the rental car counter. They agreed to accompany her to the mortuary in Bend so Emily could sign the appropriate documents for not only the autopsy, but for the final disposition of Wilbur's body. They would then make sure she was checked in at a nice motel nearby. As the rest left the airport, Richmond called Sheriff Larkin and was told he had discussed their situation with the State Police Captain in charge of the State Police facility in Bend. He was able to engage a pathologist from Klamath County who was now on her way to Bend to perform the autopsy.

DR. BARBARA MCELROY was a no-nonsense woman in her sixties with bright, alert eyes underneath a mop of dark, curly hair. When she removed the sheet from Wilbur Martin's body, she looked up at Deputy Richmond and said, "Heart attack, my ass! Just look at his face! He couldn't have sustained those injuries if he'd fallen face first from the roof!"

Further examination revealed how severe the frontal injury to the upper half of the face was, resulting in bone fragments being driven into Wilbur's brain. Dr. McElroy called Wilbur Martin's physician to see what meds he was on. His doctor was as surprised as anybody that Wilbur supposedly died of heart disease. Subsequent results of the autopsy concluded that Wilbur's heart had been healthy without any buildup of plaque in his coronary arteries. He had some osteoarthritis in his neck and spine and took an over-the-counter anti-inflammatory medication. Other than that, he was remarkably fit for a man of 76.

An examination of the burned corpse of Emil Emerson revealed the same frontal damage to his skull as Wilbur Martin's. Dr. McElroy suspected the murder weapon had been a round rod or pipe, maybe even a baseball bat.

"These men were robbed of many more years of life, Cyril. It's clear to me that they were murdered."

AS SOON AS Cyril Richmond returned to his office in the Camp Sherman Fire Station, he called Shawn Avery in Portland. He told Avery what the pathologist had said about Wilbur Martin and Emil Emerson being murdered. He also asked what, if anything, the Portland police knew about the medical examiner who signed the autopsies in question.

Shawn Avery knew nothing about the doctor, Herman Diggs but, after completing his call with Cyril Richmond, Avery summoned Corporal Jerry Banning into his office. Banning, in keeping with his long and lanky physiology, was in Avery's office and folded into a chair as quickly and smoothly as a zephyr.

"Jerry," Avery began. "Find out all you can on this Doctor Diggs who signed these autopsies as well as these two Cyril Richmond sent me a copies of." Avery passed across his desk the fat file he had compiled. "We need to know what this guy's capacity is with the State Medical Examiner and if there is any connection, no matter how remote, between him and Andre Sullivan. Use any resources you need."

Banning tucked the file under his arm, rose from the chair and said, "I'm all over it!" He was gone as quickly as he had arrived.

Corporal Jerry Banning, known throughout the state for his talents with a sniper rifle, was also the department's computer guy. He quickly found in an Oregon State government directory that Herman Diggs was the leading pathologist in the Multnomah County Medical Examiner's office. He was 45 years old, a divorced father of two and had been with the Medical Examiner's office for 15 years. He studied medicine at the University Of Washington School Of Medicine in Seattle. He was the third son of a prominent Washington State legislator, now retired.

Banning then tapped into a genealogy website out of Salt Lake City, Utah and started the meticulous process of building a family tree for both Diggs and Andre Sullivan. It didn't take Banning long to find that Sullivan and Diggs were second cousins. Their grandmothers had been sisters. He double and triple checked the lineage backwards and forwards with three other genealogy websites until he was certain he had the right information. He then gathered all the data he had compiled and returned to Avery's office.

"Second cousins, Shawn. I'm sure of it." Banning stood in Avery's office doorway because he predicted just what his lieutenant would do next. Avery flew out of his chair, scattering the piles of papers on his desk into a bigger mess, yanked his coat from a hook by the door and told Banning to have Sergeant Kowalski bring a car around. The three of them would pay a visit to Dr. Herman Diggs.

From the Justice Center in downtown Portland, the three policemen crossed the Willamette River on the Hawthorne Bridge. They turned south on US 99E and soon entered the town of Milwaukie. From there, they worked their way east to Clackamas and SE 84th Street. Sergeant Kowalski backed the car into a visitors parking place and the three officers entered the medical examiner's building.

The reception area was clean and institutional. The young female receptionist smiled broadly and asked almost gleefully if she could help them. Corporal Banning felt she seemed too perky to work in a building full of dead people, but who was he to judge?

Lieutenant Avery presented his card and asked to see Dr. Herman Diggs. She took his card and, excusing herself, disappeared through a coded locked double door similar to those used in hospital operating rooms.

While they waited, the policemen looked around the room. On the walls were a few lovely photos of Oregon scenes; a rocky coastline, Multnomah Falls in the Columbia Gorge, and Crater Lake. Also prominent behind the reception counter was the Oregon State seal.

After what seemed like forever, the double doors suddenly opened after a lock buzzed and a middle aged man in a white lab coat appeared. Looking somewhat frustrated, he strode up to the three policemen standing before him. Shawn Avery stood with his feet comfortably apart, his hands is his pockets, and his dress shirt typically hanging half-untucked out of his pants.

His tie was also askew. He was flanked by tall and wiry Jerry Banning on one side and Trevor Kowalski who towered over all of them and looked as though he could pick up the reception desk one-handed and give it a fling.

Avery, without offering a hand shake, introduced himself and the other officers and asked, "May we speak to you for a moment?"

Diggs blanched and stammered that he didn't have time. Avery repeated that it wouldn't take long and then asked if they had a conference room they could use. Diggs, his reluctance telegraphed by his grumpy countenance, led them across the reception area and into a small conference room. Shutting the door behind them, he offered them seats. Avery and Banning sat at the table, Banning with his notebook on his knee. Kowalski stayed standing beside the door. Diggs wondered if the big sergeant was guarding the room from entrance from the outside or escape from the inside. Diggs then took a seat and asked, "What is this all about?"

Avery clasped his hands in front of him on the table and asked, "Dr. Diggs, you recently did an autopsy on a Wilbur Martin from Jefferson County. Do you remember that?"

"Lieutenant, I perform a lot of autopsies. No, I don't remember a Wilbur Martin specifically."

"I have a copy. Maybe it will refresh your memory." Avery pulled the autopsy copy he'd received from Cyril Richmond from a file Jerry Banning had carried.

"How did you..."

"You determined that Martin died of heart disease."

"So? What of it?"

"Dr. Diggs, the Jefferson County Sheriff's office ordered a subsequent autopsy to be done on Wilbur Martin because they had reason to believe that a crime had been committed. A crime which contributed to Martin's death."

"They did what?" Diggs was gobsmacked.

"Their autopsy determined that Wilbur Martin died of blunt force trauma to the face. I saw pictures of his body, Dr. Diggs. The entire forehead had been smashed, driving bone fragments into his brain."

"That's preposterous!" Diggs grappled up the copy of his autopsy. Reading it, he said, "Sure, there were contusions caused by him falling face down on the floor." Diggs looked somewhat down his nose at Avery and said with an irritated air of superiority, "That's common when someone experiences a massive heart attack, Lieutenant."

Avery continued, "Their autopsy also could find no history of heart disease in Wilbur Martin. In fact, despite his age, Martin was known in the area for his stamina in climbing many mountain peaks in all western states as well as British Columbia."

"Well, I wouldn't know about that," Diggs huffed.

"Did you call Wilbur Martin's physician, Dr. Diggs, to discuss his known medical conditions?"

Diggs's lack of a response to that question was enough to tell the policemen the answer. "Listen, Lieutenant," Diggs continued, "we do many autopsies on old people. They frequently die alone. If Jefferson County suspected a crime had been committed, I must have missed that on the autopsy request. I have an entire morgue filled with known crime victims whose autopsies the police, as you should know, are waiting for. We can't be nickel and diming each and every old person's report. They are old and are going to die anyway. Everybody expects it. Nobody cares."

"They don't?" Avery's eyebrows raised in astonishment at the doctor's comment. He leaned toward Diggs until their faces were a mere two feet apart and said pointedly, "*Somebody* cares, Doctor. Somebody *always* cares!" Avery leaned back and let that statement soak in for a moment then added, "One more question; do you know Andre Sullivan?"

Startled at the change of subject, Diggs stammered, "Do I know him? I know the name. He's some sort of sleazy politician, isn't he? I don't know him personally."

"You don't know him yet he's your second cousin?"

"Huh?"

"Your grandmothers were sisters."

"How did you... I don't know anything about my grandmother Cassie Linfield. Her family never lived close to the rest of us and I probably have all sorts of cousins I don't know about."

"Okay, Doctor. That's all we wanted... for now." Avery stood as did Banning, who tucked his notebook into his jacket pocket.

Back in their unmarked car, Avery settled into the back seat and asked the other two officers, "Well, what did you think?"

Kowalski snorted and said, "He's lying and he's scared shitless that we're on to him."

Banning said, "Everybody is blood related to two grandmothers. According to the research I did, both of Diggs's grandmothers lived in the same area he did for all of his youth. I think it was rather revealing that he knew which of his two grandmothers we were talking about."

CHAPTER 15

THE MORNING DAWNED with lazy sun beams making their way through the Ponderosa pine forest. The beams briefly poked their noses into Aunt Phil and Conrad's windows then rolled on over their cabin to continue their mission of awakening the rest of the Camp Sherman community. Aunt Phil opened her eyes and stretched. She could feel Conrad stir beside her. She felt that any day she and Conrad woke next to each other had to be indeed a blessed day.

After their breakfast of toast and jam followed by a bowl of cereal and fruit, Aunt Phil dressed in her favorite T-shirt that said, *"Don't Piss Off Old People! The Older We Get, The Less Life in Prison Is A Deterrent."* Denim capris, hiking boots and dangling blue earrings completed her attire. Conrad had already left the cabin that morning to take Fido for a walk up to the Camp Sherman Store. She knew he would soon be settled onto the bench in front of the post office to chat with Mick and Dave. This was getting to be an every morning practice for Conrad and she encouraged it. She felt fortunate they had developed good friendships since they had purchased this historic cabin along the Metolius River.

The previous night had passed uneventfully but with anticipation that it wouldn't be long before Andre Sullivan and his henchmen would be creating more havoc in their area. Ironically, as soon as that thought popped into her head the phone rang.

"Phyllis," the booming voice of Tommy Jax came over the line. "They are on the move! One car is going off towards Madras, but the other is headed our way. I called both Mick and Dave's cabins but nobody answered. Do you know where they are?"

"I bet they are at the post office, T.J. I'll jump in the car and head up there so we can get into position."

"Okay. Be sure to take your radios."

"Got it!" Aunt Phil was out the door and behind the wheel of the Volvo but not before she hurriedly grabbed a sack of hats, dark glasses, and other disguise odds and ends they had prepared for emergencies like this. The Volvo left tracks and a great deal of dust behind it as Aunt Phil stormed up the lane towards the Camp Sherman store and post office.

True to her prediction, outside the post office she found Conrad along with Mick and Dave, sharing the bench with Old Bowels. Aunt Phil brought the Volvo to a stop and lowered her window. "Come on, you guys! T.J. says that one of Sullivan's cars is heading this way. We have to get into position!"

The four oldsters piled off the bench with such speed that a few residents who had come to the post office to pick up their mail watched with amazement. Conrad, clutching Fido in the crook of his arm, climbed into the Volvo with Aunt Phil. Mick and Dave made a bee line for Mick's orange 1950 Chevrolet pickup, closely followed by Old Bowels, who wouldn't be left out of anything if he knew what it was about or not. Dust was all that was left in the parking lot once the Geezer Underground got moving.

The group had previously decided that in order to protect all of the Camp Sherman area on both sides of Green Ridge from Sullivan and his minions, they would have to stake out positions here and there so at least one of them would see anyone approaching. Aunt Phil and Conrad's assignment had been to position themselves near the fork in the paved forest service road coming in from the main highway. The right hand fork led to major campgrounds and the headwaters of the Metolius. The left hand fork went directly into Camp Sherman itself. Once they had approached the fork, Aunt Phil backed the Volvo into the dirt lane which led to the garbage dump, leaving them with a great view of the road.

"Good thing it's not garbage day," Conrad said.

"Or our turn to volunteer as Dumpsteers," Aunt Phil added.

Mick, Dave, and now with Old Bowels also stuffed into the seat of Mick's pickup, headed to an area on the east side of Green Ridge where they could see if anybody approached either Beth and Arthur's cabin or Wilbur's cabin on Green Ridge Road. On their way, Old Bowels was filled in on what both law enforcement and the Geezer Underground suspected Andre Sullivan was up to.

Old Bowels was aghast that Sullivan could be so heartless. "I knew he was a self-worshiping ass, but not a murderer," O.B. sputtered. He then added that Wilbur's daughter, Emily, had said she planned on visiting her dad's cabin today to begin going through his things. O.B. tried to call her to warn her not to come but was able to reach only her voicemail. They all hoped she wouldn't come while Sullivan or his henchmen were on the prowl.

Tommy Jax and Oliver drove out of Black Butte Ranch and turned to the east on US 20 to cover the intersection of the highway and Green Ridge road. While Oliver drove, Tommy Jax called Beth and Arthur to warn them of what was happening.

"What should we do, T.J?" Arthur asked with apprehension in his voice. Knowing what had happened to Wilbur Martin, Arthur was not only terrified, but was furious that a psychopath like Sullivan, through his own self-interest, would remorselessly take innocent people who should be enjoying every precious twilight moment of their lives and make them feel victimized, vulnerable and then kill them in cold blood.

"Shelter in place, for now, Arthur," Tommy Jax answered. "You know you will see on your computer monitor anyone who gets close to your cabin. Just be vigilant and if you feel you need to, manually set off the alarm. Let's hope that whoever is driving this car is on their way to Salem or somewhere else in the Willamette Valley, but I sincerely doubt that."

Biceps was not on his way to Salem, but that didn't stop him from enjoying driving this luxurious Mercedes SUV. He appreciated that his boss had expensive taste in cars. He also appreciated that he was alone on this particular mission. Sullivan and Bailey had gone to a campaign rally in Madras. Their constant bickering drove him nuts. Now he could take his time scoping out the remaining cabins on Green Ridge Road so that later, after dark, he would reduce them to cinders. Or, if the conditions were right, he'd do it now.

When he turned off the highway at the Indian Ford Campground sign he noticed the Bentley parked in the trees a few yards off the highway. The big car drew no real concern from Biceps. He surmised some rich yahoo was in the bushes taking a leak.

Upon seeing Biceps and the Mercedes pass in front of their hiding place, Tommy Jax called Arthur to tell him that Biceps was definitely on his way. He also told Arthur that it was time to use his land line to call Deputy Richmond.

Cyril Richmond was at his desk in a corner of the Camp Sherman fire station. He was spending the morning working on what he least liked to do: month end reports. As soon as he finished, he would reward himself with a lunch of one of the Camp Sherman store's to-kill-for deli sandwiches. Arthur's call came just as Richmond was getting ready to hit the "Send" key to fire his reports off to the sheriff's office in Madras. When Arthur said that Sullivan's henchman was making his way to Wilbur's cabin and described the car he was driving, Richmond said, "Holy crap, Arthur, how do you know..." The Deputy's question remained unfinished as it dawned on him that somehow the Geezer Underground knew more about what was going on than he did. "I'll be there as soon as I can," he said as he hung up his phone and legged it out the door.

With lights flashing and dust billowing out behind his truck, Deputy Richmond made heads turn at the Lake Creek Lodge as he stormed past. He roared toward the garbage dump where Aunt Phil and Conrad were keeping vigil. Richmond, knowing the back roads like he did his own house, reached the intersection then veered off onto a primitive dirt road that led to the summit of the south end of Green Ridge.

As Richmond's truck blew past them, Conrad and Aunt Phil exchanged looks as if to say, "What are we doing staying here? The action is where he's going!" Aunt Phil fired up the Volvo and they blasted off after Richmond.

They followed the deputy, albeit not with the gutsy abandon of Richmond, up this dusty track they didn't even know existed. To say this was a primitive road was an understatement, as rocks, tree roots, and gaping holes impeded their progress. The road intersected with several other tracks and the only way to tell which way Richmond had gone was to follow the trail of dust.

Nearly bouncing his head off the ceiling, Conrad said, "If it wasn't for the urgency of the situation, this could be fun!"

Aunt Phil, clutching the steering wheel and easing the Volvo over yet another rock, grinned at her husband and said, "We'll have fun anyway but we just won't tell anybody."

Richmond, dragging a dust cloud behind him like a parachute, came out on the east side of Green Ridge not far from where Mick's pickup was parked in a thicket of small trees. Spying the three oldsters in Mick's truck, Richmond came to a sliding stop. He lowered his window and quickly asked them what they knew. Mick said they saw Sullivan's henchman go by not three minutes ago. Richmond then floor-boarded his rig, sending dust and gravel everywhere in his haste to catch up with the man.

Not too much later, Aunt Phil and Conrad came bouncing out of the woods and stopped next to Mick's pickup. After a quick conference as to what to do now, it was decided that Aunt Phil and Conrad would continue on cautiously.

Tommy Jax and Oliver had already gone past and, using the Bentley's GPS, noticed the road the cabins were on was a loop. They continued on in the opposite direction so that if they had to, they could cut off an escaping Biceps.

Mick, Dave and Old Bowels decided they would stay where they were to try to intercept Wilbur Martin's daughter if she was on her way to her dad's cabin. What no one knew was that Emily Martin was already there.

EMILY MARTIN HAD spent most of the previous evening at the mortuary. According to her dad's wishes, she had his body cremated and then sat in a quiet room with his urn on her lap. Although she was all grown up she felt like an orphan now that both of her parents were gone. She knew that in the natural way of things, we are born into this world to become orphans at some period in time. However, nothing prepares a person for being without their parents.

Emily was alone. She had never married and had been an only child to parents who were fraught with the strife of a difficult marriage. Knowing that his presence was making the tension in the household worse, Wilbur Martin knew his only alternative was to leave the marriage. The failure of the marriage turned Emily's mother into a simpering, needy casualty. So, from about the age of ten, Emily felt she had to be a mother to her own mother. Emily's mother had passed at age fifty-five from early onset Alzheimer's disease. As the woman's mind faded away, Emily had to say goodbye gradually to the mother who was never really a nurturing factor in her daughter's life.

During Emily's childhood, Wilbur had tried to be a good dad, but Emily's bitterness over her father leaving was a huge stumbling block for both of them. Now, sitting in the half-darkened room, she remembered the sweet little bay mare her dad bought for her when she was twelve. At the time, she did not understand this was her dad's way of demonstrating love for a daughter who was too damaged by the strife of her parents' relationship to even recognize love. Now that she thought back to those times, she hoped she had thanked him for the horse.

During her high school years, he would host ski parties for Emily and her high school buddies. When she was working, he would show up at her office with a cupcake and a candle on her birthday. When her work took her to the East Coast, her contact with her dad consisted of periodic phone calls that he would initiate. When he retired to Camp Sherman, he would talk of his mountain climbing and fishing and tell her he wished she could come and share what he loved about this place and its people. She would always say, "Someday, Dad." Now Emily knew all too poignantly, if you promise "someday" to a person, you better not waste any time. As her tears dropped unashamedly from her cheeks to splash gently onto the urn in her lap, she whispered, "I'm sorry, Daddy."

Emily took her dad's urn and returned to her motel but hardly slept. Just before dawn, she finally got dressed and taking the urn with her, drove her rental car through the dark to Sisters where she had breakfast at the venerable restaurant, The Gallery. Then she ventured on through the gradually lightening morning to her father's cabin. Upon unlocking the door, she slowly stepped inside. Flipping on a light, she tried to imagine what her father's life had been like here in this isolated place. The huge lava rock fireplace, now dark and cold, would have warmed and brightened this room with its massive beamed ceiling. She also remembered with sadness how her father's life must have ended at the hand of a murderer here in this very place he had called home.

She placed his urn on the fireplace mantle and ventured down a short hall to a small spare bedroom, bath, and a master bedroom. She knew she needed to get to work and sort through things and ready the cabin for sale. That is, of course, if she decided to sell. Right now, it was too soon for her to make that kind of a decision, a decision that she might regret. Life already had too many regrets for Emily Martin in her relationship with her father. She didn't want to set herself up for more.

An hour later, Emily was in her father's bedroom going through a dresser when she heard a car pull into the short driveway and stop. She looked out the window to see a man turn off the engine to a Mercedes SUV and step from the car. He was muscular and tattooed and did not look familiar to Emily, but then she knew few of her dad's friends. However, this man did not give the impression of belonging in Camp Sherman. Sensing the beginnings of fright, she wondered if her dad had a handgun in the cabin and she urgently began opening drawers in the bedside tables looking for one.

Biceps, in the maze of dirt roads on Green Ridge, had no trouble finding Wilbur Martin's cabin. After all, he'd been there before. Because of the winding and twisting nature of the road, he had not noticed that the Bentley had pulled out and was cautiously following him. However, the old dusty orange pickup parked in the dense trees and brush at an intersection not far back did spark his attention but only long enough to conclude the truck had probably been left there years ago when it just quit running. He had passed Beth and Arthur's cabin and gave it a cursory glance as he went by, knowing he could check on it after he torched Wilbur's cabin. What he didn't notice was Adam Carson sitting on a rock in the trees near Beth and Arthur's driveway with Arthur's double-barreled shotgun across his lap.

Biceps was surprised to see a car in Wilbur's driveway. Regardless, he pulled in behind it and got out of the Mercedes. He reached in the back of the SUV and took out the cutoff pool cue. He had no idea who was inside the cabin, but he was prepared to eliminate them, for that's all that killing ever meant to him. In walking past Emily's car he took a moment to peer inside. He spied her purse on the passenger seat. The slimebag gene ran deeply in his genetic makeup and he was also so good at being stupid, he quickly opened the car door and snatched the purse.

Emily Martin had been watching Biceps through Wilbur's bedroom window. Gripped in both her hands was a fully loaded 45 caliber Smith-Wesson revolver she had found in the top drawer of Wilbur's bedside table. She knew if she had to fire it, it would probably knock her off her feet, but as soon as Biceps grabbed her purse, she ran to the front door, flung it open and with both hands, aimed the gun at Biceps' chest and shouted, "Drop it, you son of a bitch!"

At that moment, with his truck's lights flashing and engine roaring, Cyril Richmond came steaming along the road. He veered into the driveway and hemmed in the Mercedes. Seeing the scene in Wilbur's front yard, the deputy was out of his truck the instant it slid to a stop. He had drawn his Glock handgun when he sternly yelled at Biceps, "Drop it! On your knees! On your knees! Hands behind your head!"

Keeping her gun aimed at Biceps, Emily watched until Cyril Richmond had things well in hand and Biceps was in handcuffs. She relaxed her stance and said, "Thank you, Deputy Richmond. It's nice to see you again."

CHAPTER 16

OLIVER DROVE THE Bentley cautiously around the loop. If Biceps spotted Deputy Richmond in his rear view mirror and would come flying around a sharp curve trying to escape, he could hit the Bentley head on. Jax and Oliver agreed that was certainly one way to stop the man.

They had nearly completed the loop when they came upon Wilbur's cabin and saw Aunt Phil and Conrad watching from the Volvo as Richmond helped a handcuffed Biceps into the back seat of the Deputy's truck. Mick, Dave, and Old Bowels were in the orange pickup and were right behind Aunt Phil and Conrad. Oliver continued on and stopped parallel to the Volvo.

"Be sure to check out that Mercedes," Aunt Phil leaned out the window and told the Deputy. "We suspect that he starts fires by soaking a tennis ball with barbecue lighter fluid, then tosses the ball with a dog toy ball launcher."

Richmond took another gander at the Mercedes and then said, "Really?" Then with a double-take he took in the Bentley with Oliver sitting stiffly behind the wheel like a man made of sticks, and the huge fellow in the back seat who had a wide grin on his doughy face and asked, "Who are these guys?"

Aunt Phil gestured to the Bentley and smiling, said, "Just more of our team."

Cyril Richmond raised one eyebrow.

"They're from Seattle," Aunt Phil added, as though that explained everything.

Richmond raised the other eyebrow.

If Deputy Richmond recognized Tommy Jax as a notorious underworld crime figure, he gave no indication. However, being a smart lawman, Richmond made a mental note to check on the large man whose face seemed familiar.

Aunt Phil sensed the hesitation in Richmond's countenance, but rather than go through all the explaining at that moment, she merely said, "Don't forget about the Mercedes."

"Right-o. Thanks for the tip." Richmond gave Aunt Phil and Conrad a nod and with a backward look over his shoulder at the Bentley, returned to the Mercedes. Peering into the luggage compartment of the SUV, he spied the ball launcher. Also, when he had yelled at Biceps, the man had dropped what looked like a three-foot long piece of the large end of a pool cue. Remembering what the pathologist had said about Wilbur and Emerson being killed with a blow of a hard round object like a bat or pipe, the hair stood up on his neck. He returned to his own truck to call Madras and then wait for a tow truck to come to Green Ridge to haul Biceps' car into the State Police crime lab in Bend.

EVENTUALLY, OLIVER, JAX, Aunt Phil and Conrad, Mick, Dave, and Old Bowels all reconnected at Beth's and Arthur's cabin. Mick, Dave, and Old Bowels were the first to arrive. Mick, as he climbed out of his pickup, said to Adam who was still sitting on his rock, "The war's over, at least for now."

"Who won?" Adam asked.

"We did," Mick answered. "Richmond has Biceps trussed up like a turkey and ready for grilling."

"Good!" Adam replied.

Dave spied the shotgun still in Adam's arms and asked, "Gee, Adam, where did you get the cannon?"

"It's Arthur's. I thought I'd look really scary holding it if Sullivan's man tried to come in here."

"You're scary, all right. Does Arthur really shoot that thing?"

"No. He says it was his dad's who only used it to kill mosquitoes in the spring."

"Ah. I hope it wasn't inside the house... that is, where he killed the, you know, mosquitoes."

"Don't know. You'd go through a lot of windows and walls and stuff doing that sort of thing indoors with a shotgun."

"Yup."

Beth and Arthur came out of the cabin with Max following. Max took his greeting duties very seriously and received lots of pets as he wagged from person to person.

After everyone was up to date with what transpired at Wilbur's cabin, the next thing to do was to find Andre Sullivan. Oliver's phone showed the Lexus parked at the Jefferson County Fair Grounds in Madras.

"There is some kind of a campaign rally going on there today," Tommy Jax said. "While we were driving over here, I went online to the Madras Pioneer newspaper. There is supposed to be a whole string of politicians talking, kind of an outdoor forum, so to speak."

"Well," Aunt Phil said. "Let's get on over there and get in-forumed. First though, you guys slip into some of this stuff." She carried a large bag from the car to the driveway and started pulling out bits of costuming. A western shirt, dark glasses, and cowboy hat went to Mick. Conrad was tossed a pair of bib overalls. Dave was given a baseball cap and a phony self-stick mustache which he plastered to his upper lip and hoped it would indeed self-stick. Aunt Phil kept for herself a straw sun hat, dark glasses, and bright pink lipstick which she applied liberally, not being too cautious about staying within the lines. "You guys," she said addressing Old Bowels, Oliver, and Tommy Jax, "are okay the way you are. They haven't seen you... yet."

Conrad held up the overalls and asked glibly, "Do I have to wear anything underneath these?"

Aunt Phil gave him a look which clearly telegraphed, *Did you just fall off the turnip truck?* This sent him and everyone else into gales of laughter. Fido must have also thought this was funny because he ran circles around

Conrad's feet and barked.

"What do we do with this little guy?" Conrad asked, pointing down at the dog. "We don't want to happen what happened at Black Butte Ranch."

"Oh, I don't know," Aunt Phil mused. "That might be kind of fun!"

Just leave him here with us," Beth offered. "We're glad to watch him until you get back."

"You want yet another dog?" Aunt Phil queried. "You have Max, Adam's two bulldogs, and now Fido?"

Beth said cheerfully, "I'll use your line, Phyllis; what's one more dog?" She reached down and said as she took Fido into her arms, "Come here, you little scamp." He wagged his tail and, to Beth's laughter, licked the end of her nose. "We'll have a barbecue ready for you guys when you get back," Beth said to the Geezer Underground as they piled into their cars. One by one, the cars roared off down Green Ridge Road on their way to Madras.

"Well," Arthur said, gazing after the last taillights to disappear down the road. "They'll be gone for a while. It's about an hour to Madras from here."

"Yes, I'd like to be a fly on the wall," Beth said as she, with Fido still in her arms, returned to the cabin.

"I think it's best," Adam chimed in, "that we stick around here just in case Sullivan has any other henchmen out there."

"You're right, Adam. Can't leave the homestead unprotected." Arthur held the cabin door open as Beth and Adam went inside. Arthur followed with Max bringing up the rear, hammering the door jamb with his happy tail.

Beth put Fido down onto the floor and Adam's bulldogs, Duncan and Noodles scurried up to reacquaint themselves with Fido. Max wagged his approval as, in the way of dogs, he approved just about everything.

Someone who wasn't approving was the cat. Booger was watching from high in the cabin's rafters.

Egads! Another dog? What on earth are they doing with another dog? What's worse, nobody asked me. No sir, no one asks the cat if anything is okay. The cat is just supposed to go along with everything like a dumb animal. Well, we'll see about this.

With this thought, Booger carefully descended from his perch in the rafters with the idea of inspecting this minute furry creature everyone was calling Fido.

Fido? Really? What kind of a name is that? It sounds like a Hobbit!

As though the little dog read the cat's mind, Fido came bounding up to Booger with nothing but play on his mind. Booger had other ideas and took a mighty swipe at Fido's nose. Fido was too fast and turned away just in time. Booger, rare for a cat, was caught off balance mid-swing and nearly fell over. He immediately acted as though he had meant to miss and began casually licking his paw. *I'm cool. I'm cool.*

Fido, rear end in the air and front end to the floor, wagged his tail and barked at the cat as if to say, "Let's play!"

Mid-lick, Booger looked at the dog with disdain and narrowed eyes. The cat then sauntered away with his tail on high. He jumped into the chair Beth had been occupying when the Geezer gang, in a cloud of dust and excitement, had showed up at the cabin. Settling down in the chair, the cat made a great effort to ignore Fido who, by now, was half nuts and continuing to bark.

"Fido! Stop that!" Beth admonished from the kitchen where she and Arthur were mixing a batch of potato salad. By this time, Max and Noodles had followed Beth and Arthur into the kitchen to help with the meal preparations. Duncan, the elder statesman of the dogs, always analyzed what was worth moving his arthritic body for. Consequently, he chose to stay in front of the fireplace and raised only one eyelid to watch the exchange between Fido and Booger.

Booger curled his forepaws under his chest and tucked his tail alongside his body. Because of the efficiency of a feline, there was no movement except for the very tip of the tail which twitched back and forth. Back and forth. With ears flattened out to the side and eyes squeezed into slits, the cat clearly telegraphed his disdain for the yapping little creature on the floor in front of the chair.

Why must they make so much noise? Surely the great god of beasts was distracted or drunk when it came to the fabricating of the dog. Beth needs to come in here and throw this thing out the door! Surely she knows I'm un-happy and my happiness should be priority one, always. After all, don't I dust the rafters for her? She calls me her rafter duster. Didn't I show Arthur my approval of her when he caught her stealing corn from his garden? I jumped right into her lap, didn't I? He had to know if I liked her, she belonged in this cabin with the rest of us. Now we are a family. Plain and simple. All because of the wisdom of the cat.

As if she was telepathic, Beth strode into the great room, snatched Fido up from the floor and holding him in front of her face said, "Why don't you come into the kitchen and help us with lunch, little guy?" He licked her nose again. She hugged the dog to her and laughed, a sweet tinkling sound that Arthur loved.

Booger closed his eyes. So did Duncan.

CHAPTER 17

TO DAVE AND Old Bowels, it would have made more sense to walk to Madras. Riding in Mick's truck, they had the wind in their faces and were beginning to get cold. This was not due to the windows being open because they weren't. It was the holes in the floorboards which were making the trip most unpleasant. Mick didn't seem to be bothered enough about the floorboards to get them fixed. He claimed you could easily see who you ran over, and if the brakes ever failed, you could just put out your feet.

This 1950 Chevrolet pickup had belonged to Mick's dad. He was the one who had it painted orange. He would put his black Labrador retriever in the bed of the truck and claim he was going to "air out the dog." Mick and his sister always suspected their dad was really going to the liquor store. Built before autos had electrical turn signals, their father tried to install turn signals by himself on the four fenders of the truck. However, when he activated the turn signals, the license plate light flashed on and off.

Mick's sister, now married to Dave, used the pickup to drive to high school. She would often chauffeur a pickup bed full of buddies on their own version of a night time hay ride and spook groups of necking teenagers parked on remote streets. They would startle them with whoops and hollers and a spot light mounted on the pickup's drivers' side door. Her dad would invariably find the pickup returned to the driveway but out of gas.

Years later, Mick was given the truck and never could part with it. It always reminded him of the goofy and fun side of a father too often inebriated to relate to. Mick kept the truck in his garage for years. When he retired from his radiology practice in Puyallup, Washington and moved to Camp Sherman, he brought the truck with him. Now that he was a widower he only needed one source of transportation, so he sold the two SUV's he and his wife had used and kept the truck. Mick was no more of a mechanic than his father had been, so Old Bowels kept the truck running for him.

The three men rattled along US 20, following the Bentley and Wardwell's Volvo. They drove through Sisters, making their way slowly through crowds of tourists enjoying the glitzy western town. Once clear of Sisters, they all turned off onto the highway to Redmond. They drove through miles of tidy alfalfa farms and cattle ranches. The highway descended a canyon near Eagle Crest Resort where the Deschutes River spilled over Cline Falls. In Redmond they picked up US 97 which led them to the north and eventually into Madras. A little over an hour from leaving Beth and Arthur's cabin, they arrived at the Jefferson County Fair Grounds where a crowd had gathered around a pavilion set up in a grassy grove of trees. There was a podium on the stage which was currently empty.

In expectation of a day-long rally of politicians, the crowd had made themselves at home. They brought lawn chairs and picnic goodies, blankets and pillows. Aunt Phil took a quick gander at the number of people and estimated several hundred were sitting or standing in anticipation of what the speakers would have to say.

The members of the Geezer Underground spread out and positioned themselves here and there around the audience. Thinking it was a possibility that Sullivan would recognize them if the original Geezers who were at the Black Butte Ranch banquet stayed together, Conrad teamed up with Old Bowels, Aunt Phil stood with Tommy Jax, Dave paired with Oliver, and Mick stayed by himself.

They didn't have to wait long before Brenda Bailey appeared on stage to introduce Andre Sullivan. She went on and on about the man's attributes and how he was going to open Oregon up for business once he was voted into office. The man himself then strutted out to the podium to enthusiastic applause from the crowd. Sullivan stood with his arms spread out to his sides as though he was the second coming and soaked up the adulation.

He began his speech by saying a prayer thanking God for the opportunity to serve the good people of Oregon as their senator in Congress. Members of the audience clasped their hands together, closed their eyes and bowed their heads as though Sullivan was gifted with a direct pipeline to the Almighty.

When Sullivan was finished with the prayer and the amens finally died off, he went on to list the disastrous circumstances created by previous administrations in the name of conservation. He told how he had been approached by business people, the very titans of industry, who begged at his feet for help in restoring what was rightfully theirs but was now denied by land use laws and the enormous restrictions to mining, logging, and other enterprise. After long sole searching and contemplation, as well as fervent prayer, he accepted, most humbly, that he was God's finest choice to restore the People's Land to the people of Oregon.

"The first thing I'd work for is to abolish the Endangered Species Act!" Sullivan paused while the audience cheered. "I'll tell you who the endangered species are. It's the American farmers, the loggers, the fishermen who need to feed their families." This comment was met with more amens from the audience.

"We'll open up all government lands so you, the people, can benefit from the trees and minerals that have been kept from us for a hundred years! We'll have booming businesses working in the woods bringing prosperity for all! The economy will always be more important than the environment!" More loud cheers and hurrahs came from the crowd.

"As for immigration, we'll just cut it off! Let the world know we're full! Send the Statue of Liberty with its 'Bring me your tired, your poor' nonsense back to France and see how they like it. This is our country and it's about time we say who stays and who doesn't!"

The crowd roared their consent, oblivious to the irony that they stood in near proximity to the Warm Springs Indian Reservation, a captive home to the original settlers of the land who remain powerless as to who stays and who goes.

Sullivan again spread his arms wide and appealed to the audience that he needed their help to get elected and that each and every one of them should open their hearts and wallets to augment his campaign.

Conrad said to Old Bowels, "That bastard should use his own money. He has more than god."

"Why should he," Old Bowels answered, "when he can get these suckers to give him theirs?"

Sullivan ranted on, "Speak to your neighbors, your families, your fellow workers and parishioners to spread the word that Andre Sullivan will save Oregon for Oregonians! I need their votes and dollars to send me to Washington, D.C. to straighten out that hell hole of government waste and degradation."

Cheers and applause filled the air as Sullivan strutted around the stage acknowledging the praise. Standing next to Aunt Phil was a woman who was clapping so enthusiastically that all her flaccid body parts were sent flapping. She turned to Aunt Phil and cooed, "Oh, isn't Andre Sullivan just wunnerful? He was sent to us by God, ya know."

"He was?"

"Oh yeah, he's goin' to save us from them environmentalists, ya know, them evil tree hugger people and all them furriners who take our jobs and rape our wimmin."

"Really? How do you know immigrants do that?"

Gesturing towards the stage, the woman replied, "He told us so."

Surrounded by Sullivan's adoring fans, Oliver quietly said to Dave, "The next time Sullivan says something totally preposterous the Geezers should, on cue, collectively barf."

This struck Dave as funny, not only what was said but that Oliver had said it. Dave started to laugh, and he laughed, and laughed until he could hardly stand up. Oliver snickered, then said, "Don't laugh so hard, you'll blow off your mustache." This sent Dave into new gales of laughter. Bending at the waist, he took off his cap and covered his face with it. Oliver stood stock still, Jack Benny-like, with his arms folded and holding one hand to his chin, his eyes turned to Dave in mock disgust.

Dave finally got control of himself but still laughed every time he glanced at Oliver, standing there with a stoic expression on his face but with eyes alive with humor. Dave understood now why Tommy Jax liked this man.

Conrad and Old Bowels moved away from the crowd and talked to each other in hushed tones. O.B. asked, "How does Sullivan attract so many people with this drivel? Are these people planted by his campaign?"

"It's rumored he busses them in but I don't think all of them are." Conrad said, eyeing the crowd. "I think a lot of these people seem to be from the surrounding communities. What I suspect Sullivan has done is bring the promise of a return to the life they grew up with; of fishing, hunting, farming, logging anywhere they want and to any extent. They don't recognize that the world is a more crowded place than it was forty or fifty years ago. They are also people who are suspicious of anybody of a different culture because they were taught to be that way by parents who were taught to be that way. Prejudice that deeply seated doesn't get changed easily."

Mick, in his western shirt and cowboy hat, chewed on a blade of grass and stood at the far edge of the crowd but near the pavilion. He stopped paying attention to what was going on with the crowd as they rustled around and prepared for the next speaker because he could overhear yelling coming from the back of the pavilion.

Mick pulled his hat down low on his head as he took his cell phone out of his pocket. Faking a call, he casually turned around so he could meander, cell phone to his ear, closer to where the argument was coming from. Bunched together were several vans and trailers used by the politicians as dressing rooms. He could see Andre Sullivan at the edge of the encampment with a cell phone to his ear. He was slowly walking towards a parking lot. The words coming out of his mouth and shouted into the phone completely destroyed the pious image he had depicted on stage.

"You fucking idiot! Whaddya mean you filched a purse? With all we have at stake here, you stole a goddamn PURSE? You were supposed to torch the place and now the police have the CAR! Do you realize what this is going to do to us? No! I'm not going to bail you out! You can rot in there as far as I'm fucking concerned!"

Sullivan's expletives faded away as he got further and further away from where Mick stood faking his own phone call. Soon, Mick put his phone away and turned back towards the pavilion. He had heard enough to know that Biceps' one allowed phone call from jail had been a colossal flop.

CHAPTER 18

DEPUTY CYRIL RICHMOND didn't have to wait long at Wilbur Martin's cabin for a tow truck. An available one was found in Sisters and it left right away for Green Ridge. As Richmond continued to wait for the tow, he also wanted to make sure Emily Martin was okay before he left her alone at her father's cabin. She had sat down on the top step of the cabin's porch and was holding the revolver in her lap.

Richmond approached her and asked if he could sit down with her. "Sure, Deputy." Emily looked up at Richmond with kindness in her eyes. She moved over slightly to make room for him.

As he sat down, he gestured toward the gun and asked, "Do you know how to handle that thing?"

"No," she answered with an embarrassed chuckle. "I'd hoped that guy," indicating Biceps, now securely locked into the back seat of Richmond's truck, "wouldn't be able to tell I didn't know how to operate it. All I know is that it's a big gun and it would probably knock me off my feet if I fired it." She fingered the revolver in her lap and gingerly picked it up asking, "Can you take it, please? I've scared myself with it."

"Sure," Richmond answered with a smile. He gently took the gun from her, broke open the cylinder and saw that it was fully loaded. Pushing the ejector rod, the bullets fell out of the cylinder and into his hand. Snapping the cylinder closed, he said, "You know, it wouldn't be a bad idea for you to know how to use this, if you are going to be staying here. Then you don't have to be afraid of it."

"I really don't know what I'm going to do, Deputy Richmond." The dejected tone of her voice touched him.

"Call me Cyril. Please." He smiled at her.

She gave him a shy smile and continued, "I don't know what my plans are. Everything, so far, has been a shock since I got that call from dad's friend Old Bowels. Yesterday dad's attorney told me how much my father's estate is worth. I was shocked! If I didn't want to, I wouldn't have to go back to my job. At this point, I don't know what to think."

"You don't have to do anything right away, do you?"

"No. I'm fortunate in that respect."

"What is it you do professionally?"

"I'm a CPA. I do mainly taxes and financials for individuals and small businesses."

"Well, there could be a market for that in Camp Sherman. I may be speaking out of turn here, but I've heard a few complaints, mainly from the seniors, of having to go into Sisters or even Bend to get their taxes done. It would be mostly seasonal, I would suspect."

"That'd be okay," Emily said thoughtfully. "It would be just enough to keep my hands in the pie, so to speak, keeping up with changes."

"Well, maybe Old Bowels could introduce you to his friends," Richmond said as he stood up. "There is quite a community of folks his age who have retired here. You could get an idea of who you would be dealing with. Believe me, there is nothing 'old' about the way those people think. Oh, let me give this gun back to you but first let me show you some things about it."

"Is that thing the safety?" Emily asked, pointing to a button on the side of the gun.

"No. Revolvers don't have safeties. That thing opens the cylinder, like this." He showed her how it worked. "It's best to store the gun without it being loaded. All you do to load it is pop the cylinder open like this... then stuff the bullets it, see? If you do want to keep it loaded, don't store it with the hammer resting on a bullet. Just leave one bullet out and let the hammer rest on the empty chamber. Now, for a safety, you just half-cock the hammer like this."

"Oh, okay. That's kind of scary. Won't it go off easier that way?"

"No, you have to let the hammer down gently before you can pull the trigger."

"Oh," Emily brightened. "Hence the expression 'going off half-cocked!'"

He laughed then said, "Right! There are some gun safety classes you should consider getting involved in. They are free and well worth the effort." He pulled out his wallet and took out a business card. "Call the number for the Sheriff's office and they can set you up. You don't have to go clear into Madras. I think they have them at the fire station in Sisters."

"Thank you, Cyril." She smiled at this no-nonsense lawman who yet had a gentle and thoughtful way about him. He returned the gun to her, and she got to her feet and took the gun inside to return it to the bedside drawer.

The tow truck could be heard grinding its gears up the slope to Wilbur's cabin. Richmond walked out to speak with the driver and watched while the Mercedes was loaded onto the back of the tow truck. Within a few minutes, the truck pulled away and Richmond was ready to haul Biceps into Madras. He briefly returned to the porch where Emily had been leaning against a post and watching the activity in the driveway.

Approaching her again, he said, "You have my card. We'll keep in touch. If I run across Old Bowels, I'll tell him what you and I talked about, that is, if you don't mind."

Looking at his card and then smiling at him, Emily replied, "No, of course not. I appreciate your help. I really do."

"Good luck with what you have to do here," Richmond said, gesturing toward the cabin. "I had to do that to my parents' house and it can tear your heart out."

"Thanks," she said simply. She then watched the deputy drive away until his truck was out of sight.

DURING THE DRIVE into Madras, Biceps kept kicking the bullet proof barrier between the back seat of Richmond's truck and the front seat. He screamed that he had to take a piss and if Richmond didn't stop, he'd pee all over the inside of the truck.

Richmond opened the small window between the front and back seats just enough to tell Biceps if he peed in his truck, he'd never pee again. He slammed the window shut and continued on his way, with Biceps now shouting for him to hurry.

In a remote part of the drive between Black Butte Ranch and Sisters, Richmond spotted a dog lying on the side of the road. Alarmed that someone had perhaps struck the dog and left it there, the deputy pulled over and backed up close to where the dog was now sitting up.

As Richmond got out of his truck, Biceps yelled, "Goddammit, Richmond, what are you doing?"

Richmond ignored him and knelt in front of the dog, an old chocolate Labrador. Its face was mostly gray. Talking softly, Richmond said, "What's going on, buddy? Are you okay?"

The dog slowly worked his way to a standing position and stiffly waddled to Richmond who took the dog's face in both his hands. Looking the animal over for obvious injuries and not finding any, he asked, "Are you hurt or did someone just leave you here?"

The dog weakly wagged its tail and licked at Richmond's hands. Richmond looked around the area for a house or trailer or barn and saw nothing. Fearing if he left the dog there, it would get hit by traffic or die some other horrible way, Richmond helped the dog into the front seat of his truck. He gave it some water by pouring it out of his own water bottle and into his hand where the dog lapped it up, thanking him by again wagging its tail.

"I think someone abandoned you because you're old and they didn't want to take care of you," Richmond said. The dog huffed and nuzzled the deputy's hand. "Or, maybe you're the missing dog from Emil Emerson's cabin. Okay, we'll take you into the humane society in Madras and see if you have a chip. That's a start."

"RICHMOND!!!" Biceps bellowed, "CAN YOU FUNKING HURRY UP?"

Okay, you son of a bitch. I can do that. If not for you, then for the dog. Richmond flipped on his lights and siren and mashed the pedal to the floor.

Immediately the dog perked up and looked at the scenery as it rushed past. Richmond opened the passenger side window a few inches so the dog could stick his nose out and now with tail wagging enthusiastically, it began to howl along with the siren. With lights flashing, siren blaring, dog howling and Biceps yelling, "RICHMOND, I GOTTA PEEEEE!" Deputy Cyril Richmond steamed towards Madras.

At the Jefferson County Sheriff's Office, Richmond left the dog in his truck and booked Biceps, turning him over to the jail warden with instructions to confiscate his shoes. Richmond wanted to compare the pattern on the bottom of Bicep's shoes to the footprint left in Wilbur Martin's kitchen. The warden looked at the booking documents the deputy had handed him and reading the prisoner's name, looked up at Richmond and said, "Percy Lumpsucker?" Richmond just raised one eyebrow and shrugged.

Richmond then walked down the hall to the Sheriff's office and asked one of the computer techs if they could look up an owner of a late model Bentley with a Washington State license plate, most likely in the Seattle area. Richmond gave the tech the plate number, hoping he had remembered it correctly or at least most of it in the brief encounter with the Wardwells and their friends at Wilbur Martin's cabin.

Deputy Richmond then proceeded into Sheriff Gary Larkin's office to update him on the investigation. When Richmond finished his story, Larkin asked, "How the heck did you know where to find this guy?"

"That group of oldsters who live right there in Camp Sherman gave me a tip," Richmond replied. "How they knew, I have no idea. I'm not sure I even want to know."

"Well, God bless old people," Larkin said. "They do keep their eyes and ears open. The rest of the population is too busy dealing with work and raising kids and paying bills to notice anything else going on around them." Larkin looked at his deputy and wondered how Cyril Richmond accomplished so much stuck up there by himself in the far south-west corner of the county. The Sheriff wished he had another dozen deputies just like him. "Carry on, Cyril. Keep me posted on what the state crime guys find in that SUV. The guy's a suspected murderer and with you seeing that pool cue in his hand, plus the ball thrower in the SUV, that's enough probable cause for a warrant."

On his way out, Richmond stopped by the desk of the tech who was researching the ownership of the Bentley. He looked at the printout she handed to him, studied it for a moment and said, mostly to himself, "Well, I'll be damned! That's who I thought it was!"

Before he returned to Camp Sherman, Richmond stopped by the Three Rivers Humane Society. Knowing that humane societies were on a state-wide network they should know if the dog had been reported missing. He learned that no, the dog was not microchipped nor had it been reported missing. Also, the clerk told him, the dog appears to be so old that most likely it wouldn't be adoptable.

Richmond knew what that meant for the dog so he said he would just take it with him and find a home for it. Surely one of the Geezers would take in an old dog and if not, he'd just take it home himself. His wife would go along with that. After all, he'd been bringing home critters in need of care for their entire marriage.

AT BETH AND Arthur's cabin, the Geezer Underground was a sub-dued group after they returned from the Madras political rally. They should have been ecstatic knowing that Biceps had been captured and was now gathering dust in the Jefferson County jail. However, the enthusiasm of the crowd at the rally towards Andre Sullivan and his campaign promises had put them all in a depressed mood.

"It was scary how those people treated Sullivan like he was the second coming," Aunt Phil said to Sophie who had joined the group. The two women carried bowls of salads and platters of barbecued chicken to the dining room table. "What he said about closing the borders to immigrants, sending the Statue of Liberty back to France, doing away with the Endangered Species Act and that the environment wasn't important was so bizarre. Then the way the crowd all went along with it was, well, it was just deplorable! I'm stunned! What has gotten into our world, anyway?"

Arthur, Adam, and Conrad also carried dishes, plates, silverware, and napkins while the rest of the Geezers, Jax and Oliver included, lounged around on the porch, having been shooed out of the kitchen when they all crowded in and offered to help.

Once the food had been placed in the dining room, everyone trooped into the cabin to load up their plates then trooped back outside to settle either at the picnic table or at lawn chairs placed here and there around the cabin's porch and front yard. The discussion continued regarding Sullivan and the favorable reaction he had received from the crowd in Madras.

"Here for decades we've been trying to clean up the pollution of our air and rivers," Conrad said. "Now a few idiots like Sullivan want to reverse all of that effort and that crowd just went along with it. Don't they recognize that we are destroying our planet and once it's irreversible, there is no other planet to go to? Do they really believe the problem doesn't exist or that it's someone else's problem? No one in their right mind would consciously leave that mess to their kids."

"They should have shouted him down!" Mick said angrily. "If that happened often enough, that would be the end of him."

"My take is that Sullivan and his ilk have awakened a latent element in our society that is racist, money grubbing, and wanting it all for themselves," Arthur mused. "Now that they have a spokesman in Sullivan, it's like someone left the gate open and it's okay to verbalize what in the past had been socially suppressed."

"Maybe we were the ones who should have shouted him down," Old Bowels added.

"But then we'd be revealing ourselves to him," Dave said.

"True, and we may have more work yet to do. At this point, we don't know how long this project will take," Adam added.

"All I know is that I could hardly believe what I was seeing and hearing." Aunt Phil poked at a pickle, then picked it up with her fork and placed it on Conrad's plate.

Mick got to his feet to get more potato salad saying, "If the police bring him down for murder, people will see him for what he really is. When the crime guys go over that SUV the henchman guy was driving, they will be able to connect it with Sullivan, even if it is owned by a rental company. There will be a record of who rented it. That will open a can of worms." He then paused as he was walking toward the cabin, turned around, looked at the rest of the Geezers and said, "You know what?"

Everyone stopped chewing and stared at him when he said, "The police will also find the tracking sensors we put on that Mercedes"

CHAPTER 19

THE SOUND OF tires on gravel turned all eyes from Mick onto Cyril Richmond's truck as the deputy pulled into Beth and Arthur's driveway. Then, wordless looks were exchanged between Beth & Arthur, Conrad and Aunt Phil, Mick and Dave, Tommy Jax and Oliver, and Adam and Sophie. Old Bowels grimaced with the expectation that Richmond was here to scold them about the tracking sensors.

The deputy opened the door to his truck and slid out. He said, "Arthur, what are you doing? You are either throwing a party or going into the used car business."

Arthur laughed and said, "Good evening, Cyril! Are you hungry? We have plenty of food here."

Richmond wove his way through the cars to where everyone was sitting in front of the cabin. "Thanks, but no. I have to get home. I just have a question for the entire group and then I need to talk to Old Bowels for a sec."

The Geezers all tensed as Richmond turned toward the group. But instead of mentioning the sensors, he told them about finding the dog beside the road, taking it to the humane society in Madras and what they told him about it being too old to adopt.

"It may have been abandoned or it may even had been Emil Emerson's dog. As far as we know, Emerson has no family. Someone might turn up, but, in the meantime, this dog needs to be cared for."

Mick perked up and said, "Well, let's meet it! Do you have it with you?"

"Yeah, he's in my truck." Richmond looked around at all the dogs:

Duncan lying next to Adam's chair, Noodles in Sophie's lap getting a belly rub, Max on the porch, and Fido in Conrad's lap. "Well, why don't you come with me to the truck, Mick? We don't want to start a dog fight here."

"Okay."

Dave watched Mick as he and Cyril Richmond walked out to Richmond's truck. With a smile in his heart, Dave knew this could be a significant healing step for the loss of Mick's wife.

Richmond also knew this was a much larger step for Mick than simply adopting a dog. This was a recognition that, yes, life does continue on and maybe it's time to go along with it. Richmond casually said, "So you think you might be interested in giving this dog a home?"

"Well, yeah, maybe." Mick remembered an instance last year when he took care of Max for Beth and Arthur. He took Max on a hike to the top of Green Ridge. Mick had lost his wife not a year before and had been paralyzed by the loss. After getting involved in activities with the Geezers, he was finally feeling some enthusiasm for life. When he and Max had reached the top of the ridge, he sat on a stump looking out over the Cascade Mountains, a scene which had been in his life forever. He then had a discussion with Max about the possibilities of getting a dog.

"You'll need to come with me to the shelter to pick it out," Mick had told Max while ruffling the dog's ears. "The two of you will have to get along so we can all do things together." Now Mick was thinking whatever dog he adopted will also have to get along with two English bulldogs and a Chihuahua.

"A big concern anybody my age has in getting a pet, Cyril, is if I croaked or became unable to care for it, what would happen to it?"

"You have a shit load of friends, Mick. They are all good people. They would do for you what you would do for them." Then looking at Mick's worried face Richmond asked gently, "Don't you think?"

"Yeah," Mick looked into Richmond's all-knowing eyes. "I guess you're right." Brightening, Mick then asked, "Well, tell me. What do you know about this dog?"

"Nothing. It was lying beside the road a few miles the other side of Black

Butte. I thought it was dead, at first. By the time I stopped and backed up, the dog had sat up and was looking at me. I knelt down and it came right to me. No collar, no nothing and, of course, it couldn't tell me anything. But it licked me and wagged its tail. I think it's a nice dog."

By this time, the two men reached the truck and Richmond opened the passenger side door and was greeted by the dog with licks and tail wagging. Having Mick there seemed to be an extra treat for the dog. Richmond moved out of the way so Mick could reach in. He took the dog's head in both his hands and said, "Hey, Buddy, how are ya?"

"Funny you should call him Buddy," Richmond said, watching over Mick's shoulder. "Because that's what I called him." Richmond could tell by the light in Mick's eyes that this dog had struck a chord in his heart. The deputy smiled as he said, "Why don't you take him over to meet everybody?"

"Okay." Mick took off his belt to use as a leash. "Now, I hope my pants don't fall off."

Richmond helped the old dog out of the truck. "You may have to build a ramp for him to get in and out of your pickup."

"I can do that." Mick and Buddy headed back to Beth and Arthur's cabin.

"Heads up you guys!" Mick announced to the group. "Take a hold of your dogs because here we come!"

Buddy walked politely beside Mick as he approached the yard full of people and other dogs. He first came to Conrad who was still holding Fido. The two dogs sniffed noses and Fido's tail wagged frantically. However, the little dog seemed content to stay in the safety of Conrad's arms. Noodles bounced to the ground and waited for Duncan to struggle to his feet. They approached Buddy and did their doggy sniffing without resulting in any traumatic reactions so Mick and the dog moved on to where Arthur and Max were waiting on the porch. Max was ecstatic with joy as he was ecstatic with most everything. Although Max obviously wanted to play, Arthur kept a firm hold on his dog's collar to keep the dog's enthusiasm in check. Buddy sniffed at Max, simply wagged his tail, and made no indications he was afraid of or intimidated by the larger dog.

"Well," Arthur scratched Buddy's head and said to Mick. "I think you have a winner here."

"I think Buddy has a winner in Mick," Richmond added, his arms folded across his chest while he watched what had just transpired. "Hey, Mick, I put a starter kit in the back of your truck for you. It's just a couple of bowls and a sack of dog food I picked up at the dog pound in Madras so you'll be all set to go."

"How did you know it was going to work?" Mick asked. Without waiting for a reply he looked at Richmond's grinning face and added, "Gods, you're great, Cyril!" Mick shook the deputy's hand and slapped his shoulder. "Thanks ever so much!"

"All the best, Mick!" Richmond then turned to Old Bowels and said, "O.B., can I speak to you for a minute?"

"Sure!"

The two men took a few steps towards the woods for a little privacy. Richmond said, "I spoke to Wilbur's daughter earlier today at her dad's cabin. She's unsure of what she is going to do but one possibility is to move into the cabin. She talked about setting up a small CPA practice doing taxes and stuff. Do you suppose you could introduce her to the Geezers so she can get to know some people around here? They may be potential clients and, knowing the Geezers like I do, they'll also be friends."

"Oh, sure!" Old Bowels agreed. "That's a great idea. Do you suppose she's still there, at the cabin?"

"I don't know but you could drive up there. You know it's not far."

"You're right. I'll take one of the girls with me. Maybe invite Emily down here for some chicken."

"Okay, O.B. I knew you'd take care of her."

Before Richmond left, he walked over to where Tommy Jax and Oliver were sitting at the picnic table. The deputy approached Jax with his hand extended. Jax stood and took the deputy's hand in his big paw.

"Tommy Jax, I'm Deputy Cyril Richmond." The two shook hands. Richmond continued, "I thought I recognized you this morning up at Wilbur's cabin. I saw you in the news a few years back. I took it for granted that you were in the slammer."

"Nope," Jax laughed. "I had a good lawyer: Phyllis."

"Ah, I understand," Richmond said, looking into Jax's dark eyes, eyes which had seen a lot of evil during Jax's notorious criminal career. Tonight, however, Richmond read nothing more in Tommy Jax's eyes than friendship and a quiet peace.

"Now I've turned my life around, Deputy. I'm just doing good deeds. Me and Oliver here."

Richmond shook hands with Oliver who remained pleasant, but silent.

"Good for you, T.J. Are you keeping these guys out of trouble?" Richmond tossed his chin back to where the Geezers were all gathered around Mick and his new dog.

"We're trying," Tommy Jax answered with a smile.

"Good, because I can't."

Tommy Jax laughed and even Oliver gave the deputy a small smile and nod of his head.

Richmond returned to his truck and, with a weary sigh, slid behind the wheel. A day's worth of good work was behind him and a loving home waited for him on the other side of the ridge. Cyril Richmond, Jefferson County Deputy Sheriff and guardian of all that is Camp Sherman, fired up his truck and headed for home.

CHAPTER 20

"HE DIDN'T SAY anything about the sensors," Conrad said as Richmond drove away.

"There probably hasn't been enough time to obtain a warrant," Adam replied.

"So, do we disguise ourselves and sneak into the State Police compound and snatch the sensors off the car?" Dave asked.

"Not unless you want to see the inside of a jail," Aunt Phil snickered.

"Oh, darn."

"So what do we do when they find them, the sensors? They will find them, eventually," Beth asked.

"We can act dumb," Mick suggested, ruffling Buddy's ears.

"That won't be hard," Dave added with a chuckle.

"Richmond is too smart," Tommy Jax said from his seat at the picnic table. Everyone turned to look at him. "He also knows you guys too well. You may as well tell him the truth, even where you got them, because he'll ask or he'll figure it out on his own."

"Unless Andre Sullivan presses charges against us," commented Aunt Phil, "there is nothing the law could do to us and why would they? We delivered Sullivan's henchman to them on a platter."

Tommy Jax said, "Sullivan is going to be in so much poop, he'll be too busy trying to save his own ass to even think about those sensors." Jax added laughing, "Besides, you have a good lawyer!"

"So do we know where Sullivan's other car is now?" Arthur asked.

Oliver looked at his phone and said, "I've been watching it on my phone ever since we left the fairgrounds in Madras. The car went back to the Oxford Hotel and hasn't left." Everyone stared at Oliver as that was a really long speech for him. Another reason for the stare was that Booger was asleep in Oliver's lap, having left his sanctuary in the rafters, slipping out the cabin door while people were coming in and going out.

Arthur and Beth, sitting on the porch with Max, exchanged amused looks. To their surprise, Booger then woke up, enjoyed a stretch and enormous yawn and casually stepped over to settle down in Jax's copious lap. Tommy Jax shared a grin with Oliver and gently stroked the cat's head between the ears with one doughy finger. Arthur and Beth then noticed Old Bowels approaching.

"Beth, Arthur, would you mind terribly if I ran up to Wilbur's cabin and if Emily is still there, invite her down here for a bite and to meet everybody?"

"No! Of course we wouldn't mind!" Beth and Arthur said almost simultaneously, their words stumbling over each other.

"Thanks. Actually it was Cyril's idea. He had talked to her earlier today and thought she may decide to move here."

"That would be great, O.B!" Beth said. "Poor woman! That had to be terrifying for her today with that thug showing up." Then she added, scolding herself, "Why didn't I think of that? She needs to get to know people around here. But, wait, O.B., you don't have your truck. Why don't I drive you up there and we'll see if we can persuade her to come back with us."

"I have a better idea!" Aunt Phil had overheard this conversation while she was taking a few plates back into the kitchen. "I'll go too. We can take our car so we can fit four of us." She then turned to the group to tell them what they were going to do.

"Gee, too bad we don't have a bus and we could all go."

"A whole bunch of old people hanging out the windows of a bus, whooping and hollering."

"That would be a hoot!"

"That wouldn't make her want to stay here. It would scare her off."

"She'd be on the first plane outta town."

"Yeah, probably better leave the bus home," Beth laughed as she and Old Bowels followed Aunt Phil to her car. "We'll be right back," Beth said over her shoulder.

EMILY MARTIN HAD finished her work in the back part of Wilbur's cabin. She still had the living room and kitchen to do but was consciously avoiding that area because that was where her dad had died. The police told her to go ahead with what she wanted to do in the cabin because they were finished with their work. Due to Deputy Richmond's determination that a thorough investigation of the scene where Wilbur died be completed, they had all the information they needed from the crime scene to put whoever killed Wilbur behind bars.

Regardless, Emily found it difficult to even enter the kitchen, let alone go through its drawers and cupboards. She knew she would be able to at some time, but, in the meantime, she spent most of the day going through bed and bath linens and her dad's clothes and personal effects. She sorted out what she wanted to keep, what could go to a homeless shelter and what should be thrown out.

What finally motivated her to quit for the day was in a bottom drawer in her dad's bedroom dresser. The dresser was part of a bedroom set which had been in Wilber's family for at least four generations. It was a lovely piece with a matching mirror built in the 1870's. Having been kept inside Wilbur's poorly insulated cabin since he retired years ago, the drawers were terribly warped. Emily tugged and twisted with a great deal of effort before the drawer opened to reveal its treasure of family pictures. As Emily began going through each one, she realized most of them were pictures of her; as a baby, a toddler, when he taught her to ride a bike, taking her to her first day of school and on through every childhood experience imaginable. Also in the drawer were every birthday, Christmas and Father's Day card she ever gave him.

Emily's mother had done everything she could to convince her daughter that her dad had left because he didn't love them. Emily always found that difficult to believe. It was the things he did, now that she was remembering, that spoke volumes for a man who could not speak openly to his daughter about his love for her. He always seemed to be present for things he knew were important to her. If she ever had the slightest inkling that her dad didn't love her, she now realized how very wrong she had been.

Overwhelmed with emotion, Emily just couldn't face going through those pictures and cards now. It was early evening and she was exhausted. She wearily got to her feet, bundled up the remains of a sack lunch she had purchased that morning at the Gallery Restaurant in Sisters, and was just locking the front door behind her when Aunt Phil, Beth and Old Bowels drove into her driveway. The three piled out of the Volvo and walked with smiles to greet Emily as she stood on the front porch.

"Emily," Old Bowels said as he noticed the fatigue in her face and the redness of her eyes, "I'd like you to meet some friends of mine and your dad's."

As he introduced Beth and Aunt Phil, both women detected the strain in Emily's face. Beth said warmly, "Emily, we know this day has been very hard for you. We'd like to invite you to my cabin for some dinner and to meet more of your dad's friends. We're just down the road."

"It's no fancy deal," Aunt Phil added. "Just come, have a bite and relax a bit. We're just a bunch of old shoes and want you to know we'll support you in any way we can."

Emily wiped at her eyes and then dusted off the knees of her jeans. She said, "Gee that sounds like heaven!" She looked down at herself, cautioning, "I'm a mite dirty."

Beth smiled, "Don't worry about it. This is Camp Sherman country. Dust is the badge of acceptance."

"Okay," Emily said brightly. "Why don't I just follow you in my car? I'll go back to my motel from your place. I've done all I can do here for now."

BACK AT BETH and Arthur's, Emily met the people who made up her father's life in Camp Sherman. A warmer and more loving bunch couldn't have been found anywhere. She felt her weariness melt away and she spent more time than she had originally planned, talking, laughing, playing with the dogs, snuggling Booger and taking a tour of Arthur and Beth's cabin.

When Beth pointed out the pieces of furniture Arthur had built, Emily mentioned the antique bedroom set of her dad's. "It's really lovely, I mean it was, at one time. My Great-Grandmother grew up with it and brought it to her marriage with Great-Granddad. It's had better days. The finish has suffered and the drawers are warped. It takes all I can muster just to open them."

She added, "I don't know how Dad lived there in that cabin, with just the caulking between the logs to keep out the cold. If I do decide to move here, I'll have to have the cabin modernized... a lot!"

"That would be fun to do that, don't you think?" Beth asked encouragingly.

"Yes. I've given it some thought. The first thing would be to replace the roof and insulate the ceiling and walls, however you insulate log walls. Next the bathroom and kitchen would need work, a forced air furnace or baseboard heat would make it livable in the winter. You do get cold winters here, don't you?"

"Yes, they can be quite cold," Beth answered, "but once it snows, it will turn sunny and dry. It's really beautiful after a snow!"

"If I come back in the spring or summer, the first thing I'd do is stop at that nice farmer's market in Sisters I noticed and buy pots of red geraniums to hang from the porch." Emily found she was enjoying talking about decorating the cabin. "Maybe paint the front door red and add shutters to the windows. Flower boxes on the windows would be cute too, if the deer couldn't reach them."

"Arthur could rebuild those drawers for your dresser. He built quite a woodworking shop on the other side of our clearing."

The use by Beth of the expression "your dresser" was not lost on Emily. Somehow it gave her a feeling of ownership toward her dad's cabin and the things in it, not just the heavy burden of having to take care of it now that her father was gone.

Late that evening, the Geezers began to depart for their own cabins. Tommy Jax and Oliver also left to return to Black Butte Ranch. Emily had helped clean up the dishes and put away the chairs. As she drove out to US 20 to start the drive back to her Bend motel, she felt a sense of belonging. She had experienced a shift of fate among the warmth of these people from Camp Sherman. She was now certain she would make a home for herself here in her dad's beloved mountains. Once she had sorted out his things, she would return to New York but for only a short while; long enough to say goodbye.

CHAPTER 21

THE NEXT MORNING, a weak sun struggled to break clear of the heavy cloud cover. Unsuccessful, the sun sighed and went back to bed, leaving a grey day for the planet Earth. Rain drops made cold ticking sounds at the Wardwell's cabin windows and tree branches bobbed and danced in rhythm with the swirling wind. Autumn was making itself known to Central Oregon.

Aunt Phil padded into the kitchen to turn on the coffee pot. She had set it up the previous evening with grounds and water. Snuggled in a long flannel Minnie Mouse nightie with matching robe and slippers, she still felt a chill as a gust of wind rattled the shutters.

The previous evening at Beth and Arthur's cabin, the Geezers decided they needed to find out what Andre Sullivan was doing in light of his henchman now taking up space in the Jefferson County jail. It wouldn't be long before Biceps would spill all the beans. Things were looking bleak for the aspiring Senate candidate Sullivan. In any event, Andre would need to react, most likely by leaving town. A plan was hatched to park the Geezers near the Oxford Hotel and watch for any sign of Sullivan and to keep track of his movements. Hopefully, they would be able to plant more sensors if Sullivan decided to abandon his other vehicle.

Aunt Phil had just taken the butter and jam out of the refrigerator when Conrad emerged from the bedroom. He had on his robe and slippers and his hair was askew. Still half asleep, his eyes were open but barely focusing. He looked like a wooly bear which had staggered from its den and wasn't sure to do so was a very good decision. She thought he looked so cute she wanted to hug him. So she did.

"Are you awake?" she asked as she wrapped her arms around him.

"Hmmph," he said onto the top of her head.

"I didn't think so. Come get your coffee, sweetie."

"Hmmph," he said again and followed her back into the kitchen. He clambered onto a stool at the breakfast bar.

"You know we have a big day today, spying on Andre Sullivan." She filled a mug with coffee and set it before him.

"Oh, God! That bastard!"

Now she knew he was awake. She said, "We can't dawdle around much this morning because Sophie is going to come over and help me dress like an old lady." That statement struck them both as funny and they started to laugh.

"I mean, some old lady other than me. Sophie is bringing over a wig, an old fashioned dress, some goofy slippers..." Aunt Phil looked down at her own slippers which had Minnie Mouse ears and pink polka-dot bows proudly perched on the toes. "I mean some other goofy slippers."

"I'll love you anyway," Conrad said around a huge bite of toast and Beth's huckleberry jam. "You know," he added, "I should be the one to dress up. I'm not comfortable with you having to be that close to Sullivan. Why don't you let me be the old lady?"

"With your mustache, you'll look like a walrus in drag. Besides, he may recognize you. You and Fido got really close to him at the banquet toss-up at Black Butte Ranch. And, we'll be fine. All of the other Geezers will be close by. I'm not afraid of that mutant."

"So, tell me, what are you and Sophie going to do?"

"You know we talked last night about the possibility of Sullivan getting rid of the other rental car. We need to get a tracking sensor on something else of his, like a suitcase or briefcase or something."

"His nose. That's something. Or, slap it on his ego, it goes everywhere with him and is certainly large enough."

"I'm not sure what we'll put it on, but we hope to have an opportunity to do so if we engage him in conversation or trip over him or whatever we find to do when we encounter him. Sophie and I will be an old lady and caregiver. I'll use the walker and she'll fuss along beside me."

"Just like for real," he said smiling and flicking toast crumbs from the front of his robe to be caught by Fido. The little dog had planted himself at the foot of Conrad's stool.

Aunt Phil continued, "Maybe I'll trip and fall on him or stumble into him. That's the first act."

"Oliver is going to play the chauffeur, right?"

"Right. That's in Act 2. Oliver will drive up in the Bentley like he's come to pick us up. We want Sullivan to think I'm a rich old hag and maybe he'll show some interest, you know, a source of easy money to exploit. Anyway, the idea is to slow him down long enough for one of us to plant a bug."

"Too bad you can't plant a real bug, like a brain eating bacteria," Conrad chuckled.

"It would starve," she countered.

"Hoof and mouth? He's mouthy enough."

"But no hooves. It will be best if he gets indicted for murder. Then his adoring followers should come to their senses," Aunt Phil said hopefully.

"The police need to find sufficient evidence first and then be able to find him."

"Oh they will find sufficient evidence, alright. It was all in that SUV that Biceps drove. Finding Sullivan? That's where we come in," Aunt Phil smiled knowingly.

"Yup!"

BEFORE TOO LONG, there was a rapping at the door. Conrad, now dressed in jeans and a sweater, opened the door to what appeared to be an enormous pile of laundry with legs. Up over the top of the pile popped the perky face of Sophie.

"Good morning, Conrad!" Sophie chirped as she bounced in with what was an armload of costumes. She was dressed in a nurse's white outfit, complete with an old fashioned starched cap and white nylon stockings. Her kinky mop of red hair was contained into a severe bun at the back of her neck.

"I have just the outfit for you, Phyllis!" She said as she dumped the pile on the sofa. "Somewhere in here..." she rummaged and pulled out a bleakly old-fashioned dress of a dreary midnight blue color and a fur stole made from the hide, head and front legs of an ill-fated, beady-eyed critter. The stole had been gleaned from the estate of some long deceased matriarch who wore it only to church during the 1940's. Along with the stole came a dark blue hat with a tiny veil and short, dingy white gloves. She also had a pair of extra-large nylon stockings which, Sophie declared, would sag and bag appropriately. Completing the outfit was a frowsy white wig and bunny slippers.

Aunt Phil squealed with delight and gathered the dress and other paraphernalia into her arms and bustled into the bedroom to try them on. While she was doing that, Mick and Dave rattled up in Mick's truck with Mick's new best friend, Buddy, happily tied in the pickup bed. Conrad, recognizing the clanging commotion of the truck met the two old codgers, with Buddy at their side, at the cabin door.

"Come on in, you two. May I caution you to enter at your own risk." Laughing, Mick and Dave stepped inside and as Fido bounced over to greet Buddy, the two men approached the pile of clothes Sophie had dumped on the sofa.

"Mick! Dave! Boy, do I have great getups for you!" Sophie exclaimed. She held up a black suit jacket and matching pants and told Dave he was going to be a priest.

"Boy, that's a stretch!" Mick said wryly.

Sophie then handed Dave a black, collar-less shirt with a separate white priest's collar which buttoned in the back. She had told him to wear black shoes which completed the look.

Mick looked him over and said, "Put in a few words for me, would you, Father?"

"I'll try but I doubt it'll do any good."

"And you, Mick," Sophie declared, "are going to be a be-fuddled old university professor!"

Dave said, "That won't be too far off the beaten path... I mean the befuddled part."

Sophie untangled the rest of the clothes in her pile and produced a brown, herringboned patterned wool jacket with suede patches on the sleeves, a grey turtleneck sweater, a rumpled pair of Dockers pants which were too long, a pair of loafers, stretched out sloppy grey socks, and a Greek fisherman's hat. She added a pipe to finish off the outfit.

"Cool!" Mick whooped as he grappled up the clothes. "This is what I always wanted to be until I flunked bonehead chemistry at the U of O."

"You didn't flunk anything at the U of O!" Dave admonished, knowing Mick graduated in pre-med in three years instead of the usual four.

Mick, picking up his costume, snickered, "They never knew I Googled all the answers."

"When you were in school, the Google guy hadn't even been born yet!" Dave declared to Mick's back as he marched to the small bathroom off the cabin's entryway to don his new duds.

Once the guys were dressed, Aunt Phil made her grand entrance. Shuffling along in the bunny slippers, she leaned heavily on the walker as she shoved it ahead of her. She was hardly recognizable. She had put on a real pale shade of makeup and accented her lips with a bright red lipstick, slopping it outside the lines of her mouth. The wig was tousled and matted and hung in her eyes. The dress was on backwards and a long slip hung below the hem, the nylon stockings bagged and sagged as promised, and the ratty fur stole was casually slung over her shoulders. The bright eyed varmint appeared to be laughing.

The three stood together as Sophie crossed her arms over her chest and seriously viewed her handiwork. She picked up a wooden cane and handed it to Mick who leaned on it appropriately. He said, "Don't make me look too doddering or someone will swoop me up and put me away in a home somewhere."

Dave quipped, "That may happen anyway."

"Speak for yourself, Your Eminence."

CHAPTER 22

THE SAME GREY cloud cover which blanketed the Cascade Mountains over Camp Sherman also hung drearily over the city of Portland. With his mood matching that of the sky, Lieutenant Shawn Avery entered his office and plopped down in his desk chair. Disheveled, he was a mess before the day had hardly started. So was his desk. He barely had time to scan which pile of paper he would work on when his phone rang.

"Lieutenant, this is Cyril Richmond." Deputy Richmond had been at his desk at the Camp Sherman Fire Station since 6:00 AM.

"Cyril! What do you know?" The sound of Richmond's voice brought Avery's mood up a notch. Avery liked this back woods lawman from Jefferson County.

"We have a possible murder weapon, a sawed off pool cue with what we think is blood and tissue remains on it and a suspect in custody. His shoes match a footprint we found in the cabin where we found Wilbur Martin murdered. The guy is not talking, yet. Protecting his boss, I suspect. The State Police lab in Bend is working on connecting the blood and tissue samples with our deceased."

"Damn, you're good!" Avery's mood went up another notch.

"The lab isn't finished yet, but what we'd like is a more positive link between Andre Sullivan and Doctor Herman Diggs. All we really have is the fact they are cousins.

"Oh, another thing," Richmond went on, "you said you had several burned houses which you thought were linked to Sullivan and Diggs working in Portland."

"Right, there were thirteen in this one area of Northeast Portland we concentrated on." Avery's mind was like a file cabinet and he rarely forgot a factor in a crime. Remembering family birthdays and to get a haircut were other matters.

"I'd like to know if any of the Fire Marshall's reports showed that there was a tennis ball at or near the source of ignition. That would help in connecting our cases with yours. In our two murders, one of the cabins was torched and a tennis ball which had been soaked in charcoal briquette lighter fluid and tossed into the cabin is suspected to be how it was ignited. In the car, along with the pool cue, were a dog's ball launcher, several cans of tennis balls and a can of barbecue lighter fluid."

"No shit?"

"No shit."

"Okay, I'll get my guys on it. Have you nailed down Sullivan?"

"Not yet. The car we've impounded was rented to a Brenda Bailey. We think she's the side kick, campaign manager, and the spokesperson who covers his ass at press conferences. Her whereabouts and Sullivan's are currently unknown. Unless his hired gun talks to us, we can't yet go after Sullivan."

"Got it. I'll get back to you as soon as I can about the cousin."

"Okay, thanks, Shawn."

AVERY GATHERED BANNING and Kowalski for a brief meeting. Corporal Banning was to research the Fire Marshall's reports on the burned homes while the other two drove out to Clackamas to again talk to Diggs.

Using a patrol car with the lights flashing, Kowalski and Avery quickly covered the distance to the Medical Examiner's facility. When the two policemen entered the building and approached the reception desk, the young woman who had previously greeted them when they first came to talk to Diggs quickly picked up her phone. After saying a few quiet words, she addressed the policemen with, "Our acting director will be right out to speak to you." When she said "acting director," Avery and Kowalski exchanged looks.

The acting director was a short young woman in a white lab coat which hung below her knees. Avery, who felt every year of his middle fifties, thought she looked about eighteen years old. She approached him with her hand outstretched.

"Lieutenant! I'm Dr. Wagers."

Shaking her hand, he said, "You know who I, er, we are?" He gesturing over his shoulder to Sergeant Kowalski.

"Yes," she said simply. "Can we talk over here in the conference room?" She held out her arm in the direction of the same conference room where the policemen had met with Dr. Diggs just a few days ago.

They were soon settled in the room; this time Kowalski no longer stood guard at the door but sat with a notepad on his knee.

Dr. Wagers spoke first, "I know why you're here."

Avery looked into her pleasant dark eyes and said, "Dr. Diggs."

"He hasn't been at work since your visit with him last week."

Avery raised his eyebrows, knowing full well there was more she was going to say.

"He has not answered his phone. I've tried to call him several times. However, he has done this before; just hasn't shown up for days at a time."

"Oh?"

"Dr. Diggs has addictions, Lieutenant. Gambling is one; alcoholism is another, drugs too. He seems driven by them and, unfortunately, it affects his work. However, it's my personal feeling that this time he won't be back."

Avery and Kowalski exchanged glances.

Dr. Wagers continued, "After he met with you, he left shortly afterwards. He went straight to his office and cleaned out his desk of some personal things and then left. He didn't say a word to anyone but seemed nervous. Frantic is a word I'd use to describe his state of mind, the way he went through his desk and hustled out of the building. When he didn't show up the next day I tried to call him but got no answer. It's my gut feeling he's abandoned his job here and we won't see him again."

"Do you think he could be in danger?" Kowalski asked. "Gamblers who run short of cash can get in debt quickly with the wrong people."

157

"I have no idea, Sergeant. I do know that Dr. Diggs is not intimidated easily. His leadership style has been, shall I say, most inflexible. The only time I ever have seen him act the least bit unconvinced of his superiority was when you officers talked to him last week. That was the first time I've ever seen him act scared."

"Don't like him much, do you?" Avery asked with a wry smile.

Wagers leaned toward Avery, looked him in the eye and said pointedly, "No. I don't."

"Would you share with us his telephone number and address? We can get it ourselves, but if you could give them to us, it will save us time."

"Of course. I'm glad to help."

"One more thing, Dr. Wagers. You don't happen to have a picture of Dr. Diggs, do you?"

"There should be one in his employee file. Give me a minute, okay? I'll make a copy for you." She stood, left the conference room, walked briskly across the lobby and disappeared through the big double doors leading to the laboratories.

Both policemen stood and headed for the lobby. Kowalski said quietly to Avery, "Boy, did we luck out with her!"

ARMED WITH A photo and a residence address for Dr. Diggs, Avery and Kowalski set out towards Beaverton to visit his home.

"She didn't pull any punches, did she?" Kowalski asked while he entered the address into the patrol car's GPS.

"Not at all. She had some pent up aggression towards Diggs that she felt justified in sharing with us. She has probably suspected the worst from her boss for a long time and has had to take up the slack due to his absences and is royally pissed off."

"Lucky for us. It helps our investigation when people are honest and try not to protect someone."

"Yeah," Avery sighed and put his hand over his eyes. "If people would just tell the truth, it would make our job so much easier."

Shawn Avery was tired. The day had hardly begun and he already felt worn to a frazzle. He knew he was burning out. He'd spent half of his life with the Portland Police Bureau and sometimes he wondered how he could hang on until retirement.

He'd known men who had been with the bureau for thirty to forty years and who had essentially retired years before they officially did. In his young, gung-ho days he had always said he would never be that way but as he aged, he could relate to those men. He had seen just about everything evil humans could bestow upon one another and he was just plain sick of it.

He felt fortunate that he had good men to work with. As a team, they made mayhem the job brought into their lives easier for all of them to deal with.

Kowalski, a skilled driver who had spent several years with the patrol division, expertly maneuvered through the traffic towards the Vista Ridge Tunnel. Avery looked up at the city's West Hills. The cloud cover had lifted, revealing the wooded slopes which were changing colors with the season. Avery thought, before winter set in, he should take a few days off. Cyril Richmond had once invited him to do some fly fishing on the Metolius River right there in Camp Sherman. Maybe he'd just do it. If it worked out, he'd take Banning and Kowalski with him. It would give all of them a break. Yup, that was a good idea.

As Avery was musing about fly fishing, Banning called. He reported that the Fire Marshall's reports on the causes of the fires involved with this case were inconclusive. From gas stoves catching something aflame to electric lamps being knocked over by the victim falling and the broken light bulbs subsequently setting a shade on fire to hot coals being disposed improperly in garbage cans. No mention of the remains of tennis balls. The killer was definitely good at covering his tracks.

DR. DIGGS'S HOUSE was not what they expected of a medical professional. A small, ill-kept square built in the 1950's, the little house sat forlornly in the middle of a messy lot of mostly dead grass and blackberry vines. A sagging single car garage stood separately to the side of the house. The garage door had been left open and the building was empty with the exception of an old reel lawn mower and a few garden tools, all draped with spider webs.

As Avery and Kowalski stepped from their car, Avery remembered what Dr. Wagers said of Diggs, that he was plagued with addictions. The state of this sad little house was the typical collateral damage of an addicted soul.

Avery started for the front door and Kowalski headed towards the back. Avery mounted the crumbling concrete porch, knocked at the door and listened carefully for the sounds of someone coming to the door. He heard nothing. He knocked louder and then rapped heavily on the door. "This is the police, Dr. Diggs. Open up please."

Getting no response, Avery backed away from the front door to see Kowalski come around from behind the house.

"Nothing going on back here, Shawn. I looked in some windows and I could see dresser drawers in a bedroom are standing open. A closet door is open with some empty hangers lying on the floor. It appears to me he hurriedly packed and left. We could gain entry by way of a welfare check but I think it's a waste of time."

Avery responded, "Let's get some uniforms up here to do that. They can also find out what the neighbors know. In the meantime, let's get back to the office and put out an APB on Diggs and his car. Banning will be able to find out what he's driving and the license number."

Shawn Avery knew he would also have to place a phone call to Deputy Richmond that Richmond was not going to like: Herman Diggs could not be found.

CHAPTER 23

IN CAMP SHERMAN, the geezers were getting into their costumes for the day's encounter with Andre Sullivan. In Portland, Lieutenant Avery and Deputy Richmond were conversing on the phone. In Bend, a peculiar but ferocious argument was transpiring in Sullivan's room at the Oxford Hotel.

"What the hell are you doing here?" Andre Sullivan was pissed and was backing away from the door. His cousin, Dr. Herman Diggs, had knocked at Sullivan's door and then bulled his way inside when Andre opened it.

"You are never hard to find, Andre. You always stay at the most expensive places." Diggs sneered and stood in the entryway into the suite of rooms. Brenda Bailey was seated on a small settee and remained oddly quiet as though she wished she could dissolve into the upholstery. She was rendered speechless by Diggs's sudden presence.

"Well, get out!" Sullivan looked like a hobbit up against the looming figure of Diggs.

"Call the cops, you feckless wonder," Diggs laughed. "But first, I have something to say to you. Your game is up, Andre! The Portland Police have my number and I'm not going down without you going with me."

"One for all and all for one, huh, Hermie? Just like when we were kids and did your sister?"

"You can't threaten me with that anymore, you're just as guilty as I am."

"Tell me, did they ever find her?"

"No, and they won't unless someone wants to dig up an old John Doe in that pauper's grave."

"Fit her in there with him, did you?"

"Yeah."

Both men were quiet for a bit and stared at one another. Brenda was horrified at what she was hearing. Did these two murder Diggs's sister and dispose of her body? Worse, what did they do to her before they murdered her? This must have been when Diggs was an intern at a mortuary while in medical school. Could these two get any more evil?

"So what are we going to do?" Sullivan appeared oddly meek in the presence of this larger and more formidable man. Could it be that Andre Sullivan, the obsessed warrior of all that was money grubbing, was actually out of ideas?

"Run. Like we always talked about when we were kids."

"Butch Cassidy and what's his name, right?"

"That's right. It looks like you're packing." Diggs looked around the room at the suitcases open on the bed.

"Yea, with Biceps behind bars, our campaign is toast, at least for now. As soon as he squeals to the police, they'll come after me. I made him swear to me that if he got caught, he wouldn't rat out the others. Of course, he's dumb enough to think that applies to all of us. He'll figure out soon enough that he's been a patsy and then he'll talk. We're going to leave Oregon for a bit. Wait for stuff to cool down. It might take some time, but I'm thinking that's the best thing to do."

"I'll go with you."

Andre looked at his cousin. They hated each other but needed each other, especially now. He asked, "Okay, you have wheels?"

"Yeah."

"Good! We'll use them until we can get something that can't be traced to us. Come on, Brenda, get your ass off the couch and finish packing your stuff. We gotta get out of here, now!"

BY THE TIME Sullivan, Bailey, and Diggs exited the hotel, the Geezer Underground was ready for them. They had been parked a half a block away in the Volvo with Adam behind the wheel. Oliver was a block away in the other direction waiting for the signal that he was to drive the Bentley to the hotel with the pretense of picking up Aunt Phil and her "nurse."

Although none of them knew who the tall, dark man was with Bailey, it was obvious he was a foil. Sullivan left the hotel first carrying no luggage but a briefcase as though it was just another day on the campaign trail. That was the only way he could get away without paying his bill.

Brenda and Diggs left together as if they were a couple, hauling the luggage with them. Brenda kept her head down and walked on the side of Diggs away from the registration desk. Diggs, of course, was unknown to the hotel staff and brought no attention from the employees at the desk. The lobby was busy with other guests coming and going.

As soon as Sullivan reached the sidewalk, he hovered near the curb where Diggs had parked his car, an older model Ford Taurus. The car was of the era where many automobile models looked as though they had been squeezed out of a tube. It hadn't been washed since the last time hell froze. The finish was dull and splattered with bird droppings as Diggs's garage had become a favorite roosting place for a large flock of pigeons.

As soon as they spotted Sullivan, Aunt Phil and Sophie exited the Volvo. Aunt Phil slowly pushed the walker and with Sophie holding onto her arm, made their way down the street towards the hotel. Not far behind but definitely separate from Sophie and Aunt Phil was Mick, leaning heavily on the cane and limping convincingly. Dave crossed the street and jauntily walked down the sidewalk, a simple parish priest on his way to the book store across from the hotel.

At the same time Aunt Phil had reached the proximity of Sullivan, Brenda Bailey and Diggs exited the hotel dragging several pieces of luggage behind them. Aunt Phil stopped, pointed to Sullivan, who had moved to help load the luggage into the Taurus's trunk, and said, "Don't I know you?"

Sullivan looked at her and said, "Huh?"

Aunt Phil started towards him with her walker and peering at him myopically said, "Yes! You're Walter, my fourth husband!"

Sullivan looked around for an avenue of escape. He found none since he was between Aunt Phil and the Taurus. Bailey and Diggs were loading the luggage and were effectively blocking the rear of the car and now Mick was approaching from the other side. Sullivan's venues of escape had been cut off. He stammered, "Sorry, lady, you're mistaken."

As Aunt Phil continued to approach Sullivan, Sophie was tugging on her arm, all the while explaining to Sullivan, in a British accent, "I fear, Sir, that Madam gets confused. You mustn't be alarmed. These spells don't last long and then she's right as rain, she is."

Aunt Phil faked tripping in her bunny slippers, which wasn't hard to do and in so doing, shoved the walker into Sullivan. The man slammed into the car and started to fall. Aunt Phil managed to fall on top of him, effectively knocking the wind out of his lungs. Sullivan lay on his back on the sidewalk, gasping like a beached carp as Mick, Sophie, Diggs and Brenda tried to lift Aunt Phil to her feet.

Dave came out of the book store where he had been watching and as he crossed the street, he said quietly into the radio in his shirt pocket, "You're on, Oliver." Leaning on the fender of the Taurus, Dave placed a tracking sensor on the underside of the bumper. He managed to place another underneath the fender before he dove into the mix of flailing arms and legs. With many "Oh my's" and a few "Tut-tut's," he tried to help as folks grabbed and pulled Aunt Phil's arms this way and that. Mick dropped his cane, a shoe kept coming off, and he lost his hat repeatedly. He generally got in the way while he grappled with all the things which he kept losing.

Aunt Phil purposely gave no assistance to those trying to get her upright. She sat there like a sack of clams on Sullivan's stomach, her legs, baggy socks and all, sticking straight out in front of her like a little kid in a really big chair. By the time Sullivan's eyes began to bulge, Aunt Phil was finally brought to her feet. Sophie straightened Aunt Phil's hat and stole and brushed her off while Diggs and Brenda tended to Sullivan.

Oliver neatly whisked the Bentley to the curb and got out. Muttering, "Madam, madam, are you all right?" he took Aunt Phil by the elbow to help her to the car.

Sullivan, by this time, had gotten to his knees and angrily sputtered, "Is *she* all right? What about me? She could have killed me! I'll sue, that's what I'll do!"

Diggs grabbed Sullivan's arm and boldly lifting him to his feet, hissed, "Andre! Come on, we have to get out of here!"

Sophie then said to Sullivan, "Mrs. Vanderbilt is so sorry if she hurt you Sir, but she's not herself these days and loses her balance on occasion. It was so lovely of you to break her fall."

Sullivan did a mental double-take and said, "Vanderbilt? Did you say Vanderbilt?"

Again Diggs snarled, "Leave it, you nincompoop, before the cops come."

The word cop got Sullivan's attention and abandoning the urge to sue Aunt Phil or at least ask for a campaign donation, he scurried to toss the remaining baggage into the trunk. With Bailey and Diggs, he piled into the Taurus and the three roared off down the street, leaving a tail pipe worth of black exhaust in their wake.

BY NOW, A crowd had gathered and watched as Oliver and Sophie helped Aunt Phil into the back seat of the Bentley. Sophie also got in the back seat as Oliver folded the walker and stashed it into the trunk.

Someone from the crowd could be heard saying, "Did ya know she's a Vanderbilt?"

All eyes turned to the speaker as someone else exclaimed, "Really? Here in Bend?"

Oliver then got behind the wheel and calmly moved the Bentley into traffic. They waited until they were well away from the Oxford before they all erupted into laughter.

Meanwhile, Mick and Dave crossed to the bookstore side of the street and made their separate ways further on down the block and around the corner where Adam waited with the Volvo. They too enjoyed a few whoops and high fives as they worked their way through town towards a pre-planned rendezvous with the other Geezers at Drake Park.

CHAPTER 24

AUNT PHIL LEANED over the back of the Bentley's front seat and peering at Oliver's phone, asked, "Where is Sullivan going? Can you tell?"

"Oliver glanced at his phone and handing it over the seat to Aunt Phil said, "It looks like he might be headed for the Redmond airport."

Sophie said while looking at the phone in Aunt Phil's hand, "Wow! Look at that cluster of sensors! We must have planted a bunch!"

"We better cue O. B. They're headed his way."

Old Bowels was sitting in his pickup near the intersection of US 97 and US 20. He heard on his two-way radio, "O.B! This is Phyllis. Sullivan is headed your way. They are in an old, dirty grey Ford Taurus. There are three of them; Sullivan, Brenda Bailey, and another guy, tall and wearing a dark suit. He's the driver. They may be heading for the airport in Redmond, but we don't know for sure. We're trying to get in touch with Deputy Richmond."

"Okay," Old Bowels replied. "I'll keep watch for them." The importance of Old Bowel's mission was not lost on him. He could feel his heart rate quicken and all his senses were on alert. It wasn't long before he spied the Taurus as it went by. As he pulled his old pickup onto the highway and sped to catch up, he realized he hadn't had this much fun in years.

IN THE TAURUS, the three fugitives didn't notice when they whizzed past a rattle-trap 1947 Ford pickup with a bumper sticker which said, "Honk if anything falls off!" They also didn't notice when it pulled onto the highway behind them. They were preoccupied with the continuing snarl-fest which had begun in Sullivan's hotel room.

"All right, genius, where are we going?" Sullivan had regained his composure and growled at his cousin.

"To the airport," Diggs snapped back. "How else are we going to get out of here?"

"Don't you think that's the first place they'll look?" Brenda said from her distasteful position in the back seat. The seat was strewn with empty take-out tubs and wrappers, drink cups, lids, straws and other assorted garbage. The headliner was hanging in loose drapes as it disintegrated from a robust moldy growth. Not only was Diggs a crook, he was a slob. "If we're going to fly out of here, we need an airport that isn't so obvious to the law, like Klamath Falls or Eugene."

"Holy shit woman!" Diggs exclaimed over his shoulder to Brenda. "Both of those are miles away. It'll take us hours! How are we going to do that without being noticed?"

"We stick to back roads," Brenda said as she leaned over the back of the front seat. "Let's go on up here to Redmond, hit that highway that goes to Sisters, and then take the McKenzie Pass highway over the mountains to Eugene. They will be looking for us to go either to the Redmond airport, or towards Portland."

Diggs glanced over to Sullivan. Sullivan shrugged and said, "Sounds good to me."

As they hung a left onto OR 126 at Redmond, Old Bowels radioed to Aunt Phil, "They're not going to the airport! They just turned off towards Sisters. I'll hang back a ways but continue to follow them."

"Okay, O.B., be careful!"

"Will do. Have you been able to reach Richmond?"

"No. Not yet. He doesn't answer his phone. He has always told us we can call 911 if it's an emergency because they'll know where he is. If Sullivan is running, this is an emergency!" Aunt Phil proceeded to call 911.

DEPUTY CYRIL RICHMOND was firmly planted in an interview room at the Jefferson County Jail in Madras. Biceps, or as he was known to the law, Percy Lumpsucker, was gloomily shackled to the table opposite Richmond. His court appointed attorney, a young woman, was at his side. Sheriff Gary Larkin was watching through a one-way window from a room next door. Percy was fidgeting and looking nervously everywhere around the room except at Richmond.

"Listen, Percy, you are going to go down for not one, but two murders, maybe more. We have the weapon with your prints on it, we have the DNA from at least one victim on the weapon, and we have your footprint at a murder scene. It can't get much worse for you, Percy. The only way you can improve your position is to cooperate with us. It's called turning State's Witness. It can save your life, Percy. You are going to go down with a minimum two counts of murder in the first degree from Jefferson County. If you cooperate, you might get twenty-five years with a possibility of parole. If you didn't cooperate, you could go in for life with no possibility for parole. Then, if we find you did murder for hire, that's considered aggravated murder in Oregon and subject to the death penalty."

Biceps blanched but continued to avoid eye contact with Richmond. Biceps was a thief, a bully, and a cold-blooded killer. He was also a man who would never be able to direct his own life. He needed someone to tell him what to do and when to do it. As long as he did what he was told and obeyed the rules, he could rely on being taken care of by Sullivan. As a consequence, the one thing Biceps was adamant about; he was blindly faithful to his boss. Sullivan had told him to keep his mouth shut and, by cracky, shut it would stay.

There was a rapping at the door and when Richmond opened it, a deputy handed him a note. The message said: *Phyllis Wardwell says Andre Sullivan and two other individuals are west bound in a Ford Taurus on Highway 126 between Redmond and Sisters. They have luggage with them and appear to be leaving the area.* The Taurus's license plate number and Aunt Phil's phone number were at the bottom of the note.

Richmond said to Percy, "I'm going to step out of the room for a minute.

Discuss with your attorney what we talked about turning State Witness." Richmond then paused the recording. When Richmond stepped into the hallway, Sheriff Larkin was there to meet him.

"Whatcha got, Cyril?"

When Richmond told him, the sheriff said to the deputy who brought the note, "Get an APB out on this Taurus." Then, to Richmond, "Let's go back in there," indicating the interview room in which Biceps still pouted.

Both policemen returned to the room. Larkin didn't bother to sit down but put both his big hands on the table top and glared at Biceps. "Percy," Larkin barked, "I'm Sheriff Larkin. We have Andre Sullivan in our sights. This is your last chance to come clean with what you know. When we talk to Sullivan and he tells us what you won't, you're gonna be toast. Do you understand?"

Biceps looked at his attorney then up at the sheriff's piercing blue eyes and understood. He spilled his guts.

THE GEEZER UNDERGROUND, minus Old Bowels, reconvened at their favorite picnic table at Drake Park. The table was strewn with wet but brightly colored fall leaves. There were few other people enjoying the park because, although the rain had stopped, it was cool and breezy. The Deschutes River was reflecting the slate grey of the sky. Wind ripples ruffled the surface of the water as it slid by.

"Where is the Taurus now, Oliver?" Mick asked.

Oliver held up his phone so everyone could see the colorful cluster of sensors which were moving west along Highway 126 towards Sisters. They knew that Old Bowels and his pickup would not be far behind.

"Hey, O.B., can you hear me?" Dave said into his radio.

"I can!" Old Bowel's cheerful but garbled voice was hard to discern among the clatter and rattling of his truck.

"Sullivan shows up on Oliver's phone like a Christmas tree," Dave continued. "Phyllis has notified Deputy Richmond where they are but we haven't heard anything back from him yet. We're going to head toward Sisters via

US 20 in just a few minutes."

"OK," Old Bowels voice warbled over the radio. "I'll keep the vigil."

"Gee, O.B.'s truck out-rattles mine," Mick said somewhat disappointedly to no one in particular.

"Boy that Taurus does light up the phone!" Aunt Phil now had Oliver's phone in her hand. "You guys must have planted lots of sensors."

"I dropped one in Brenda's purse!" Sophie beamed proudly. She added, "No girl ever goes anywhere without her purse so even if they ditch the car, we'll be able to see where she goes."

"Good job, Sophie!" Aunt Phil said adoringly, as she noticed Adam was also beaming at Sophie.

"Won't she find it in her purse?" Mick questioned.

"Probably not," Aunt Phil answered. "It will settle to the bottom and I, for one, haven't visited the bottom of my purse in years."

Everybody laughed.

"I slapped a sensor onto the bottom of Sullivan's shoe," Mick said. "It was up by the heel so he won't be walking on it. The tall guy, whoever he is, stepped on my hand as I was crawling around so I shoved his foot off and put a sensor on his heel. I hope it stays on."

"Was that when you were down on all fours chasing your own shoes?" Aunt Phil asked, laughing.

"Was that an accident, your losing shoes and hat and stuff, or on purpose?" Dave asked. "Whichever, it was pure genius."

"Thanks. It just kind of happened but it went along with the befuddled professor thing. I also put a sensor on the bottom of Sullivan's brief case. However, the way they threw stuff into the trunk, I'd be surprised if it stayed put."

"How is your hand, Mick?" Adam asked.

"It's okay. I pushed him off really quickly. Anyway, it's anything for the Geezers."

They all shouted in unison, "ANYTHING FOR THE GEEZERS!"

"Okay, gang," Aunt Phil interrupted the cheering. "We can whoop and holler later. Let's get on to Sisters." She paused as she looked at her phone.

"Oh, Richmond just sent me a text," she announced. "They tried to put an APB on the Taurus and found there was one already, put out by the Portland Police Bureau. I don't know what that's all about, but Richmond also said he doesn't want to know how we know where the car is."

Laughing, they all returned to their cars.

CHAPTER 25

DESCHUTES COUNTY SHERIFF'S Deputy Greg Leese sat in his patrol car at Cline Falls picnic area on OR 126. He wondered if he should take the time to pee. He had listened to the updated All-Points Bulletin about the grey Ford Taurus and that it was seen traveling on OR 126. If he left his car to use the restroom facility at the park, he might miss the Taurus as it passed the picnic area. On the other hand, it may have already gone by and he could sit here forever having to take a leak. He knew full well that if he stood next to his car to relieve himself, someone would see him and report him to the Sheriff's Office in Bend. It had happened before. Reluctantly, he heaved his six-foot, five-inch frame out of the car and ventured to the restroom.

Old Bowels rattled over the bridge on the Deschutes River at Cline Falls. Since they had left Redmond, he had been following the Taurus at a discrete distance, but close enough to notice if Sullivan and Company turned off at any of the many possibilities. From the bridge, he could see the Deschutes County Sheriff's patrol car parked next to the restroom in the park. O.B. pulled over, did a quick U-turn, crossed back over the bridge and hung a sharp right into the picnic area. He pulled up right next to the empty patrol car. O.B. slid out of his pickup at the same time Deputy Leese exited the restroom facility.

"Deputy!" Old Bowels scurried up to Leese. "Deputy, did you hear the APB on a Ford Taurus?" Not waiting for an answer, O.B. continued, "It just crossed the bridge going towards Sisters. I've been following it since it left Bend."

"Thanks!" Leese said over his shoulder as he raced to his car. Dirt and gravel flew everywhere as Leese sped out of the picnic area and onto the highway. With its engine screaming, the patrol car was soon out of sight behind its own cloud of dust.

Old Bowels said into his radio, "Geezers! A Deschutes County deputy is after Sullivan. He just left the Cline Falls picnic area and is in hot pursuit!"

The Geezers were now on US 20. The two-car caravan was making its way towards Sisters. Dave, who had his radio on in anticipation of hearing updates from O.B. said, "Good job, O.B! Are you still following?"

"Yup! I'm on my way." Old Bowels clamored into his truck and sped off, adding his own dust to the desert air.

DEPUTY LEESE DIDN'T want to turn on his lights and siren until he was closer to the Taurus. He needed to make sure it was the right car. He also didn't want to spook them into flight since they already had a big head start.

However, it wasn't long before Herman Diggs looked in his rear-view mirror and said, "Uh-oh!"

Both Brenda and Sullivan turned around in their seats to see the distinctive look of a police car far behind them.

"Oh, shit!" Brenda exclaimed as she watched the patrol car quickly close the gap between them. "What are we going to do?"

"He may not even be after us," Sullivan offered.

"Oh, yes he is," Diggs said when the patrol car slowed down but kept pace with them. "Now he has to be checking to make sure we're the car they are looking for. I'm going to do something. Hold on!"

Coming in the opposite direction, on their way to Redmond to do some shopping, Earnest and Madeline Kemper tootled along in their older model Honda CR-V. After spending a busy life raising three children while they both held down full-time jobs, they were now retired and hardly ever in a hurry to go anywhere. Today they were looking forward to enjoying a lunch at Diego's in Redmond. However, when the grey Ford Taurus crossed the center

174

line and came right towards them, their pleasant world abruptly changed.

To avoid a collision, Earnest Kemper swung the CR-V's wheel to the right. The little car clung to the gravel shoulder for a heart-stopping moment then plunged over the edge. It rolled once and came to rest against a huge gnarled juniper tree.

The shrieking inside the Taurus as Diggs jerked the car back into the west-bound lane was enough to raise hair in places where hair was never meant to grow. Brenda and Sullivan's eyes and mouths were wide in utter disbelief of what Diggs had done.

"You could have killed us, you fucking fathead!" Sullivan ranted at his cousin. Diggs laughed in response.

Brenda Bailey watched out the back window of the speeding Taurus as Deputy Leese pulled his patrol car to a stop where the Honda had gone off the road. He leapt out of his car, raced across the highway and down the embankment after the CR-V.

"The cop stopped," Bailey reported.

"Of course he did," Diggs replied, happy his maneuver worked.

OLD BOWELS SAW what happened and pulled his pickup onto the shoulder of the road behind the patrol car. He too, slid out of his vehicle and raced to the opposite side of the highway. He would never forget what he saw at the bottom of the embankment.

The Honda was in ruins. The roof over the driver's side was caved in. Deputy Leese was dragging an unconscious Earnest Kemper out from behind the steering wheel.

"Let me help you!" Old Bowels yelled as he half-fell, half-scrambled down the rocky slope.

"Thanks!" Leese yelled back, struggling with the large and inert Kemper. "There is a woman still in the car! I can smell gas. This thing's going to blow!"

By the time O.B. reached the bottom of the bank, Leese had managed to drag Earnest Kemper free of the car. Old Bowels, his own safety not a concern, dove into the remains of the Honda to find Madeline Kemper struggling with her seat belt. Old Bowels managed to snap the belt open and took the woman by the shoulders. He thought if he was ever going to suffer another hernia, it would be now. With a mighty heave, he pulled her out through the driver's side door as though the car had given birth. With O.B.'s help, she gained her feet and the two managed to get some distance from the car just as a massive explosion rocked the earth around them. O.B. and Madeline ducked their heads and Leese covered Earnest Kemper's body with his own until pieces of the Honda stopped falling from the sky.

"Was there anybody else in the car?" O.B. asked Madeline who shook her head no as they all looked horrified at the charred mess that was the Kemper's Honda.

Madeline tended to her husband as the deputy radioed for an ambulance and fire crew. O.B. suffered no ill effects from pulling Madeline out of the Honda and scrambled back up the embankment to grab the fire extinguisher from his pickup. With the deputy's keys in his hand, he also retrieved the extinguisher from the patrol car. The two then worked to put out a fire in the dried grass and brush around the remains of the Kemper's car. Then Old Bowels used his own radio to inform the rest of the Geezers what had happened.

"Why that filthy son-of-a-bitch!" Dave muttered as he heard what Diggs had done. Dave then conveyed to the rest of the crew what Old Bowels had told him.

Mick shook his head unbelievingly and said, "That mother fucker is going down even if we are the ones who have to do it!"

With renewed determination, the Geezer Underground sped towards Sisters to try to intercept the Taurus.

REACHING SISTERS FIRST, Diggs veered off the main highway onto North Locust Street. He continued on Locust to West Barclay where he hung a left.

"Where is he going?" Aunt Phil was looking at the Taurus's track on Oliver's phone.

"It looks like he's taken the bypass," Sophie answered, being familiar with Sisters. "He probably wants to avoid the crowds on the main highway."

Sisters was a small resort town with US 20 being the main thoroughfare through the center of town. There were several blocks of shops and restaurants along this road and traffic often slowed to a standstill as groups of tourists trooped from one side of the highway to the other. Getting through Sisters on US 20 was often an exasperating exercise.

Thinking that taking the bypass through town was not a bad idea, the little caravan of Geezers followed in the path of the Taurus. They watched Oliver's phone as the Taurus approached the roundabout on the west side of town.

"They are heading over the Santiam Pass, I'll bet." Aunt Phil said as she communicated over her cell phone with Mick, Dave, and Adam in the Volvo.

Much to her surprise, the Taurus didn't turn onto US 20, but went straight through the roundabout and headed into a shopping center around a Bi-Mart.

"They are going into a shopping center! What do you suppose they are doing? Are they out of toilet paper?" Aunt Phil said as the Bentley approached the roundabout. Oliver had to bring the car to a halt because of a semi-truck with two trailers which had become stuck in the roundabout. It had tried to negotiate the circle but was unsuccessful getting the second trailer clear of the hub in the center. This gave Mick, Dave, and Adam a chance to catch up in the Volvo as a long string of cars formed behind the semi waiting for it to maneuver out of the way. Since lines of cars had formed in all directions, it took quite a while for the Geezers to make their own way through the roundabout.

Meanwhile, Diggs, Sullivan, and Bailey had made it through the shopping center and out the back, negotiating several blocks of neighborhood streets until they came out on the McKenzie Highway. Once free of the town of Sisters, Diggs put his foot down and the Taurus shot towards the west and the McKenzie Pass. By the time the Bentley and Volvo followed the Taurus's path and reached the nearly deserted McKenzie Highway, the Taurus was well out of sight.

Just before Oliver turned onto the McKenzie Highway, Aunt Phil, who had been watching the progress of the Taurus on his phone, said, "Wait a sec, Oliver. It appears the Taurus has stopped. "

"Where?" Sophie asked as she looked over Aunt Phil's shoulder at the phone.

Oliver pulled the Bentley over to the side of the street and Adam parked the Volvo behind it. All three men in the Volvo got out of the car and gathered around the Bentley."

"What's going on?" Mick asked.

"Well, we're not sure," Aunt Phil answered. "The Taurus seems to have stopped about five miles up the highway."

"Maybe someone has to pee," Dave suggested with a chuckle.

"Well, it appears as though the sensors we placed are staying with the car, or just outside it. It's hard to tell with this small scale."

"Maybe they are having a pee-in." Mick chortled.

"Phyllis," Dave said, "maybe you should call Deputy Richmond and tell him what we have going on here."

"You're right, Dave. I did call him when we were stuck at the roundabout. He said he was on his way but I'll call him back. I don't know what we should do now that the Taurus has stopped."

While Aunt Phil called Cyril Richmond, the rest of the Geezers watched Oliver's phone as the strangest thing happened; four of the sensors began to move away from the Taurus and into the forest.

"Maybe something happened to the car and now they are on foot and are going to hide in the woods?" Sophie offered.

SOPHIE WASN'T FAR off the mark. At about the same time Sullivan, Bailey, and Diggs thought they had smooth sailing towards the McKenzie Pass and on to Eugene, the Taurus's engine abruptly quit, bringing the car to a halt. An "Add Oil" light had been on for some time and had been joined with a "Check Engine" light. Diggs couldn't tell how long either light had been on since he paid little attention to that sort of thing. He rarely bothered to have his car serviced and couldn't remember how long it had been since the last oil change.

"Hermie, you are such a fucking slob!" Sullivan snarled at his cousin as he got out of the car. "You let your car get like shit and now we're stranded out here miles from anywhere."

Diggs had tried to lift the hood, but it was so hot, he couldn't put his hands on it.

"If we had any eggs, at least we could fry them on the hood." Brenda was starting to feel very hungry and looking around her, saw no homes or ranches where they could get help. There was nothing but forest in sight and the sound of wind high in the tree tops made the day feel even colder.

"Well, we can't stay here. They'll find us as soon as someone reports this car beside the road." Sullivan paced up and down on the graveled shoulder. He was furious and ready to skin his cousin alive.

"I know what we can do," Brenda looked to the north where she could see the top of Black Butte looming in the distance. "We're going to walk to Black Butte Ranch."

"We're going to what?" Diggs stammered.

"Are you crazy, woman?" Sullivan looked to where Brenda was focused on Black Butte.

"Sure," Brenda continued. "The police are going to be looking for us on the McKenzie highway. What we'll be doing is walking through the woods towards US 20. From looking at this map, it's about five miles to the north of us. If we just keep Black Butte in sight, we can't miss the ranch. Once there, we can steal a car or whatever and head to the Willamette Valley on US 20."

Sullivan looked at Diggs. What Brenda had proposed made sense. The McKenzie Highway was rarely used this late in the year and they hadn't seen any other cars since leaving Sisters. Now, tourist season was over for the most part and all of the main traffic was staying on Highway 20. They were indeed stranded by staying where they were.

"Well, let's get to it," Diggs said. "We can't stay with the car, that's for sure."

CHAPTER 26

"PHYLLIS, WHERE ARE you?" From his speeding truck, Jefferson County Deputy Cyril Richmond barked into his phone. He was just one mile east of Sisters on OR 126 and he was burning up the highway, running with lights and siren. Hot on his heels was Deputy Leese of Deschutes County. Two counties; two deputies; one mission: bring in Andre Sullivan.

"We're on McKinney Butte Rd. at the McKenzie Highway." Aunt Phil had to lean over the front seat of the Bentley to read the road sign of the cross street.

"Okay. Don't go anywhere. We'll be right there."

In order to bypass the congested main street through Sisters, both policemen veered off onto Hood Avenue which paralleled the main street. The lights and sirens of both vehicles effectively stopped oncoming traffic so they could negotiate the left turn onto Hood. From there they cautiously made their way down Hood as quickly as possible. Pedestrians scurried to the sidewalks and autos went anywhere they could to get out of the way. The two police vehicles went by Sisters Coffee Company in a blur and were soon on West Cascade Avenue. In a heartbeat, they were parked behind the Bentley and Wardwell's Volvo.

Cyril Richmond exited his truck and walked up to the Bentley. He looked at Mick and Dave in their costumes. They were casually leaning on the Bentley and Richmond did a double take. When he reached the driver's window, he leaned down to look in and took a gander at Oliver in a chauffeur's uniform, Sophie in a nurse's outfit, and Aunt Phil in a rumpled dress, fur stole, frowzy wig, and red lipstick smeared generously in the vicinity of her mouth. They were all smiling at him.

"Going to a costume party?" he drawled.

"Yes!" Aunt Phil answered. "Pre-Halloween warmup!"

By now, Deputy Leese had left his patrol car and joined Richmond at the Bentley but not until after fixing his eyes on Dave looking like a priest with his hands together as if in prayer and Mick in his sloppy clothes, sucking on a dead pipe.

Richmond said to Leese, "Don't be alarmed, these are friends of mine."

"Whatever you say, Cyril."

"Okay," Richmond addressed the group in the car. "We need to know where Sullivan is and how you know."

"Show him your phone, Oliver," Aunt Phil said.

Oliver held his phone out the window so that both officers could see it. What they saw was a contour map of a five-mile radius around a pile-up of colorful blips. To the west of the Bentley and five miles up the McKenzie Highway, there were two stationery green blips, representing the Ford Taurus. A tiny bit north of the Taurus, two red, one blue, and one yellow blip represented the sensors on Sullivan's shoe and briefcase, the sensor in Brenda's purse, and the sensor on Diggs's shoe. Oliver pointed out that it appeared they had left the car on the highway and were now on foot in the woods, working their way north.

Richmond and Leese exchanged looks. Richmond then said, "Uh, those blips are caused by tracking sensors, right?"

The Geezers all nodded. Richmond took a deep breath and let it out. "You can tell me later how those sensors got where they are." He then asked, "Do you happen to know if Sullivan and these other people are armed?"

"We didn't actually see any guns, Cyril," Mick answered. "That doesn't mean they don't have some somewhere."

Richmond nodded and then said to Oliver, "Uh, can we use your phone when we go in to get these guys?"

"Better than that, officer," Oliver replied. "Let me have your phone number and we can put your phone on our system."

Again the two deputies looked at one another, both asking the same silent question, *what is the risk? Is there sensitive Sheriff's Department information Oliver and Jax can access?"*

As though Oliver read their minds, he said, "I understand your concern. It won't give us access to anything on your phone. You're just going to have to trust me on that." Oliver knew that was a hard step for these deputies to take, especially considering they were clueless as to who he was.

The two deputies again looked at one another.

Richmond, with a look to Aunt Phil's encouraging face, gave Oliver his phone number.

Oliver said, "Okay. Let me call T.J."

TOMMY JAX SPRAWLED on Conrad's couch. He took up all of it. He had both a laptop computer and a Chihuahua on his lap. When his phone rang he snatched it from the end table, saw who was calling, hit "speaker" and answered.

"T.J!" Oliver's voice came over the phone. "Where are you?"

"I'm at Wardwell's cabin, helping Conrad dog-sit." Jax replied cheerfully as he scratched Fido behind one ear. Conrad, in his chair in front of the fireplace, chuckled. Buddy was curled up in front of the fire.

"Do you have your computer with you?" Oliver asked.

"You bet. We're watching everything Sullivan does except it doesn't look like he's doing much right now."

"Put this phone number into our tracking system. It belongs to Deputy Richmond. There are two deputies who are going to use it to follow Sullivan. It looks like our illustrious senator wannabe and those with him have abandoned their car and have gone into the woods. We're going to let the law take it from here."

"Okay. Good idea. Give me a moment." Jax removed Fido from his lap and drew his laptop closer. Jax made a few entries into the computer, hit "enter" and then said, "There. That should do it. Give it a second."

"O.K.," Oliver answered. Then he said, "Hey, wait a sec," Oliver could be heard talking to someone and then he came back on the phone. "Put this number in too." Oliver then recited Deputy Leese's phone number. "That's the Deschutes County deputy. He decided it would be a good idea to have two phones showing where Sullivan is in case they need to separate."

"O.K. Good! This'll take just a minute." More tapping came from Jax's laptop. "O.K., they're all set."

Oliver could be heard telling the officers that when the subject moves more than 50 feet at any one time, their phones would beep an alarm. The alarm would also sound on Jax's computer. The system will compute how fast each subject is moving, indicating whether the person is walking, running, or has commandeered a vehicle. He also showed them how, with just placing two fingers on the screen, they can widen or make smaller the size of the map.

Jax then asked Oliver, "When are you guys coming back to Camp Sherman?"

Oliver looked to the others in the car and said, "Probably soon. There's not much more we can do now but stay out of the way."

"Okay. Meet us at Beth and Arthur's. We're supposed to eat up the leftovers from the party the other night."

DEPUTY LEESE SAID goodbye to the gang in the Bentley and made his way back to his patrol car. As he approached his car, Old Bowels rattled up in his pickup and rolling down his window, stopped to talk to Leese.

"What's going on?" O.B. asked.

"Your friends tracked that Taurus. It appears to have been abandoned about five miles up the McKenzie Highway. Richmond and I are going to check it out. Did the Kempers get taken to the hospital okay?"

"Yeah. Mr. Kemper had come to and seemed alert when the EMTs wheeled him into the ambulance. Mrs. Kemper climbed in after him. I think they'll be okay. Your backup took care of some of the paperwork but he says you'll have to complete the report when you get back."

"Yes, I know. Thanks for staying at the scene and helping me. I could hardly believe my eyes when that Taurus ran Kemper's Honda off the road. I don't think I remembered to thank you for what you did. When my backup arrived, I took off as soon as I could."

"Anybody else would have helped. Just catch those bastards."

"We're going to try." Leese shook hands with O.B. and continued to his car.

Before Richmond left the Geezers, he gave them all a thumbs up. "Good job, you guys. Now, I want you to go home. We're going to try to get a S.W.A.T. team to go after those guys. They have night vision goggles and the whole works. Bullets may be flying and I don't want you anywhere around."

Mick said, "Hey, if you don't have to go into the woods tonight, come to the party at Beth and Arthur's. I'm sure there will be plenty of food."

Dave accentuated this statement by blowing a toot on a paper party horn which unrolled and bleeped when he blew into it.

Richmond laughed and said, "If we don't go into the woods tonight, I may do just that. I'll come disguised as a cop."

As Richmond walked back to his truck, Adam looked at Dave who still had the party horn in his mouth. Adam rolled his eyes and asked, "Where'd you get that?"

Dave answered around the horn, "It wath in that pouch behind the pathenger theat of your aunth' car." He then tooted the horn again.

Adam shook his head and said, "Only Aunt Phil! She's always ready to party."

RICHMOND AND LEESE proceeded up the McKenzie Highway and traveled a little less than five miles before they came upon the Taurus. It was leaning tiredly onto the shoulder of the road. The trunk and passenger side doors were hanging open. There was debris shattered around the ground in the vicinity of the trunk. Richmond got out of his truck and put his binoculars to his eyes. He scanned the surrounding territory while Leese watched the blips on his phone.

"If we can trust this system," Leese said, pointing at his phone, "this would indicate they are all currently about a mile into the woods. They're still moving in a northerly direction. When I zoom in on the blips, they are all walking like they're drunk."

"They are probably working their way through the manzanita. It's really thick in there," Richmond replied. "Well, it will be dark soon. They are going to have to stay put. I can't imagine them stumbling around in the dark."

Putting away the binoculars, Richmond said, "Let me call Sheriff Larkin. "We need backup before we go after these guys. Two against three are not good odds as far as I'm concerned."

Richmond's call was short and left him unprepared for the answer. The Tri-County S.W.A.T. team was on an incident in Crook County. No backup was available until the morning and maybe even not then.

"I'm calling my sheriff," Leese said. "This is still Deschutes County and we have our own S.W.A.T. but he'll need to authorize it to come out here. They'll have night vision goggles. *They* can follow these bastards through the woods."

BRENDA BAILY WAS regretting her idea of walking through the forest to Black Butte Ranch. She had her purse slung over her shoulder and was dragging a small roller suitcase through the brush and rocks and over downed logs. The underbrush was scratching her arms and face as she fought her way along. She was wearing high heels which made walking in the dirt very awkward and her feet were killing her.

She and her cohorts had gleaned just about everything they could carry from the Taurus. After they had decided what they would take with them, Diggs had tossed everything else out of the trunk and tore into the spare tire well where he had secreted a broken down Remington twelve-gauge shotgun.

As Diggs put the barrel and the loaded stock of the shotgun together and was stuffing extra shells into his pockets, Sullivan sneered at his cousin. "Wouldn't you know, you would give a shotgun priority over a spare tire."

"Shut up, Andre! Just shut the fuck up!" Diggs growled. "If you hadn't been so damned greedy, we wouldn't be in this mess. A spare tire isn't going to get us out of it, either." He then hefted the gun in his hand and said, "Maybe this will."

"Blame me, will you? You were always willing to take money for faking those autopsies. If you weren't hooked on booze and gambling..."

The argument carried on as they stumbled through the woods. Brenda finally had her fill, stopped in her tracks and bellowed, "Listen, you two, you both need to shut up! We have a lot of ground to cover and it's getting dark. I'm hungry and my feet hurt. Come on!" With that, she stomped off, dragging the awkward suitcase behind her.

The two cousins looked at one another, shrugged, and followed Brenda into the darkening forest.

CHAPTER 27

DEPUTY LEESE CALLED his sheriff. While he talked, Cyril Richmond inspected the items left strewn around the Taurus. He knelt beside a small empty paper box and turned it over with his pen. The top of the box revealed what Richmond suspected it had contained, 12-gauge shotgun shells.

Leese terminated his phone call and slammed the device back into his pocket. He was disgusted and angry. "Well, we're it!"

"We're what?" Richmond got to his feet and looked at Leese's stormy face.

"We're IT! We'll get no help from the department. The sheriff says he can't spare a man. Some idiot went into a Safeway brandishing a gun, there is a huge wreck out on Highway 97, a climber has fallen at Smith Rock... he went on and on."

"Well, shit!" Richmond looked around himself unbelievingly. "And that box," Richmond said, pointing to the box on the ground, "proves they're armed." The two deputies looked at one another for a moment before Richmond concluded, "Okay, Greg, if we're it, we're it. Let's get to it."

Both deputies retrieved small survival packs from their patrol vehicles. Donning the packs and checking their firearms for readiness, the two men waded into the forest.

Cyril Richmond led the way. He held his phone in front of himself as though it was a compass. Even though this was still Deschutes County, it was close to the part of Jefferson County for which he was responsible. For that reason, he was more familiar with this part of the woods than Leese was.

It didn't take long before the deputies were able to pick up the fugitives' trail. Even in the fading light, they found the distinctive track of a suitcase being dragged. It was easy to follow over the prints of a woman's high heels which left holes in the volcanic dust. There were also two trails of what appeared to be men's dress shoes either alongside the woman's or over the top, indicating the woman was leading the way.

The track scrambled out of the underbrush and onto a dirt road that Richmond knew as Forest Service Road Number 1028. There were many such roads which crisscrossed this area of the forest. The deputies were able to lengthen their stride as it was obvious Sullivan's band had followed this road.

They soon came upon a fork in the road and the confused prints in the dust indicted Sullivan's crew was uncertain of which way to go. The fugitives had made up their mind to stay on the same road because the tracks continued on. The road headed uphill and to the northwest. Both deputies looked at their phones which revealed that the sensors were off to the right of the direction this road currently headed. Richmond knew this road didn't turn to the north and so he surmised the fugitives must have left the road at some place about another mile and one quarter ahead.

Following the road, they continued on until the tracks veered off to the right into the brush. Richmond looked around him and could barely see the rounded top of Black Butte in the greying light of dusk. The butte was now off to the northeast.

Deputy Leese looked at the tracks and said, "Do you get the same feeling I do, that they are working their way towards Black Butte?"

"Yeah. Like towards Black Butte Ranch."

"Or, Highway 20."

"Maybe Camp Sherman?"

The two deputies looked at one another.

"Either way, they have to go through Black Butte Ranch to get there. There are lots of opportunities there to commandeer a vehicle or to take a hostage."

Leese nodded and said, "I better call Eric. He needs to know what may be headed his way. He may be able to give us a backup. He helps the county out once in a while."

ERIC CONROY HAD been on the Black Butte Ranch police force for seven years. A retired Crook County Sheriff, he and his wife of fifty years lived in a one story house on Foxtail Lane not far from the club house at Big Meadow golf course. Any uneventful day at Black Butte found Conroy whacking golf balls with his buddies. Other than a few unauthorized stays at cabins, searching for a lost child, car and bicycle accidents, life went fairly smoothly for Chief Conroy. That is, until he received the call from Deschutes County Deputy Leese.

"You gotta be fucking kidding!"

"I wish I was, Chief," Leese replied. "They're on foot and barely making their way, but it does appear they are headed directly towards you. Right now, the sensors indicate they have stopped, probably for the night, somewhat southwest of Five-Mile Butte. They haven't moved in a while, anyway."

"I'll get a word out for everyone to secure their vehicles and to stay inside with doors locked until we know more." Conroy asked with trepidation, "You say they're armed?"

"At least with a 12-gauge."

"Aw, shit! So, are you guys going in now?"

"If they start moving again, we will; we'll have to. However, if it appears they have stopped for the night, we may bag it and come back tomorrow, unless we know for sure they're on the move again." Leese briefly explained the G.P.S. sensors, how they worked with their cell phones, and that they would send an alarm if the subjects start moving.

"So how did the sensors get on their luggage and shoes?" The Chief asked.

Leese looked at Richmond and said, "Some people from Camp Sherman. I just barely met them. A bunch of old folks."

"Old folks? Really? Vigilantes?"

"Kinda. Behind the scenes. Does it matter?"

"Nope. As long as they don't get in the way, more power to 'em."

The Black Butte community had a network of property owner emails and group text messages used for news, events, and warnings such as this.

Conroy tapped out an emergency email on his computer then used his phone to activate a group text message. He also called the resort headquarters, restaurants, and both golf pro shops in case they wouldn't see the text right away. Their employees would be going home soon and needed to be careful coming and going from their cars and especially in the morning when they arrived at work.

Chief Conroy then rousted out his entire police force. He had seven sworn officers, one with a police canine. They would establish a protective boundary along the southern edge of Black Butte Ranch. That was a lot of territory for seven officers to secure, but with the help of volunteers and the G.P.S. systems on Leese's and Richmond's phones, they hoped they could concentrate their force and prevent the suspects from entering Black Butte Ranch property.

The officers were to be on standby all night until Conroy got the word from Leese or Richmond that the fugitives were on the move.

CYRIL RICHMOND AND Greg Leese stood in the shadowy forest; waiting and listening. A waning moon which flickered in and around the clouds did little to penetrate the darkness. The little birds and other forest creatures had stopped making their twittering and rustling sounds as they settled for the night.

The sensors had not moved in several minutes and the deputies were hoping Sullivan's gang had stopped because of darkness. It was so dark that movement through the woods would be dangerous and nearly impossible.

As Richmond and Leese waited in the rapidly cooling night, Richmond studied his phone again and again. He said, "You know Greg? I have a hunch exactly where these guys are. It doesn't look like they're going to move any time soon so I'd like to check something with the guy who set this system up for the Geezers, Tommy Jax."

Greg Leese looked off into the darkness for a bit and then asked, "Tommy Jax. Tommy Jax. That name is familiar. Isn't he an underworld guy from Seattle?"

"The very same."

"Really? No foolin'? He's in the slammer for murder, right?"

"No. His lawyer got him off. Now he's supposedly doing good deeds."

"You're shittin' me. Who's his lawyer?"

"One of the Geezers."

Leese's jaw dropped. "My, you have an interesting beat out here in the woods, Cyril."

"You can say that again."

The two deputies then returned to their patrol cars.

CHAPTER 28

BRENDA WAS FALLING. Down into blackness she went. It was all so sudden. She had been trudging along through the forest, barely able to distinguish in the darkness shadows from trees and shrubbery. She had been dragging all she had left in the world in a small roller suitcase when the earth dropped away.

The landing was worse. Sharp rocks pierced her skin and pain in her right calf grabbed her so intensely, she couldn't even breathe. As soon as she caught her breath, she took in a lungful of the musty, stuffy air that enveloped her and screamed. And cursed. She screamed and cursed enough to strip bark from the trees.

Sullivan and Diggs stopped in their tracks. They could barely see in the darkness but they were suddenly aware that Brenda, who had been in the lead, was gone. Then the screaming started. Diggs pulled out his cell phone and using what precious battery power it had left, trained the light in the direction of the screaming.

What the two men saw took their own breath away. Just a few feet from where they stood was a black, yawning gap in the forest floor. A lava tube with the ceiling partially fallen away was known to the locals as Skylight Cave. For eons, there had been legends told about this cave. More recent history had books, both fanciful and academic, written about this cave and many other such lava tubes in this wild, volcanic area of Oregon. Although there were no roads nearby, the cave was in several hiking publications which could get the adventurous close to Skylight Cave and then leave them to wander about through head-high manzanita and thickets of trees to find or not to find a cave which had captivated the curious for centuries. Who would have guessed that these three bumbling fugitives, not even knowing about the Skylight Cave, would come upon it in the dark?

Still using the light from his cell phone, Diggs crept toward the edge of the gap and shone his light down the ten or twelve feet to the bottom. There was Brenda Baily, crumpled, bleeding, and whimpering, her right leg twisted grotesquely beneath her.

Seeing the men's two faces peering over the edge of the cave, Brenda lashed at them with a new wave of profanity. "Get me outta here, you fucking idiots! My leg is broken!"

"If your leg is broken, we're not going to be able to get you outta there," Diggs shouted to her.

"Look, Herm," Sullivan said, spying the top rungs of a ladder which descended into the hole. "There's a ladder. We can get down there."

"Yeah, but she's not going to be able to use it to climb out. Not with that leg."

"We may as well go down there to join her, at least for the night. It's starting to rain and we can't see well enough to go any further." Sullivan swung his leg over the top of the ladder and worked his way downward.

"Shit!" Diggs exclaimed as he soon followed.

WHILE THE THREE fugitives huddled together in the coldness of the cave, the Geezers were gathering at Beth and Arthur's cabin. Still in costume, Aunt Phil and Sophie had fun surprising Beth in the kitchen as she was removing warmed chicken from the oven.

"Oh, my gosh, Phyllis! I didn't recognize you in that get-up. And Sophie, what a cute nurse you make." The three women laughed together as they put on the table a quick dinner of leftovers.

Tommy Jax and Conrad had also arrived, bringing the two dogs, Conrad's Fido and Mick's Buddy. The men all stood in the cabin's front yard while the dogs milled around, doing the doggy things that dogs do when they get together. Old Bowels rattled up in his pickup and was sharing with the other men how Diggs had driven a small car off the road in order to disrupt the pursuing police car.

The men's rapt attention was interrupted when Deputy Richmond pulled into the driveway with Deputy Leese right behind him. The two policemen exited their patrol vehicles and Richmond introduced Leese to the Geezers.

"These are the folks, well most of them, who found Sullivan and his cohorts for us," Richmond explained. There was much shaking of hands and slapping of shoulders as the men did those manly things men do when they get together.

Richmond then introduced Greg Leese to Tommy Jax. The two men shook hands and Greg stood rather gobsmacked in the presence of the notorious organized crime figure while Richmond talked to him like he was the neighbor next door.

"T.J., if you have your computer with you, can you give me the compass coordinates for the sensors we have been following? They appear to have stopped for the night. I'd like to put the coordinates into Google Earth because I have a hunch I know where they are."

"Sure," Jax said amiably. "I left the computer inside."

The two deputies followed the lumbering Jax into the cabin and were soon joined by the rest of the Geezers. Everyone gathered around while Jax noted the longitude and latitude coordinates of the sensors and then pulled up Google Earth onto his computer screen. When he entered the coordinates into Google Earth and hit enter, the image of the earth whirled around and zeroed in exactly where Cyril Richmond thought it would; at Skylight Cave.

Luckily, the cave was noted in the Google Earth program, along with many other natural phenomena of the scenic mountainous region. Richmond and Leese then discussed the possibility of using the manpower that the Black Butte Police Department could offer and lie in wait at the cave until the suspects emerged in the morning. Richmond knew that although there were other parts of the cave's ceiling which had collapsed, hence the name "Skylight," the only feasible escape from the cave was the hole where the ladder had been placed years ago. He, Leese, and the officers from Black Butte would approach Skylight Cave from the north, traveling the forest service roads from Black Butte Ranch. Now that Richmond was assured of the suspects' exact location, he knew he could get his little posse there in a short amount of time, even in the dark.

The Geezers had all gathered into the cabin's great room and had their curious ears cocked to overhear what the deputies were planning. Richmond, using the sixth sense he seemed to have with regards to this bundle of old folks, turned around and said to the crowd, "Okay! I know what you are thinking and you are NOT to do anything but stay out of this! I don't want any of you running around out there in the woods when we know these guys are armed." Richmond made eye contact with each person then said, "Am I making myself clear?" Everybody nodded their agreement and although he could read disappointment on most of their faces, Richmond felt he had done everything he could to keep them safe shy of locking them all in the back seat of his truck.

"Before you go Cyril," Beth said from the back of the room, "you might as well have something to eat as it's going to be a long night for both of you."

The two deputies gave her grateful smiles as it had indeed been a long day with little time for refreshment. The entire roomful soon had plates of chicken, salad and garlic bread and were seated every which way that worked around the room and front porch.

Deputy Leese took a huge bite of homemade garlic bread and as the taste and smell of melted butter, garlic, and grated parmesan cheese filled his sinuses with warmth and his soul with well-being he said, "Oh, that's good stuff! We won't need to shoot those bastards, we can just breathe on 'em."

Once he was finished with his meal, Deputy Leese phoned Chief Eric Conroy of the Black Butte Ranch Police Department and shared with him the plan he and Richmond had devised. Conroy agreed the plan would work and that he and Sergeant Evans with his police dog, Lola, would go with Leese and Richmond. The rest of his crew would stand at strategic points along the south-western perimeter of the ranch in case any of the suspects escaped the trap and managed to get far enough to be a threat to the ranch. With this plan of attack cemented, deputies Leese and Richmond returned to their patrol vehicles, leaving behind their thanks for the meal.

As the two deputies drove off into the darkness, the Geezers stood together watching them leave. Sharing a mutual wish that these two dedicated lawmen would return unscathed from a successful mission, the Geezers then parted company to return to their respective cabins for the night... well, not quite.

CHAPTER 29

"WAIT A MINUTE!" Mick stood still as the rest of the Geezers started to leave. "We can't just turn our backs and leave those policemen to capture Sullivan's band of pirates. There are only four cops and a dog against Sullivan's three. That's not the best odds in the world."

"You heard what Cyril said, Mick," Dave argued. "He'd boil us in oil if he finds out we are out there thrashing around in the woods."

"Dave's right, Mick," Old Bowels added. "In fact, we could spook Sullivan's bunch early and they'd have a head start and maybe get away."

"Or, if we got caught in a crossfire and end up dead, Cyril would really be pissed." Conrad noted, dryly.

Arthur commented, "Boy, he'd never forgive us if that happened!"

"Okay, wait, gang," Aunt Phil interrupted, "being collateral damage was never on my bucket list either but let's hear what Mick has in mind."

The drizzle had stopped for the moment and a weak moon brightened the sky as Mick sat on the edge of the porch. The rest of the Geezers gathered around. "Here's the deal. We're not going out there towards Skylight Cave or anywhere close. What if we keep our eyes on possible avenues of escape in case any or all of Sullivan's crew gets past Cyril and his men? We'll only be augmenting the Black Butte Police by backing up their guard of the southern edge of the ranch. There is only going to be a small handful of officers so they can't see everything. We'll patrol the northern perimeter of the ranch, including any roads that leave the area. They'd have to eventually come out on Highway 20."

"We'll know," Oliver said as he held up his cell phone, "if they start to move. If they are on the run, they'll probably separate anyway. We'll be in touch with each other with our radios so we can concentrate our forces wherever Sullivan's crew happen to be headed."

Tommy Jax smiled. It pleased him that Oliver was feeling comfortable enough with the Geezers to open up.

"I like this," Adam said with his arm around Sophie's shoulders. "It's a good idea. If the police capture them with no incident, we melt back over here to Camp Sherman and Cyril will never know we were out there."

"As invisible as a fart in the dark," Dave said.

Aunt Phil said, "None of us will get any sleep tonight anyway. We'll be worrying about Cyril, Greg, and the Black Butte Police guys if anything goes terribly wrong. At least this will give us something to do."

"Okay, I'm convinced," Arthur said as he turned to go back into the cabin. "Let's go inside and plan who is going to be stationed where."

As the Geezers trooped into the cabin, Beth, always the hostess, said, "Who's for ice cream?"

With the Geezers, that's like asking a dog if it's hungry. Everybody put a hand in the air except Dave who put up both his hands hoping he might get two servings.

"Nice try, Dave!" Beth laughed as she counted. She then added, "Who's for coffee? It's going to be a long night."

A collective "Meeee!" came from the crowd. Still laughing, Beth headed for the kitchen.

"I'll make the coffee," Sophie said, following Beth.

"I'll help," Adam told her. "I've been staying here so I know where everything is."

Aunt Phil smiled to herself as she thought, *Nah, you just want to be with Sophie.*

The rest of the Geezers gathered around Arthur. He had spread on the dining table a topographic map of the Mount Jefferson and Mount Washington area. It included all the forest service roads from Camp Sherman south to the McKenzie Highway.

"Okay, let's see how many cars we have available." Aunt Phil started counting on her fingers. "Our Volvo, O.B.'s pickup, Mick's pickup, the Bentley..."

"Don't forget our pickup," Arthur added.

"Dave, how about your Prius?" Aunt Phil asked.

"My wife has taken it to the valley to peddle her books."

"You have that yacht yet?" O.B. asked, snickering because he knew the answer.

Dave replied, "Nah! She doesn't sell enough books to buy a row boat."

Deputies Cyril Richmond and Greg Leese traveled down Green Ridge road until it met with Highway 20. They then turned west toward the Black Butte Ranch entryway. Once inside the ranch, they hung a left toward the Welcome Center and followed the drive around to the Police Station.

When they stepped out of their vehicles, Richmond approached Leese and asked, "So what did the Chief say he could do for us?"

"He'll come with us as well as another officer who has a canine. The rest of the officers will secure the southern perimeter of the ranch."

"Oh, good!" Richmond replied, "They're bringing the dog!"

Leese then said, "You work right across the highway from these guys, do you know what kind of canine they have?"

"An English bulldog. Lola. It belongs to their Administrative Manager."

Leese paused for a second and leveled his eyes at Richmond, "An English what? Really? Can it chase somebody down and pull them to the ground?"

"Oh, you'd be surprised!" Richmond said then added, "If you are the one being chased, you don't need to be concerned by how fast the dog can run, but how fast *you* can run. And, that's not the only canine they have, another officer has a Black Lab puppy."

"Oh, good! So its job is to lick the bad guys into submission?"

"Yeah, something like that." Richmond said with a smile as he held the door of the Police Station open for Leese.

They waited briefly in the small vestibule until the interior door was opened by the Chief himself.

Chief Eric Conroy was a burly bull of a man with gnarly brows over glowering eyes. His full head of straight black hair greying at the temples belied his seventy-plus years. The weight of worry showed in the slump of his shoulders.

"Greg. Cyril." Chief Conroy had his bullet proof vest on and was strapping on his duty belt. "I don't like these bastards being on my turf! I've got a lot of people here to protect. Couldn't you have chased them off toward Sun River or Eagle Crest?"

"Sorry, Chief," the two deputies said in unison then gave each other wry smiles.

"So," Conroy went on, "we're gonna blow these bums out of Skylight Cave, huh?"

"Well, we're hoping they will crawl out and right into our arms."

"We'll sic Lola on 'em," Sergeant Jayden Martinez emerged with an English bulldog wearing a police dog harness. The dog's happy drooling smile made her look as though she should be snoozing in front of a warm fire. To the dog's credit, she was a sturdy hunk with muscular legs. The legs were admittedly longer in relation to her body than Adam's two lap potatoes.

Sergeant Martinez shook hands with Richmond and Leese and the four officers left for the parking lot. Leese and Richmond got in Richmond's truck while Chief Conroy, Martinez and Lola piled into Martinez's SUV which was especially marked for a police canine.

The plan was to approach within a mile of Skylight Cave, traveling without lights on a tangle of National Forest roads which resembled, on a map, a dumped bowl of spaghetti. Richmond knew the roads well and it helped that the rain had drizzled off to the south. The few remaining clouds allowed for a hint of pale moonlight. Once close to the cave, the officers would go the rest of the way on foot then wait for the suspects to continue their flight in daylight.

With Richmond leading, the two police vehicles made their way out to Highway 20 and traveled the two miles west to McAllister Road. It led to the National Forest roads south of the ranch and although it was a longer route, it was quicker than weaving through the many roads within the ranch.

As they turned south onto McAllister Road, they didn't see Old Bowel's pickup parked fifty yards out in the woods on the other side of the highway. Nearly invisible in a thicket of small pines, O.B. and Conrad were bundled up in winter clothing and sipping at mugs of hot coffee.

As they watched the two police cars disappear into the forest, Conrad said, "Godspeed, you guys."

CHAPTER 30

THE REST OF the Geezers positioned themselves here and there on the north side of Black Butte Ranch. Beth and Arthur, with Max riding in the cab with them, parked their pickup out in the woods where they could see the intersection of Green Ridge Road and Highway 20. Aunt Phil and Oliver in the Bentley parked near the Welcome Center where they could see the gate into the private areas of the ranch. Mick and Dave in Mick's pickup kept watch over the parking lot of the restaurant, pool, and recreation center where a few cars remained overnight. Adam and Sophie in Adam's Explorer cruised to the parking lot of the Big Meadow golf course.

Tommy Jax stayed at Beth and Arthur's cabin and from the couch kept watch on the computer he had placed on the coffee table. He also served as baby sitter to the dogs. Mick's chocolate lab curled up in front of the fire. Adam's bulldogs cuddled together in a basket bed Adam had brought with him. Fido was firmly ensconced on Jax's broad, warm stomach.

Booger had retreated to his haven in the rafters. He looked down upon Fido sleeping peacefully on Tommy Jax's expansive belly. Booger declared long ago that once someone's character qualified under the cat's rigid scrutiny, the warmth of that person's lap belonged to him. Who was this yappy little smidge of a dog to claim such important territory? Surely, there was plenty of Jax's girth for two.

Having made this decision, Booger gathered his legs underneath him with enough precision that when he launched himself from the rafter, he landed smack in the middle of Tommy Jax's stomach. Anyone who has taken high school physics knows that every action will result in an equal and opposite reaction. Fido, being the projectile of this reaction, was tossed into the air. When the dog came down, neither Jax nor Booger was there.

Once Tommy Jax came to realize what had happened, he laughed so hard he could hardly stand up. Settling back onto the couch, he picked up a bewildered Fido from the floor and placed him back on his stomach. Booger glared at Jax from about four feet away.

"Well, come on," Jax said to the cat. "There's room for you too."

Booger took that as an apology from Jax for leaving so abruptly and sauntered over, tail on high. As though he had springs for legs, the cat jettisoned himself onto Jax's belly. Accepting a gentle pet from the man's big, warm hand, the cat settled down and before long, all three of them were asleep.

Adam and Sophie parked underneath a large fir tree and watched for any activity occurring in the parking lot of Big Meadow Golf Course. Although Chief Conroy had told workers to leave as soon as possible, there still was a car parked close to the pro shop. Before too long, however, the Head Pro left the pro shop and looking all around him, hurried to his car, hopped in, and charged off like the devil might be lurking close by. Once his car had cleared the parking lot and journeyed off down Glaze Meadow Drive to Highway 20, Adam and Sophie figured everyone associated with the course had left.

Now their job consisted of watching for any individuals who might come snooping around the buildings. Their phones showed that the sensors had still not moved and the night settled around the Explorer. Sophie said, with a sideways glance at Adam, "If we were in high school, we'd be necking."

Adam sucked in air and held his breath. The time he and Sophie had spent together has been strictly casual, in a light hearted mode, and with the exception of the walk they took along the river with the dogs, always in the presence of others. He thoroughly enjoyed the association and since Sophie suggested the two of them team up for this surveillance mission,

Adam was pleased that Sophie also seemed to enjoy being with him.

Up to this point, Adam had been reserved and cautious. He didn't want to blunder into a relationship because blundering seemed to be his MO when it came to women.

However, and there always seemed to be a "however" when love affairs are concerned, Sophie was as different from other women as the sun was different than the moon. Sophie was her own woman, self-directed in her life and career. She seemed to love her life and everyone in it and was not needy for emotional support. Adam admired her for all of this and if she chose to share some of that life with him, all the better. If she didn't, he would respectfully keep his distance for he loved his own life and was perfectly content to let it roll as it had been doing for all of his sixty-plus years. There was that horrifying exception of a brief association with Gabriella Fitzpatrick, but that's another story.

Now, he didn't know what to do. Did Sophie expect him to make a move? Dang, he wished things didn't have to be so complicated when it came to women!

Sophie let him off the hook by saying, "But we're not in high school. We have a duty to perform, don't we?" She looked at him and in the dim glow of the dashboard lights, her eyes looked huge and so very beautiful.

He reached across the back of the seat and touched her shoulder. He then took a wayward lock of her hair and placed it behind her ear. The smile in his eyes told her all she needed to know.

"When all this is over, Adam," she said, "I'd like to have some time for just you and me. You are a very special man and I think we need to become better acquainted to know if we can have a relationship worth nurturing."

"Okay," he said simply.

She returned his smile and softly repeated, "Okay."

AUNT PHIL AND Oliver sat in the comfort of the Bentley and watched the gate into the private areas of Black Butte Ranch. Conrad had insisted Aunt Phil be the one to join Oliver because he wanted to make sure she was warm. The Bentley's seats were heated by a separate battery than the one used to start the car. She and Oliver would stay warm without ever using the car's engine.

Not many vehicles passed through the gate because of the warning from Chief Conroy to shelter in place unless folks were able to leave immediately. Someone driving in a car could be commandeered and it appeared most residents aimed to stay home and guard their property.

Aunt Phil tried to think of things to talk about with Oliver. Normally being quiet and reserved, he was such a different character than Tommy Jax. She wanted to know how they knew each other, how they came to be living together in that weird warehouse in Seattle. Truly, she knew that no matter what the answers may be, it didn't matter. It wouldn't change the way she felt about them. She would like them anyway. She told herself that just because she was curious didn't make their life any of her business. Oh well, what the heck? She asked anyway.

"Oliver, tell me how you know T.J.?"

If Oliver had an inkling that his relationship with Jax wasn't any of her business, he never showed it but jumped right in, seeming eager to share their story. "I met T.J. at a homeless shelter in Seattle. I was the one in the shelter. I had lived in a crummy apartment building ironically owned by the guy you Geezers have been chasing, Andre Sullivan. Although, at the time, we didn't know it was him because all the correspondence came from some sort of holding company.

"He evicted everyone in the building because he was going to renovate the apartments and then let us all move back in. Well, he renovated all right, and he didn't use a dime of his own money. He used government grants to do it. Instead of letting the former tenants back in, he sold the now empty building for a fortune. He never paid the general contractor so the guy had to sue the holding company. As a result of the suit, the holding company declared bankruptcy. The money from the sale of the apartment complex had disappeared, probably into Sullivan's vast empire of sham companies or even into an overseas bank.

"Anyway, I couldn't make enough money as a waiter to afford another apartment in Seattle so I ended up homeless. T.J. came into the shelter one day looking for a computer guy. I had some computer experience in the past so he hired me. This must have been right after you cleared him on that murder rap.

"We hit it off. I mean, you know there is something special when you meet someone who can look in your eyes and read the story of your life. That's the way it was with T.J. and me. He offered to share his home with me and we'd work together to try to make life easier for disadvantaged people. Now we are having fun doing good stuff. We cook for homeless shelters, volunteer at food banks, I volunteer at an underprivileged youth club as a basketball coach." He looked at Aunt Phil's skeptical eye and added with a wink, "I'm faster than I look."

"As for T.J., he'd followed his family into the crime business," Oliver said casually, as though Tommy Jax's family were furniture builders. "Other than amassing a fortune in dirty money, he felt he had wasted his life up to the time you got him off. He took that as a wake-up call."

"So," Aunt Phil asked, "trying to help the police stop Sullivan's evil ways is kind of revenge for you, right? I mean for kicking you out of your apartment and leaving you homeless?"

"You could say that, but because of his evil ways I was homeless and able to meet T.J. in that shelter. Funny how life works, huh?"

"Yes. Yes, it is." Aunt Phil felt as though she had turned a corner, or that Oliver had. Being the recipient of this candid background information made her feel privileged that this strange, normally private man had opened a welcoming door.

Oliver had his phone propped into a holder attached to the dash board. It was positioned so both of them could see it. When he turned on the GPS feature so they could follow the sensors, Aunt Phil noticed not only the sensors grouped together in the cave's location, but another one, this one bright orange, moving slowly along the Forest Service road.

"Oliver!" Aunt Phil said, suddenly alarmed by the strange orange light. "What is that light doing out there on the road?"

Oliver looked at Aunt Phil with a smirk and paused a second before answering, giving Aunt Phil a chance to figure out what it was. She did: "Oliver! You didn't! You put a sensor on Richmond's truck! Oh, my God! He'll eventually find it and throttle us for sure!"

"No, he won't," the thin man said confidently. "The sensor is magnetized and all T.J. has to do is hit a button on his computer and the sensor will fall off. That orange light shows only on my phone and the computer, which T.J. is watching. No one else will see it."

"Holy crap!" Aunt Phil said. "Well, it's a good thing. Now we'll know where the police are." She looked at Oliver and said, "You and Jax are something else! Never would I have thought after that effing murder trial in Seattle, you two would end up helping us do undercover work for the police."

"I leave it all to T.J.," Oliver said. "When you got him off, he changed completely. You must have said something really poignant because of the way he turned his life around. What did you do, threaten him or something?"

"Well, sort of. All I said was he better stay out of trouble because he wasn't the only one who knew hit men."

Oliver laughed so hard, Aunt Phil was afraid his bony body would shake apart. With a smile she leaned back in the Bentley's warm cushy seat and opened a sack of chocolate cookies Beth had provided. She offered the sack to Oliver then poured coffee for them both and thought this surveillance business wasn't such a bad gig after all.

DAVE SAT SHIVERING in Mick's truck. "Geez, Mick! Why don't you let Old Bowels fix those holes in the floor and put some insulation in the doors or something! It's fricking freezing in here." Dave was wearing two sweaters, a parka, knitted hat, a scarf wound twice around his face, ear muffs, mittens, wooly socks and fur-lined snow boots. He was still cold.

"Man, what a pansy!" Mick seemed perfectly comfortable in a sweater, corduroy pants and wool jacket. Beth had made sure each vehicle was equipped with hot coffee and cookies. "Gee, too bad you are so bundled up. Otherwise, you could eat some cookies. The coffee is still warm too."

Mick took a sip. "Well, that leaves more for me!"

Dave glared at him. After a moment, he ripped off the mittens and scarf and shoved a cookie in his mouth. He said around the cookie, "Thaths whas ooo think!"

After the cookie and a gulp of coffee, Dave looked at Mick and said, "How can you be warm dressed like that and it's colder than moose tits out here?"

Mick looked slyly at his brother-in-law, reached under his rump and pulled out a hot water bottle.

Dave's mouth opened so wide you could have driven a snow plow through it. Greedily he looked at the bottle and made a noise which sounded something like "Gahh!"

"Here," Mick, feeling the cold already seeping into his bones, handed the device to Dave and said, "you can use it... for a while."

Dave grabbed the thing and sat on it. "Ahhhh! Ooooo! "Man, that feels good!"

"Don't get too comfortable 'cause I'm gonna want it back."

"You'll get it," Dave said, "when hell freezes over."

CHAPTER 31

THE POLICE TRAVELED surreptitiously without using any lights. When they neared the target, they slowed, so whatever dust was left after the rain wouldn't catch the moonlight. Occasionally a few stars and the moon peeked out from behind the fleeting clouds, as though they weren't sure they wanted to watch what was going to happen.

It seemed like forever before Five-Mile Butte loomed out of the darkness. The butte was a small cinder cone the top of which bristled with antenna and was not far from Skylight Cave. The road curved around the east side of the butte and then split three ways. Richmond took the middle fork and knowing they were getting close to the cave, stopped and turned off the truck. There was no sense in getting any closer because the sound of the engines could carry on the wind.

Leese had kept his eye on his phone, ready to report that the sensors had moved, but the lights stayed static, indicating the suspects were still holed up in the cave. Worst case scenario is that the suspects had detected the sensors, tossed them into the cave, and were now miles from here. Leese didn't even want to think about that possibility. He shook it off and concentrated on the present.

The policemen exited their vehicles and closed the car doors carefully so that there was no noise. The interior lights of both vehicles had been deactivated before they ever left Black Butte Ranch. Manzanita, which had grown with abandon after the B&B fire, was now nearly head high and once the men separated, they would be invisible from each other.

They had decided to station themselves in a fan shape around the side of the cave opening where the ladder was. Although there were other parts of the cave's ceiling that had collapsed, the hole where the ladder stood was the only way out of the cave. There were four lawmen and if they were careful, they could effectively cover the opening without being in each other's crossfire if things went badly.

Chief Conroy was the first to position himself to the left of the ladder about twenty-five yards from the opening. Despite his age, he was limber enough to get into a good position underneath a small fir. He held his Glock with both hands and hoped they wouldn't have to fire into the cave. Bullets would ricochet from the rocks and create havoc. There were worries at every corner of police work, but Eric Conroy, a veteran of over forty years of law enforcement, still had plenty of fire in his gut to want to do this shit.

Greg Leese moved about twenty yards to the right of Conroy but still stayed twenty-five yards from the opening. Spaced to his right was Richmond and then Martinez with Lola. They all hunkered down in the cold to wait and listen. Lola took the opportunity to take a nap.

Ironically, Lola was the first to hear it: whimpering coming from deep within the cave. The dog lifted her head and sniffed the air. Martinez picked up on the dog's attention and he too shook off the lethargy brought on by the inactivity and cold. He could barely see in the darkness but he closed his eyes to better listen and then he heard it too. There was whining followed by a moan then whining again. *Egads, are they having sex in there?* Martinez wondered.

"Woman!" came a loud male voice from the cave. "Would you shut up? I'm trying to sleep!"

"You shit head!" Brenda Bailey's voice was high and shrill. "My leg HURTS! I wish it were YOU who had fallen in this Goddamn hole!"

"Will you BOTH shut up?" Sullivan was pissed. There wasn't anything about this escape plan that had gone right. Above all, his campaign was toast. That fucking Biceps let himself get caught by lifting a stinking PURSE! All the money Sullivan had acquired by defrauding the government and killing off those old people for their real estate would now go for attorneys' fees. Those suckers better keep him out of prison or he'd... he'd... well, he'd think of something. Humiliation and threats were how he treated anyone who crossed him. With attorneys, however, that method usually didn't go well.

Sullivan was cold, hungry, and saddled with his idiot cousin. Brenda was going to slow them down, even if there was some way they could figure out how she could walk. It would be best for the men to leave her here. They could travel faster without her. If someone found her, good enough. If they didn't, well, so what? She'd been a loyal servant, but those were a dime a dozen when one is as charming as Sullivan thought he was.

The policemen settled down as the squabbling quieted. Soon nothing but silence emanated from the gaping hole in the forest floor. So the policemen continued their cold vigilance.

ABOUT A HALF hour before dawn, Diggs woke up. He was freezing and starving. He gave Sullivan a kick and snarled, "Come on, Andre. We gotta get the hell out of here before we freeze to death in this fucking cave." Diggs slowly moved his stiff joints until he was able to stand. When he stood, there were parts of the cave ceiling he brushed with the top of his head. When he moved around, his head brushed more than just the ceiling. A large accumulation of bats had taken refuge in the cave to hibernate until the spring. The sleepy little critters, once disturbed, began to squeak and stir in the icy darkness.

"What is that?" Brenda Bailey asked, suddenly awake and aware of the twittering noises made by the furry beasts.

"It's just a bunch of bats," Sullivan said, getting to his feet.

"Bats? Did you say BATS?" Brenda was nearly hysterical with fright. "You guys have to get me outta here! BATS? You can't be serious!"

"Come on, Andre," Diggs said impatiently, we gotta get a move on."

"I'm coming, I'm coming! I gotta pee first."

"Hey, you can't leave me here," Brenda was nearly frantic by now. "I'll die in this hole!"

"Too bad, Sweet Cheeks," Diggs tossed the words over his shoulder at he started up the ladder. He made his way awkwardly because he held the shotgun in one hand.

By now, Bailey was fully aware the men were going to leave her in the cave. As Sullivan, clutching his briefcase, followed his cousin up the ladder, Brenda filled the air with screeches and enough obscenities to last a sailor a lifetime.

When the two men finally reached the top of the ladder and gingerly stepped onto the ground, the police were ready for them. "Freeze! Police!"

Diggs did anything but freeze. Not being able to see anybody in the dim light of an awakening day, he just took blind aim into the direction the voice came from and pulled the trigger of the shotgun. Nothing happened. The sludge and debris which had collected in the spare tire well of the Taurus had effectively corroded the workings of the gun so that it jammed.

He threw the gun to the ground in a disgusted fit of rage and took off running. With the direction of her handler, Lola scampered after him. With blazing speed the dog was on Diggs before he got twenty yards away. She grabbed him by the pant leg, tripping him. She then launched herself at the nearest thing within her reach, his crotch, sinking her teeth in where teeth should never be. The resulting pain rendered the man helpless. The bellowing racket Diggs made rivalled the cloud of expletives Brenda Bailey was still sending skyward from the depths of the cave.

While all this was going on, Sullivan meekly surrendered to Richmond claiming he was an innocent hostage of his evil cousin. Resisting the urge to say, "Yeah, I'll bet," Richmond cuffed him, telling him he was being arrested for conspiracy to commit murder, and read him his rights.

As for Diggs, Sergeant Martinez put hand cuffs on him while the doctor groaned in pain and whined that he was the victim of blackmail and that Andre Sullivan made him do it. Just what was the "it" was left undefined. Martinez arrested him on conspiracy to commit murder and attempted murder of a police officer. As Martinez read to him his rights, Diggs blathered on and on about everything and anything that could be used against him in a court of law.

Chief Conroy had approached the edge of the cave and peered inside. He felt fairly safe doing so because if Bailey was armed, surely she would have blasted away at her two companions as they abandoned her.

Brenda looked up at the shadow which loomed at the edge of the cave opening. Conroy was backlit by the brightening sky.

"Get me outta here!" she bellowed. "My leg was broken when I fell in this fucking hole!"

"Are you Brenda Bailey?" Conroy asked.

"Yes, you fucking idiot! Get me outta this hole!"

"Okay," Conroy said simply. "We'll get some help. In the meantime, I'm arresting you for accessory to commit murder."

As he read her rights to her, she wept the tears of the utterly miserable and muttered, "Yeah, yeah okay whatever!"

A LOUD ALARM woke Tommy Jax like a bolt of lightning. Jax's whole body jumped which dislodged both Fido and Booger from Jax's stomach. The sound came from Jax's computer, as a warning that the tracking sensors had moved. The first few rays of dawn were sneaking in the big front window of Beth and Arthur's cabin as Jax called Oliver.

"Yes, we heard it too." Oliver said into the speaker on his phone as he watched what was happening on the GPS screen. "Two of the three sensors moved, but they didn't go very far. The third one is still stationery."

"Let's give it a minute and see what happens." Jax advised. This message went out to all the Geezers on their radios. Everyone was now alert and glued to their phones.

As Aunt Phil focused on her phone screen, the machine itself rang. She looked at Oliver and they shared a questioning look as she answered.

"Phyllis!" Cyril Richmond's voice echoed both relief and exhaustion. "Sullivan and Diggs are locked into the back seat of my truck. Brenda Bailey fell into Skylight Cave and broke a leg, she says. We will send for the search and rescue crew out of Camp Sherman who will probably build a hoist over the hole to get her out and then transport her to the hospital in

Bend. The Black Butte Police will stay with her until a guard is assigned to her hospital room. Deputy Leese and I are taking Sullivan and Diggs to the lockup in Madras. After we book Diggs, he'll also be taken to the hospital for treatment for, er, some dog bites. I thought I'd give you a heads up as to what transpired overnight."

"Thanks, Cyril! I appreciate you keeping us informed. Good job and I hope you can get some rest! You must have been out there all night." Aunt Phil again exchanged looks with Oliver. "I'll update the rest of the Geezers."

"Okay. Tell them thanks for their efforts." Cyril shut off his phone knowing full well that somewhere out there in the woods was an invisible posse of Geezers who could now go to bed.

CHAPTER 32

AUNT PHIL SENT out the word that everyone was to abandon their posts and to do so quickly as Deputy Richmond was on his way out to the highway. The Geezers fired up their vehicles, retraced their routes and soon had melted out of sight. Deputies Cyril Richmond and Greg Leese stopped briefly at the Black Butte Police headquarters long enough for Leese to pick up his patrol car. By the time the two deputies pulled their respective rigs onto the highway, the forest was as empty of Geezers as though they had never been there.

Tommy Jax watched on his computer screen the progression of Richmond's truck from the location near Skylight Cave out to US 20. As soon as the truck pulled onto the highway, Jax hit a key on his keyboard and the tiny sensor Oliver had placed under Richmond's right front fender fell off and was soon lost in the red cinder rock of the highway shoulder.

Leese escorted Richmond with his load of crooks to the Jefferson County Sheriff's office and aided in removing the prisoners from the truck, then assisted in the booking process. After sharing a handshake with Richmond for a job well done, Leese traveled back to the Deschutes County Sheriff's office in Bend and filed two reports; one of Kemper's vehicle being run off the road by Sullivan's crew and the other of his assisting Jefferson County with the capture of three murder suspects. He also checked on the Kempers' condition with St. Charles Hospital to find they had both been discharged. Deciding he would look in on them later in the day, Leese gratefully went to his home and slept as though he had been drugged.

Richmond spent a few minutes briefing Sheriff Larkin on what had transpired overnight. He arranged for two other deputies to haul the ever complaining Dr. Diggs to St. Charles's ER. Then, calling it a day at 8:00 AM, Richmond drove back to Camp Sherman.

On his way home, he placed a call to Lieutenant Avery in Portland. Avery had just arrived at his desk and was silent and frozen in place while Richmond told him Jefferson County had the three suspects in custody and described how they were able to apprehend them.

Avery replied with what had become an expression of choice between the two policemen, "No shit?"

"No shit," Richmond answered. "If you want to talk to them, be my guest. Our facilities are at your disposal. Just give me a few hours to sleep."

"Not a problem, Cyril. I'd like to talk to Sullivan. We are in the process of exhuming victims of his scheme here in Portland and are developing a pretty solid case against him and his slimy cousin. Good job, you and the Deschutes County guy, Leese! I'd like to meet him, him and the Black Butte guys. An English Bull dog is their police dog, really?"

"No shit." Both men laughed.

Richmond approached the turnoff to Camp Sherman but before he went home, he swung onto the Green Ridge Road to pass by Beth and Arthur's cabin. The cabin appeared dark and very quiet. Not even Max's nose was poking out between the draperies. He then made his way over the ridge and drove by Mick's cabin. The old orange pickup was parked at the side, but the cabin was dark. When Richmond reached the store's parking lot, the bench outside the post office was empty. Its normal occupants, Mick, Dave, and Conrad, were conspicuous in their absence. Chuckling to himself, Cyril Richmond pointed his truck towards home for a much deserved sleep.

TO SAY THAT the Portland Police Homicide Division had been busy while Richmond and the Geezers were chasing Sullivan and his murderous crew all over Central Oregon would be a gross understatement. Lieutenant

Avery had shared with his Captain what Percy "Biceps" Lumpsucker had revealed to Richmond about Sullivan and Digg's operation in Portland. Captain Marc Nelson, a huge man whose military style crewcut would have made a good scrub brush, lowered his riveting blue eyes at Avery and said, "Exhume as many of those bodies as you can. Let's have a forensic pathologist take a look at them. The alleged killer has given us probable cause to do that. Get me the names and cemeteries and we'll contact the court and see if they'll expedite warrants. The first few bodies will tell us if we really have a case."

Avery wasted no time. He put Banning and Kowalski to work reviewing the death certificates they had previously researched. In just one neighborhood alone, there were three dozen properties. Although numerous other neighborhoods were involved, the investigators decided to use one neighborhood as a test section. Out of those three dozen death certificates, the method of body disposition was burial in twenty-three cases.

Armed with the proper court order, Avery, Kowalski, Banning and a forensic team headed out to where three of the suspected victims were interred, Angel's Rest Cemetery in NE Portland. The policemen were scheduled to meet Dr. Calvin Wiggins, retired Divisional Director, Oregon State Police, Medical Examiner Division. Seventy six year-old Dr. Wiggins still kept his medical license valid and now served as an expert witness in forensic analysis for court cases across the country. He admitted he also enjoyed "a good dig in the dirt" when asked to perform autopsies on post burial suspected murder victims.

At his own insistence, Dr. Wiggins did not yet want to know any particulars as to why the police wanted these specific bodies exhumed and examined. Avery didn't know if Dr. Wiggins knew Herman Diggs but Avery's research did discover that Wiggins had retired long before Diggs became lead medical examiner for Multnomah County.

Arriving at the cemetery, the police found Dr. Wiggins dressed in water proof coveralls and standing under a blue canopy previously set up by cemetery workers. Dr. Wiggins was a rumpled gnome of a man with a head of fuzzy white hair which peeked out from under the edges of a rain-proof flop hat. He had on Wellingtons and nitrile gloves. His sparkling grey eyes and toothy grin belied any doubt that Dr. Wiggins was already having a good time.

Handshakes and introductions were made all around and the team got to work. The cemetery had provided a backhoe complete with operator who made quick work of digging a hole down to the top of the coffin. The heirs of the decedent had not paid extra for a concrete vault so it wasn't long before the dirt was dug sufficiently away from the coffin. Before anyone was allowed to climb inside the grave, the backhoe operator deftly lowered reinforced plywood slabs down all four sides of the hole to prevent it from caving in. Once those were in place, enough remaining dirt was dug away so that the coffin lid could be pried open. Every team member was wearing eye guards and surgical masks to protect themselves from the fumes of decomposition. Still, the initial blast of odor escaping the coffin could, as Kowalski later exclaimed, gag a maggot.

Everyone took a step away except for Dr. Wiggins who, in his element, leaned in to get a closer look at the corpse and said, "My, my, my! This face is a mess!" He then turned his head around to address Avery and said, "Lieutenant? Without looking any further at the rest of his body, it's clear to me that before or after death, this man was struck just above the nose with something long, thin, and hard. It would be my guess, at this point, that it was something round, like a baton, a pipe, a broom handle, something like that. There is massive damage done to the frontal area of the skull. If he wasn't dead before this happened, he surely was afterwards as there are shards of bone driven into the intracranial space. Well, let's get him out and we'll do a complete autopsy of what is left of the body, but I'll bet it's a moot point."

As the forensic team dealt with removing the body from the grave, Dr. Wiggins, Avery, Banning, and Kowalski, along with the backhoe driver, moved to the next blue canopy where the process started all over again. What they found were identical injuries in the next two bodies. At this point, the detectives had all the probable cause they needed to put out arrest warrants for both Andre Sullivan and Dr. Herman Diggs.

Wiggins, after climbing out of the third grave, stood at the hole's edge and gazed down sadly at the corpse. After a moment or two he turned to Avery and said, "Okay, Lieutenant, tell me what the autopsies for these three people indicated was the cause of death."

Avery looked at Kowalski who had brought copies of the autopsies and read aloud, "Probable heart attack for the first two, and diseases consistent with old age for this last one." Kowalski added, "Each autopsy states that there were contusions on the face consistent with falling face down."

Wiggins again looked down in the grave, then looked at all three policemen and said, "Contusions? If these folks were all dead when these injuries occurred, falling to the floor would not have caused them. Someone would have to have beaten the corpses in a very strange manner and why would anybody do that?"

Dr. Wiggins was briefed on the detectives' suspicions as to what really happened to these victims. When the pathologist asked how many victims were involved, Avery said, "As far as we know, there were seventy-six properties involved in this scheme to acquire land. The process went on for many years, and the victims were all old. Old people die, hence the pieces were never put together to point to murder. We won't be able to prove all seventy-six deaths were murder because nineteen of those people were cremated. That leaves us with fifty-seven burials to investigate."

Wiggins' eyes widened and he said, "This could result in the largest number of victims attributed to one murderer in the state's history!"

"We're not yet sure there was just one murderer," Avery continued, "but we are pretty sure the killings were ordered by one individual or an agent of that individual. All seventy-six autopsies were completed by one person who is a relation of the individual who ordered the killings and subsequently purchased the properties from the decedents' estates."

Wiggins asked to see the autopsies and after much page flipping perusal accented by quiet grumblings he noted that only one pathologist's signature was on each report, indicating there was no assistant in the autopsy process. Dr. Diggs was the only one in on determining the cause of death.

"You said, Lieutenant, that the pathologist is a relation to the one suspected in ordering the killings?"

"Yes," Avery answered.

Wiggins got a faraway look in his eyes while he digested the implication of the entire picture and said more to the cosmos than anybody else, "Holy Mother of God!"

CHAPTER 33

LIEUTENANT AVERY SUMMONED Corporal Banning and Sergeant Kowalski to his office. He told them what Deputy Richmond had revealed about the capture of Sullivan, Diggs, and Bailey.

"Hot damn!" Kowalski cheered.

"Good for Cyril!" Banning added.

"Do you guys want to take a little trip to Central Oregon to talk to these people? Instead, we could just extradite them."

Banning spoke first, "Jefferson County has their own case against them and that extradition process can take a long time."

"Right," Kowalski joined in, "I think we ought to take a crack at them. Besides, I'd like to see Camp Sherman again. You know, have another of those deli sandwiches the store makes, plus a piece of huckleberry pie to go along with it." Kowalski licked his chops with just the thought.

"Get two forks," Banning quipped, "for the pie."

"Git yer own pie!" Kowalski snarled.

"Don't drool on my desk, you two," Avery laughed. "Well, those exhumations are continuing on schedule and they have given us enough for arrest warrants. Nothing much else is going on in Murder Land that the rest of the crew can't handle. I'll see if I can get us a few days out of the office. Let's get out while the getting's good."

ANDRE SULLIVAN WAS thoroughly pissed. He sat in his cell at the Jefferson County jail, crossed his arms over his chest and pouted. The phone call he was allowed to make to his attorney in Portland was a bust. The guy had the audacity to tell Andre that he hadn't been paid for the last work he did. Even if he could get paid, he didn't appreciate having to chase Andre around the block for his money. Therefore, he wasn't going to do anything else for him now or ever. Shit! Andre was stuck in this chicken shit jail having to deal with this chicken shit sheriff's department in this chicken shit little town!

"Mr. Sullivan?" The young attorney had stopped outside Andre's cell and was thumbing through the papers in his hand.

"Yeah. What of it?" With a sneer, Andre looked up and down at the man's attire; jeans, chambray shirt, and dusty hiking boots.

"I've been assigned your case by the Public Defender's Office."

Sullivan leapt to his feet and charged the bars on his cell, forcing the man to jump away. "Don't those idiots know who I am?" Sullivan snarled. "I'm a famous political figure! I'm not going to settle for any chicken shit public defender! I'll defend myself first!"

"Fine," the young man replied, smiling. He shuffled the documents in his hands and said, "Sign this waiver and you can defend yourself. That's what it says." He thrust a piece of paper and a pen through the bars at Sullivan.

Sullivan snatched the pen and scratched out his signature and stuffed the document back at the attorney. Andre sat back down on his cot and pouted some more. Surely this lawyer business couldn't be so hard that he couldn't figure it out.

The young man gave Andre a copy of the waiver he had signed, closed his briefcase, turned away and cheerfully said, "Good day, Sir!" He then muttered under his breath, "you chicken shit little pissant."

THE GEEZERS CONVENED at the Wardwell's cabin at around one o'clock. They were still tired and sleepy but elated that Sullivan and his crew were finally where they belonged, behind bars. Aunt Phil had brewed coffee and everyone sipped at the welcoming hot drink and discussed their overnight adventures.

Tommy Jax and Oliver pulled up in the Bentley and Jax entered the cabin proudly carrying a steaming pan of lasagna. He had gone to the Camp Sherman Store early that morning for the ingredients and had baked the dish while the rest of the Geezers slept.

"Wow, T. J., how did you find time to do this?" Aunt Phil asked as she made room on the kitchen counter.

"This morning. While the rest of you were on patrol last night, the animals and I got some sleep knowing that the computer would wake me up if something happened. I came to the store for the ingredients and then went back to the house at Black Butte Ranch and whipped it out."

Oliver had followed Jax into the cabin with a warm loaf of olive bread and a large container of salad Jax had also tossed together.

Dave walked up and taking a sniff of the lasagna, backed up a few steps, waved his arms around and said, "Make room! I'm going to do a swan dive face first into that pan!"

Tommy Jax laughed and removed the foil he had placed over the dish, remarking, "There is enough cheese in here to put us all in the hospital."

"Oh, good!" Mick said, taking a plate off a stack Aunt Phil placed on the counter. "We'll take over the place."

"St. Charles will never be the same."

"Two bedpans in every room!"

"Along with wide-screen TVs!"

"I'll make my room a man-cave."

"Cookies and lattes at four o'clock!"

"Wheelchair races in the hallways!"

"I win!"

"Beds are big enough for two," Conrad wiggled his eyebrows at Aunt Phil. Sophie and Adam exchanged glances and both blushed.

"They'll have to call in the National Guard to get rid of us."

"Oh good! The more to party, the better."

All this was going on while the Geezers filled their plates and settled in for lunch. Looking out the kitchen window Arthur announced, "Oh, here comes Cyril!"

"Jiggers, it's the cops!"

"Now, we'll find out how much trouble we're in."

"Or not."

Cyril Richmond was dressed in his uniform and approached the cabin with a purposeful stride. Conrad met him at the door and invited him in. "You're just in time for lunch, Cyril! Grab a plate. I guarantee T.J.'s lasagna is the best you'll ever taste."

Richmond took a deep lung full of the savory odors of cheese, rosemary, tomatoes, and sausage which filled the cabin. To the tune of his stomach grumbling he said, "Gee, thanks! I will! But I'm going to have to hurry. Three homicide detectives from Portland are coming to Madras. They want to talk to Sullivan and the rest of his gang."

"I'm guessing it's Lieutenant Avery, Corporal Banning, and that big really cute hunk, Sergeant Kowalski," Aunt Phil said.

Richmond nodded, yet again amazed at the connections the Geezers had.

"Oh, good!" Beth said. "So my hunch about the deaths of my friends panned out?"

"That's one thing they are investigating, Beth," Richmond answered. Richmond then turned to the rest of the crowd, reached into his coat pocket and pulled out a plastic evidence bag filled with a mish-mash of tiny tracking sensors. As he held it up so everyone could see what he had, he said, "These are not integral to the investigation so I thought I'd return them. We found them on the Mercedes SUV Sullivan's hit man drove to Wilbur's cabin, Digg's Taurus, and also on some personal items belonging to Sullivan's crew."

He placed the bag on the coffee table and then he headed for the door. Smiling, he said, "Maybe you can use them again." With a wink to the Geezers, Cyril Richmond opened the door and was gone.

CHAPTER 34

THE PORTLAND DETECTIVES made good time on their way to Madras. Much to Trevor Kowalski's dismay, Shawn Avery insisted on taking his personal car. Jerry Banning didn't care because he didn't have to drive the thing.

The 1970 Chevrolet Caprice Kingwood Estate station wagon wallowed through the Mount Hood National Forest on US 26's forested curves. Kowalski was at the wheel, Banning was sprawled across the copious back seat, Avery was riding shotgun but was asleep.

"Hey, Shawn," Kowalski had to speak loudly to be heard over the road noise and rattling coming from the car, "tell me again why we are driving this haven for rust."

"Careful, Sergeant," Avery cautioned, opening one eye. "You are talking about something that is very close to my heart."

"I know that, but why take this car when we could have taken a department set of wheels. After all, we are on official business. We'd have good shocks, which is better than no shocks, air conditioning that actually cools instead of spitting ice cubes out the air vents, plus we wouldn't have to be concerned about leaving loose parts lying in the roadway everywhere we go."

"Betsy needed some exercise," Avery said as if that explained everything and closed the eye.

Kowalski sighed, shook his head and looked in the rear view mirror at Banning suppressing a smile.

The back of the station wagon seemed alive with rattling fishing equipment. Avery was determined to take Cyril Richmond up on his invitation to go fly fishing on the Metolius. Avery brought enough gear for everybody as well as renting a cabin at Metolius River Resort, right across the bridge from the Camp Sherman Store. That fishing expedition, however, would have to wait a day or two as their mission this afternoon was to interview as many of Andre Sullivan's gang as they could.

Once they entered Madras, they exited the highway at NW Cherry Lane and made their way to the Jefferson County Sheriff's Office. As they pulled in front of the building, who also was parking his truck but Cyril Richmond.

Richmond stepped from his vehicle and said, "Good afternoon, gentlemen." As the Portland detectives climbed out of the Caprice, Richmond took in the car from stem to stern and said, "I remember this aircraft carrier! You drove it to Camp Sherman last summer. It was parked in front of the store. That's an amazing machine!"

Avery grinned while Kowalski said, "What's more amazing, it made it again without anything falling off."

"Yeah," Avery said, "it probably ought to have one of those diaper things carriage horses wear hanging behind them to catch crap."

After laughter and shaking hands all around, the men walked to the entrance of the building and went inside. Richmond stepped up to the reception desk and asked the duty officer to tell Sheriff Larkin he was here to see him and that the Portland homicide team also was here.

Jefferson County Sheriff Gary Larkin soon entered the reception area from a hallway behind a closed door. They could hear his boots clomping on the tile floor before he flung open the door. Larkin, a huge, well-proportioned man whose presence had authority written all over it, greeted each detective with a smile and a handshake.

"Thank you for coming," Larkin said. "Come on back to my office and let's talk about how we're going to relieve these people of their insistence that they are innocent victims of each other."

As the lawmen settled around a conference table in Larkin's office Avery asked, "So that's the story you're getting? That the other guy made him do it?"

"Well, that's pretty close," Richmond began. "Sullivan refuses to say much of anything. He waived the right for a court appointed attorney and hasn't been able to come up with one for himself. He thinks he can represent himself."

"We'll make sure we get his signature and his desire for no attorney on tape and then go at him," Larkin added. "He's delusional in that he thinks it can't be hard to get off. He also thinks he's too important to be held here in po-dunk Jefferson County and continues to proclaim his innocence."

"Of course," Richmond continued, "we have both his cousin, Diggs, and the actual confessed killer, Percy Lumpsucker. . ."

"What's the name?" Avery interrupted.

"Yeah, Lumpsucker," Richmond answered.

"That's a fish," Jerry Banning noted. "It's a small round thing. The two pectoral fins act like suction cups and it can fasten itself to stuff."

Cyril Richmond raised both eyebrows and said, "No shit?"

"No shit," Banning laughed.

"Anyway," Richmond continued, "both those guys claim that Sullivan is the ring leader and ordered the killings with the intent that he would acquire the property of the victims, eventually obtaining enough land on Green Ridge to put in a destination resort."

"What about Brenda Bailey?" Avery checked his notes for her name.

"She claims the men kidnaped her and that she had nothing to do with any of it," Richmond answered. "She does have a court appointed attorney as do both Diggs and Lumpsucker. Bailey is under guard in St. Charles Medical Center in Bend. She sustained a broken leg while the three of them were trying to escape through the woods up near Black Butte Ranch."

Then Larkin spoke to the Portland detectives, "What kind of a case have you been able to make against this bunch?"

Sergeant Kowalski opened the file folder he had carried in a briefcase. "Lieutenant Avery had gotten a hunch that Andre Sullivan may have been involved in some property acquisitions in NE Portland which involved deceased elderly property owners."

"It was an old memory regarding Sullivan pressuring the police to conclude their investigations," Avery interjected.

"Our research," Kowalski continued, "revealed that the death certificates and autopsies of all those people were oddly signed by one pathologist, Dr. Herman Diggs. The reasons for death were vague and almost all the same." Now Sergeant Kowalski referred to his notes. "Either 'probable heart disease' or 'diseases consistent with old age.'"

"I was curious," Avery added, "what they meant by 'probable' and 'diseases consistent with old age' because an autopsy is supposed to determine a scientific reason for the death, so I called the guy, Diggs. He was so condescending and evasive that I didn't get much out of him. Cyril had shared with us the autopsies of the two murder victims here in Jefferson County; the one set of autopsies done by Diggs with his causes of death being consistent with ours in Portland and the second autopsies done by the pathologist you had arranged for showing skull trauma as the real cause of death. So, the three of us went to talk to Diggs in person. But again he was evasive and aggravated that we interrupted his busy schedule. He claimed that old people die all the time so he hurries those autopsies through. I asked him if he knew Andre Sullivan and he claimed not to, even when we told him they were second cousins.

"Cyril wanted a more positive connection between Diggs and Sullivan so we went to see Diggs again. The acting director of the medical examiner's office told us Diggs had cleaned out his desk and left the office shortly after we had been there the first time and he had not been back."

"We went to his house and it appeared vacated, so that's when we put out the APB on his car," Kowalski said, "Because, at that point, we knew he was related to Andre Sullivan, but we really didn't have anything concrete to charge him with in Portland except suspicion of conspiracy to commit murder."

"That's when we started exhuming bodies," Avery continued. "Each victim had evidence of frontal skull fractures above the bridge of the nose just like your two victims did. We're still exhuming bodies."

"How many properties did Sullivan acquire?" Larkin asked.

"76 over about thirteen years," Banning checked his notes. "He then sold one chunk of land for twenty million dollars to a California outfit which put in a huge shopping center."

Larkin let out a whistle when Banning revealed the enormity of the scam. The sheriff felt a chill run up his spine with the thought that Sullivan had attempted to do the same thing on Green Ridge. Larkin again asked, "So during that time no one caught on that those properties were all purchased by the same person?"

"No," Avery answered, "not until we started to dig into the multitude of scam corporations which purchased the properties. Jerry here was the one who figured it out. Corporal Banning is our computer guy. He started peeling back the layers of holding companies and found they all traced back to Sullivan. The guy was well insulated from the dirty work but Jerry found him."

"When we get a conviction, we can follow the money paper trails," Banning commented. "Maybe the estates of those dead people can get some compensation."

Avery added, "Jerry also was the one who found the relationship between Sullivan and Diggs."

"They are cousins, I understand?" the sheriff asked.

"Second cousins," Banning answered. "Their grandmothers were sisters."

Sheriff Larkin got a faraway look in his eyes and said, "I'll bet those two women would roll over in their graves if they knew the crimes their offspring committed."

The sheriff turned to his deputy and said, "Cyril, Lumpsucker is waiting for us in an interview room, right?"

"Yes, sir."

Larkin got to his feet as did the other lawmen and said, "Well let's get to it."

CHAPTER 35

PERCY LUMPSUCKER WAS a mess. His stringy hair clung damply to his scalp and the skin on his face was pale and paper thin, looking shrunken as it stretched over the facial bones. His appearance made you think you were looking at a skull rather than a face. He was also sweating profusely and was definitely uncomfortable being shackled to the table. His court appointed defense attorney sat next to him with the unhappy look of someone too close to a foul smelling substance but unable to get away. What would have made Percy sweat even more, had he known about it, was that Portland homicide detectives were in the next room watching him through a one-way window.

Lumpsucker jumped in his chair when Sheriff Larkin and Deputy Richmond opened the door and entered the room. Percy was afraid of these policemen, but since he had turned State's Witness against Andre Sullivan, he was even more afraid of blowback from his boss. Sullivan was an obsessively vindictive man and anybody who crossed him paid a dear price. Percy knew. He often was the one who was paid to administer that price.

When the tape was set to record, Richmond identified the individuals in the room, the present date and time and then the interview began. As Percy continued to fidget and squirm, Sheriff Larkin said, "What we want to do today is start out by repeating the discussion we had after you were first apprehended at Wilbur Martin's cabin. This time, if you have recalled facts that you didn't share with us before, we want to hear them. Starting at the beginning, can you tell us in detail what led up to you being found at Wilbur Martin's cabin on October 15th of this year?"

Lumpsucker looked helplessly at his attorney for guidance as he would for every question asked. At her slight nod, Percy stammered out his story; Andre Sullivan had employed him to kill the owners of two cabins on the east side of Green Ridge, making their deaths look as though they had suffered a major medical emergency and had fallen face down, then he was to torch the cabins.

Richmond then asked how Percy knew how to kill someone like that. Again Percy looked to his attorney, who again nodded. "He fucking told me how."

"Who told you how?"

"Andre did. He had it all figured out, because we had already done..."

His attorney then instructed Lumpsucker to strictly stay with the answer.

"Oh, okay, er, he gave me this pool cue, see," Lumpsucker continued, "it was cut off so it was mostly handle and he, well, showed me where to hit someone in the face and to do it hard, you know, like fucking *really* hard. Then as I left the place, I was to soak a tennis ball in that barbecue lighting fluid stuff, and then light it, you know? I then threw the ball into the cabin with a thing you use to throw balls for a dog."

Larkin remained quiet knowing that would encourage Lumpsucker to fill the silence with more information. Percy obliged.

"I didn't get a chance to torch the second cabin because some dumb ass came to the door and knocked and called the guy's name. I hid in the kitchen until I heard him drive away. His truck made all this fuckin' noise! So I left as soon as I couldn't hear the guy's truck no more."

"So Andre Sullivan was the one who showed you how to kill people with this pool cue method?" Richmond repeated.

"Uh, yeah. Andre did, uh-huh," Lumpsucker said, glancing first at his attorney, then at the two policemen and back at his attorney. "And I was fucking good at it, you know?" A maniacal smile broke out on Lumpsucker's face, obviously proud of his grisly accomplishments. He stupidly turned the smile to his attorney. If he was hoping for a look of admiration from the woman, he was sorely disappointed.

"Percy," Richmond said conversationally, "do you know why Andre Sullivan directed you to do this?"

"Well, yeah, you see in Portland we been. . ."

Again, his attorney interrupted to tell him to keep in the present. On the other side of the one-way window, the three Portland homicide detectives exchanged looks and Avery quietly said, "We got him."

"Well," Percy continued, "he wanted to buy their fucking land and then sell it, or do something with it, like put in, like, a resort or some shit. He was going to have me hit a couple of other properties around in that same area on Green Ridge but, well, I guess you guys caught me first."

"Okay, Percy," Larkin said, "was there anybody else in on this plan?"

"Oh, sure, there was that doctor guy and the broad."

"Who?"

"A doctor who does, er, I guess you call 'em fucking autopsies and shit? His name is Hermie, er, Herman Diggs. Kinda funny name for a guy who cuts into people, huh? Diggs?" Again the maniacal smile. Again the answering scowl from his attorney.

"And what did this doctor do?"

"Well, he faked the autopsies to make it look like the people died of something else. He worked in Portland, see, and he knew that you guys in Central Oregon send stiffs to Portland to be autopsied."

"Okay," Richmond said, looking at his notes. "Percy, you said there was also a woman involved?"

"Yea! Brenda Bailey. She has big fucking boobs!" This drew another scowl from the attorney.

"Do you know what her role was?"

"Well, you see, all this time, Andre was running for a fucking senatorship or whatever you call 'em. He was going to be a big shot, like, in government. He already thought he was a big shot but I don't think he ever held an office or nothin'. Brenda, she was kinda in charge of his campaign, arranging for his speeches and shit. But she also kept me supplied with a car and a place to stay and the tennis balls and crap."

"So, if she bought the tennis balls and lighter fluid, she knew what was going on about killing the cabin owners?"

The attorney interrupted, claiming the question was heresay.

Richmond looked at his notes and said, "Okay, Percy, I guess that is all we need right now. We have informed your attorney that there are some homicide detectives from the Portland Police Bureau who are also here to talk to you." He and Sheriff Larkin then left the room.

Percy Lumpsucker was already nervous enough. Now, with this new development, he was nearly half-crazed. His attorney looked at his hyperventilating face and said, "Listen! The best thing you can do is offer to turn State's Witness with these guys. You are in this up to your neck, Percy, and unless you do, you'll fry. I'll get the best deal for you I can, but I can't do anything for you unless you confess... to all of it. Do you understand?"

Percy had shared with his attorney Sullivan's operation in Portland. What they had done on Green Ridge was miniscule compared to the scope of the Portland crimes. With the Portland police appearing here at the Jefferson County jail, it was clear that Percy Lumpsucker was on their radar and there was going to be no escaping the far-reaching talons of the Portland Police Bureau.

Lieutenant Avery entered the room first followed by Banning. Kowalski came in, filling the doorway, and closed the door behind him. He then remained standing, leaning on the door. Avery introduced himself, Corporal Banning and Sergeant Kowalski while Jerry Banning set up the tape recorder.

Avery began by reintroducing himself and his men for the recording's benefit, adding the presence of Lumpsucker and his attorney. He then spoke to Percy. "Okay, Mr. Lumpsucker," Avery began, "you know who we are and why we're here. We want to know all you know about Andre Sullivan's criminal activities in Portland and what your involvement was."

The story they heard was just as grim and grisly as they had expected it to be. Over the course of twelve or so years, Sullivan obtained possession of dozens of properties formerly owned by elderly people. Those owners had been systematically killed using the same method Lumpsucker had explained to the Jefferson County Officers.

"Andre was, what the fuck you call it, obsessive com... com somethin'."

"Obsessive compulsive?" Avery offered.

"That's it! He insisted that I do them all in the same way I done the others," Lumpsucker said. "He made me tell him how I was to fuckin' kill 'em before I did each one, just to make sure I'd do it right. He figured it was a foolproof method. No way anybody would figure out it was murder." Lumpsucker paused then leaned in Avery's direction and added, "Actually, I kinda think he liked to hear just how I'd do it, ya know? Kinda like he imagined himself doin' it, ya know... killin' those people."

Lumpsucker's interview lasted for over one hour. He also explained how Brenda Bailey would identify vulnerable elderly property owners and then after Lumpsucker eliminated the homeowner, she would quickly present herself to the heirs as a real estate agent for someone who wanted to buy the property. "She wanted to get in there fast before they even put the property up for sale. She was pretty fuckin' good at what she did. We all were pretty fuckin' good at what we did."

Cyril Richmond, in the room next door, was watching and listening alongside Sheriff Larkin, Richmond thought, *"Yeah, you think you were good but the Geezer Underground was better. They found you before you could do any more damage, you stinking sack of shit!"*

CHAPTER 36

DR. HERMAN DIGGS had been waiting forever. The interview room was beginning to close in on him. The contents of his bowels were turning into slush and he was starting to sweat. His court appointed attorney calmly sat at his side. The infuriating bastard was casually looking at his phone as though this was just another day at the office.

To the attorney, Elliott Anderson, Diggs' case really was just another day at the office. Throughout his career, Anderson had heard every lie imaginable and had been told more secrets than God. This was just one more guy trying to save his neck using smoke and mirrors. Diggs' claim he had been blackmailed by Sullivan might stand up. However, Anderson suspected there was more behind the blackmail than merely covering up and paying for Diggs' addictions. If all the reasons behind the blackmail should come forth, Anderson felt that Diggs might very well be in bigger trouble than if he'd confess criminal conspiracy with Sullivan on the murders. Smoke can veil just so much before it wafts away, exposing the evils humans horribly bestow upon one another.

If Diggs had even a shred of confidence that his blackmail story was going to save his hide, he lost the bravado very quickly when the door to the interview room opened and into the small space walked two policemen. Diggs recognized both: Sheriff Gary Larkin and Lieutenant Shawn Avery. One look at Avery and Diggs' bowels turned to more than just slush. He desperately flexed his sphincter muscles accordingly.

"Dr. Diggs," began Sheriff Larkin after he set up the tape recorder with the date, time, and named the individuals in the room. "I don't think I need to introduce you to Lieutenant Shawn Avery of the Portland Police Bureau. You and I have already discussed your case here in Jefferson County in which you claim to be a blackmail victim of Andre Sullivan, so I'm going to leave the room now and let you talk with Lieutenant Avery." Larkin left the room, took five steps down the hall and entered the room next door where Deputy Cyril Richmond, Portland detectives, Corporal Jerry Banning and Sergeant Trevor Kowalski, were watching Avery and Diggs through the one-way window.

"Hello, Dr. Diggs," Avery began pleasantly. "Do you know why I'm here to talk to you today?"

"Sure. You want to know how Andre Sullivan blackmailed me."

"Well, yes, there is that. We'll get to that in a minute. Do you remember when I and two of my colleagues visited you at your office in October of this year?"

Herman Diggs, the consummate snob, sniffed and said, "Yeah, I guess. Vaguely."

"Do you remember what we talked about?"

"Yeah, something about some autopsies," Diggs waved his hand dismissively.

"Correct. We showed you autopsies done by another pathologist on two bodies you had already performed autopsies on." Avery made a point of checking his notes, "Your determination of the cause of death was 'diseases associated with old age' for one of the bodies and 'probable heart disease' for the other one."

"Whatever."

"The second pathologist determined that both individuals had been murdered by blunt force trauma to the face."

"Look, I said Andre was making me fudge those autopsies."

"Fudge," Avery said looking Herman Diggs. "Funny word to use for falsifying an official document, especially when it involves conspiracy to commit murder. It's a Class A felony in this state, Doctor. Fudge."

"Lieutenant," Anderson cautioned.

"Sorry, Mr. Anderson," Avery said with a slight smile as he rummaged in his tattered brief case. He brought out a messy cluster of papers and put them face down on the table.

"Dr. Diggs, we went back to your office on October 20th to talk to you again and we were told that, on the day of our prior visit and shortly after we were there, you had cleared out your desk and left your office and that you had not been back to work. Is that correct?"

"I was sick of that place. I needed some time off."

"We also went to your home and found it empty and abandoned."

"So what? I was also sick of Portland."

"I see." Avery then turned over the pile of papers and untidily put them into a resemblance of a stack. "Dr. Diggs, I have here twelve autopsies done on six individuals who had died in Portland sometime during the past twelve or so years. You have done an autopsy on each of these individuals. Every one of your autopsies shows the cause of death as either probable heart disease or diseases associated with old age. We are in the process of exhuming the bodies of all these people and plan to do many more."

Herman Diggs noisily took an intake of breath. His attorney turned to look at him.

"Another pathologist," Avery went on, "performed autopsies on the bodies we have currently exhumed and determined each and every one of them died in the same way; blunt force trauma to the face. In other words, they were all murdered."

"I told you Andre made me do that!" Diggs was sweating buckets by now. "He bought the houses those people lived in so he could sell off the land. He'd rent the houses out until he had several properties together. Then he'd evict the renters for some stupid reason or another and sell the whole mess for a fortune."

"We know, Dr. Diggs. We are investigating fifty-seven cases in the Portland area where old people have died and their property was subsequently purchased by Sullivan." Avery picked up the stack of autopsies and said, "These are just the beginning."

Diggs' attorney was now staring wide-eyed at his client.

Avery paused for a moment then placed his hand on the pile of documents and said, "Dr. Diggs, tell me why you lied about the cause of death of these people."

"Andre said if I wouldn't help him, he'd tell my superiors that I was a drug addict and alcoholic. He'd ruin me! And... and I needed the money."

"To support your habits?"

"Yes!"

"Is that the only reason you did it, to finance your habits and to keep Sullivan from exposing your addictions?"

"Yes!" Diggs was now squirming in his chair.

"That's all?"

"Yes! I admit it, damn it! What else do you want from me?"

"Funny you should ask," Avery replied and gave a nod of his head.

Soon there was a soft knock at the door and Jerry Banning entered the room. As Avery introduced his corporal, Banning took a seat next to Avery. He had a sheaf of papers in his hand. One was a folded up poster-sized family tree. Banning unfolded it and placed it face up on the table and then turned it around so that both Diggs and his attorney could see it. Banning explained he had compiled the tree using three genealogy websites on Diggs' and Sullivan's family. The tree started with the set of great-grandparents which both Diggs and Andre Sullivan shared. The left side of the tree followed the grandmother of Herman Diggs, and the right side followed her sister who was the grandmother of Andre Sullivan. Diggs was gobsmacked at the tree but after studying it for a moment answered yes to Banning's question that the family tree was indeed of the Diggs and Sullivan families.

Banning said, "Now that we have established that fact, I want to point out what I really want to discuss with you. What made me curious is right here." Banning used a yellow marker to highlight a part of the tree showing that Diggs had a sister, Francine, born ten years after Diggs.

"You had a sister named Francine or Franny, did you not, Dr. Diggs?"

"Yes," Diggs swallowed heavily.

"Is she still alive?"

"She ran away," he answered hurriedly. "We don't know if she is alive or not." Diggs' bowels, by now, were screaming at him.

"I found newspaper archives reporting that at the time of your sister's disappearance, the police investigation included questioning of both you and your cousin Andre Sullivan." Banning presented copies of several newspaper clippings discussing the mysterious disappearance of twelve-year old Francine Diggs.

"Why do you think the police questioned both you and your cousin Andre?" Banning asked.

"I don't know!" Diggs replied impatiently. "I.. I guess they talked to everyone. I didn't pay much attention."

Banning slapped the table with the palm of his hand and said vehemently, "Your little sister vanished without a trace but you didn't pay much attention?"

Elliott Anderson opened his mouth to protest but before he could say anything, Jerry Banning said, "Scrap that question. Dr. Diggs, you were twenty-two years old at the time of your sister's disappearance and in your first year of medical school. Is that correct?"

"Yeah, I guess that would be right."

"Did you work anywhere during your first year of medical school?"

Herman Diggs helplessly looked at his attorney who asked Banning, "What does that have to do with Francine Diggs' disappearance, Corporal?"

"It might have everything to do with it, Mr. Anderson," Banning replied, his blue eyes boring into those of Diggs' attorney.

Anderson looked at his client and shrugged. Diggs then reported that he worked nights at a funeral parlor. Elliott Anderson's eyes widened and he gave his client a curious look as he digested this information.

"Okay, Dr. Diggs," Banning continued, "do you remember what the police asked you about your sister's disappearance?"

"No! Like I said, that was a long time ago."

"Indeed it was. Has your family ever heard anything at all from Francine? A phone call or a letter? After all, if she is alive, she'd be in her thirties by now."

"No. No, she was, er, a difficult child. They figured she ran away and never heard from her."

"Difficult? At twelve years old? Really? I interviewed another second cousin of yours," here Banning used his pen and highlighted the name of Sharon Ann Mosler She was a half-sister of Andre Sullivan. They shared the same mother. "Sharon Ann told me that she and Francine were best of friends and that Franny, as she called her, was a sweet child who loved her parents but didn't like Andre and who was afraid of you. So, tell me, in what way was Francine difficult?"

When Diggs didn't answer, Banning asked, "Can you explain why Franny would be afraid of you, her brother?"

"She, er..."

Anderson again cautioned, "Corporal! This is... "

"She what, Dr. Diggs? What were you going to say?" Banning interrupted.

When Diggs squirmed, swallowed hard and avoided eye contact with both Jerry Banning and the attorney, Banning leaned forward, leveled his eyes at Herman Diggs and said, "Doctor, I think you can tell us where we can find Francine."

All the sphincter muscles in the world couldn't keep Herman Diggs' bowels from giving way.

CHAPTER 37

THE INVESTIGATIVE TEAM gathered back in Sheriff Larkin's office. Since the day was about over, they decided to let Andre Sullivan's interview wait until the next day. With the exception of Sheriff Larkin, the team would now travel to St. Charles Hospital in Bend so the Portland detectives could talk with Brenda Bailey. Then Deputy Richmond and the Portland team would head for Camp Sherman for the night.

As they walked to their vehicles in a late afternoon sun, the discussion centered on how Banning found out about Herman Diggs' missing sister.

"When I was compiling that family tree, trying to find a connection between Diggs and Sullivan," Banning began as he walked, "I saw where Diggs had a sister with a birth date, but that was all. Usually, you can find when they died or who they married but I could find nothing else about her, no obituary, death certificate, nothing. On a hunch, I called the Sheriff's office there in King County, Washington where Diggs' whole tribe lived and where he and Sullivan grew up. Indeed, the Sheriff's Office had a cold case for a missing child dating back to 1997. Franny Diggs was twelve when she vanished on the night of December 2, 1997. The Sheriff said they never found a body and suspected Herman but couldn't find any evidence to charge him. It was a big deal in the papers because of Herman's dad being in the Washington State Legislature.

"Sullivan's half-sister, Sharon Ann Mosler, was also twelve years old when Francine disappeared, but couldn't or wouldn't tell the police much. She was twelve, after all. I found her through Facebook, of all places. She still lives up there in King County. She knew immediately why I was calling. She's never been able to forget that Franny was never found. She also was the one who told me that Diggs worked at a mortuary while he was in med school."

Banning looked off to the horizon decorated with the Cascade Mountains and continued, "She felt the same way that I do anytime a child is murdered; they never get to grow up and experience life, love, watch their children grow. Franny didn't even get to experience being a teenager! Knowing what a scuzz Herman Diggs is, I decided to shoot for the moon and all but accuse him of being the reason behind her disappearance. You all saw his reaction so I guess I scored one."

"You did!" Avery said. "His attorney was aghast. Now he's going to have a much bigger job than dealing with criminal conspiracy, fishing his client out of murder soup."

"The King County Sheriff's Office," Banning continued, "has subpoenaed the records of the mortuary where Diggs worked. They are going to try to determine who was buried during the time shortly after Francine disappeared. They'll also be doing some exhuming just like we are in Portland."

"Wow," Richmond exclaimed. "Jerry, they need you up there in King County."

"Shhhh! Don't tell him that!" Avery said. "He'll leave."

"Or get such a big head," Kowalski drawled as he unlocked Avery's car, "we won't be able to stand him."

Richmond said, "I can't believe they never pursued the half-sister now that she's grown up."

"It's most likely a matter of finding the manpower to pursue cold cases," Avery said. "We all have those we'd love to be able to get at."

"You can say that again!" Richmond said. "What about Sullivan's side of the family? What do you know about them?

"Sharon Mosler told me that her mother divorced Andre's father a long time ago. When Andre was twelve, the judge said he could decide which parent he wanted to live with. Andre chose his dad," Banning explained. "The guy had gobs of money but was a jerk. Egotist, womanizer, cruel. He was a big time investor in growth stocks. Left Andre a wad when he died."

"Kinda makes you wonder what he died of, doesn't it? I guess that's King County's problem," Richmond said as he reached his truck and swung onto the seat.

Richmond led the way into Bend and to the hospital. As the Portland lawmen followed the deputy, Avery turned in his seat and asked Banning, "Jerry, what I want to know is, how the heck you knew there is a fish called a Lumpsucker?"

"I'm a great fan of the Oregon Coast Aquarium," Banning replied. "I grew up over there in Newport and my mom volunteers at the aquarium. Every once in a while they post on their Facebook page something on a special species. A Lumpsucker is about the size of a dime and looks like a wart with fins. It has two pectoral fins which act like suction cups so it can stick itself to rocks."

"Oh," Avery exclaimed dumbly. "Trevor, did you know there was a fish called a Lumpsucker?"

Kowalski shrugged and said, "I thought everybody did."

BAILEY'S COURT APPOINTED attorney had been called earlier and told about the Portland detectives who wanted to talk to his client. When they reached St. Charles Medical Center and made their way to Bailey's room, the attorney was already there. A tall, lanky man with a neatly trimmed, white Van Dyke beard and long hair pulled into a pony-tail stepped into the hall. He amiably greeted the lawmen with eyes which sparkled with a love for life. The attorney quietly told Avery's team that his client had decided to turn State's Witness. She knew she was going to be found at least as an accomplice and hoped she could get a break in her sentence.

"That makes your job as well as ours a whole lot easier," Avery said as the Jefferson County Deputy assigned to guard Bailey's room checked the identification of the Portland lawmen. Then they went into the room to meet the suspect, Brenda Bailey.

Reclining on the bed in a darkened room with her right leg in traction, Brenda Bailey appeared drawn and miserable. She looked at the three Portland detectives with contempt in her eyes.

Richmond introduced Avery and his team. As Avery pulled a chair close to her bed, Banning set up a tape recorder, explaining it to Bailey. He, Kowalski and Richmond then stood back in the shadows. Her attorney sat on the opposite side of the bed from Avery.

Avery could also see in Brenda Bailey's eyes the pain that even drugs couldn't completely eliminate. His heart softened. Seeing anybody in pain always broke his heart and was one reason he chose the profession he did; to bring justice to those who caused pain in others. He had to get to the bottom of whether Brenda Bailey was another victim of Andre Sullivan or his accomplice. So far, it appeared she had set up those old people in Portland to die. Of course, that information came from her fellow suspects, all accomplished liars.

Bailey looked at Avery's face. Did she see kindness there or was it the drugs playing with her mind? "Ms. Bailey, do you feel like talking to us today?"

She answered by burying her face in her hands. Between sobs she said, "No. But I need to...to get this stuff out. It's all so horrible!"

Avery reached to the stand beside the bed and moved a box of tissues over to rest on the bed beside her. He waited. "Take your time," he said. "Your attorney has told us you want to turn State's Witness. Is that correct?"

"Yes. This is all my fault," she said, wiping her eyes and then staring at the opposite wall.

Avery waited for a few moments then asked calmly, "What is, Brenda? What's all your fault?"

She turned her eyes to him. His eyes were still kind. She exclaimed, "That I'm in this mess! I trusted Andre from the day I met him. What a fool I was! I thought he was the one for me. He told me he loved me. I was willing to do anything for him."

When Avery remained silent, she continued, "I found those old people for him. At first I didn't know he was going to have them killed. I thought he wanted me to find them and offer to buy their property. What I didn't know, if they refused to sell, he'd send in Lumpsucker. I'd buy up their property from their estates. I didn't know Lumpsucker was killing them. Honest! At least not at first. Once I discovered what was going on, I couldn't get out of it. Andre threatened me within an inch of my life! So I became an accomplice. I had to. By that time, I was afraid of him."

Bailey went on, "So when he decided to run for a public office, I continued to lie for him, covered his screw-ups. He claimed he wanted to make Oregon like in the old days when you could log and mine and manufacture and leave your waste and debris around without any consequences. You know, like water and air pollution and stripping the land of trees and minerals and causing erosion. Back then, you could just count your money and walk away from the destruction you made. Then came all the regulations. I discovered that all he really wanted was fame and even more money for himself. He got gobs of campaign money from the people who would benefit from opening up national forest lands for enterprise. But he had plenty of his own money! He didn't need theirs! I know because I helped him hide it in offshore banks. He's just a crook! He always used money that wasn't his. That way he'd never lose a dime on his own hair-brained schemes. He talked big but he really didn't give a shit about Oregon. He didn't give a shit about me either. He left me in that cave to die!"

"But you didn't," Avery said with wry smile.

"Right! Thanks to the policemen who found us."

Avery looked at his notes and said, "In an earlier statement to the Jefferson County Sheriff, you said you were kidnapped by Sullivan and Diggs. Is that true?"

"No. I wasn't. I could have left Andre a long time ago but I was afraid what he'd do to me. He threatened horrible things! I said I was kidnapped because I was scared and that's the first thing that came to mind. I know I'm in big trouble but by being a witness against Andre, I can get back at him, the bastard! I'll rot in prison, all right, but by taking him with me, I'll know I did the right thing in the end."

ON THE WAY back to Camp Sherman, the team from Portland was quiet for the first several miles. All three detectives seemed lost in their own thoughts. Maybe it was the immensity of the case in which they were involved; the uncanny chance of seeing Conrad Wardwell and Fido on the front page of the Oregonian which triggered their involvement into the investigation into Andre Sullivan; or perhaps it was merely the breathtaking beauty of the sun setting behind the Cascade Mountains.

Sergeant Kowalski broke the silence. "Do you believe Bailey's statement that she was afraid to leave Sullivan and she wasn't an active member in the plotting and scheming of his evil deeds?"

"Well," Avery said, "she could have notified the police as soon as she discovered Lumpsucker was killing people. She kept quiet instead. For years! Did she really fear Sullivan's retaliation? I don't know. That will be for a judge and jury to toss around, not us.

"Yup," Banning said from the back seat. "We just gather 'em up and haul 'em in."

The three were silent again for a while until Banning asked, "I wonder how much Phyllis Wardwell and her buddies had to do with the rounding up of Sullivan's gang?"

"I don't know," Avery answered, "but I'll bet it wasn't a trifle. We'll probably never know," Avery paused and then added, "but Richmond does."

"You think?" Kowalski asked.

"Oh, yeah!" Avery said, looking at his Sergeant. "He told me about the tracking sensors they found on the killer's vehicle. I suspect he's being careful because he'll be in big trouble if Jefferson County knows he knowingly let Phyllis and her crew do their undercover shenanigans."

"As if he could stop them!" Banning chuckled.

"You're right, Jerry," Avery said. "Those oldsters have been there and done it all. Nothing is going to scare them away. Just like anybody else, old people need a purpose in life." Avery then added thoughtfully, "Maybe it's even more important for old people to feel that way. The way this bunch are doing it, they do good work and have a blast at the same time."

Kowalski said as he turned off US 20 onto the Camp Sherman Road, "Probably the best thing to do about it is to just get out of their way!"

CHAPTER 38

ANDRE SULLIVAN, THE prisoner, was not having a good time! He had been in this stinking cell for days without knowing what was coming or going. Now he had been put off for another day for an interview with the police. He knew they would refer to it as interrogation, but Sullivan knew his position put him above such insulting terminology.

He would make his case known! This chicken shit sheriff's office was treating him like dirt. He was sure Sheriff Larkin was retaliating because he had given the Sheriff a run for his money in the last election. As soon as he could, Sullivan would insist that the State of Oregon launch an investigation into Larkin's operation. Nobody treated Andre Sullivan like he was a common criminal and got away with it.

Sullivan thought of himself as anything but common. His father had always told him that they were above and beyond the normal riff-raff which scuttled their way through life. The masses were suckers to be taken advantage of at every opportunity. Andre was enough of a sucker himself to believe everything his father told him.

Andre's father had always bestowed upon his son plenty of money, but no social values. Other people were just to be exploited. Go ahead and take as much advantage as you can. Andre didn't have the mental acuity to realize there was anything wrong with this. Empathy was never a part of his makeup. Therefore, everything in life was a game to him. He never felt a shred of guilt. He kept himself thoroughly insulated from crime by installing layers of those suckers his dad told him about. Give them enough money and pie in the sky promises then getting caught will always be their problem, not his. Andre would just disappear and emerge somewhere else. He had no reason to think now would be any different. This time he would make his way to Switzerland where his money languished in wait for him and he would start all over again. He just had to get out of this fucking jail.

Anybody who is successful in escaping a jail or prison has to have an accomplice, either inside the jail or outside. That person usually is a stooge, needy for money, attention, or sex, and easily sucked in by empty flattery and promises. If there was anything Andre Sullivan was good at, it was dishing out empty flattery and promises.

Now the object of Sullivan's attention was a sixty year-old county employee by the name of Benjamin Mooney. Benny had never amounted to much and drifted from one menial job to another. Sheriff Larkin hired the man because he knew Benny's aged mother was trying to support both of them on her meager Social Security. Benny was pleased to work for the sheriff, a lawman Benny had always idolized. Benny had aspired to be a lawman just like Larkin. Unfortunately, just getting out of his own shoes was somewhat of a challenge for him. So keeping the county jail clean and its inmates fed was as close as Benny was ever going to get to his dream.

Sullivan had picked up on the man's gullibility and concentrated on being friendly and supposedly interested in his life and dreams. Not too many other individuals showed poor, simple Benny much interest. Benny showed his appreciation by doing Andre little favors. He would bring him an extra dessert or slip a porno magazine onto his dinner tray.

All the time that Sullivan waited in his cell, he fostered a relationship with Benny. Sullivan convinced Benny that he was a political prisoner and desperately needed his help in righting the terrible wrong done to him by Jefferson County. Benny was to be Sullivan's right hand man in his crusade to expose county politicians for the supposed corruption and injustices they bestowed upon the citizens of Jefferson County, Benny's mother included. Benny was so sucked into believing that even his own mother had been a victim of these supposed cads that he was willing to abandon his allegiance to Sheriff Larkin in order to follow Sullivan. First though, Benny had to aid in Sullivan's escape.

The eve of Sullivan's appointment to talk to the police proved to be a perfect storm of coincidences. The night shift was short a worker so the deputy who usually stayed in the cell block had to serve in the front office. That left Benny on his own all night. It so happened that it was also the night that Benny agreed to help Sullivan escape. He had confiscated Sullivan's clothes, wallet and shoes. Since no one else was on guard, it was easy for Sullivan to change out of the county issued jump suit and slippers.

Sullivan asked Benny to give him the keys to Benny's car so that Sullivan could drive them to a special secret hiding place which, of course, didn't exist. As Sullivan took the keys from Benny, he pointed to a book he'd left on his cot and asked Benny if he'd retrieve it for him. Benny was so excited to be included in Sullivan's noble mission that he hurried over to snatch up the book. Much to his surprise, he heard the cell door clang shut as Sullivan, now outside the cell, used Benny's own jail keys to lock him inside.

Without a backward glance at the man he had duped, Sullivan slipped down the hall and was out the door in a flash. He left the hapless Benny Mooney shaking the cell bars and yelling for someone to help. Using the fob on Mooney's key chain, Sullivan located Benny's aged Toyota Corolla. He ran to it and once he urged the asthmatic little car to life, he was soon out of sight.

WELL, NOT COMPLETELY. Deputy Cyril Richmond was awakened by his phone. As he fumbled with it, he noticed the time was 3:30 AM.

"Hullo?" he answered sleepily.

"Deputy Richmond, this is Tommy Jax. It looks as though Andre Sullivan is on the run."

Richmond was suddenly alert as he sat up in bed and asked, "What? How..?"

"You missed one tracking sensor. There was one on his shoe."

"Holy crap! Can you tell which way he's going?"

"It appears he's southbound on US 26 in Madras. He just left the Sheriff's

Office. I still have your phone number. I'll set your phone back up onto our system so you can track him too."

"OK! Thanks, T.J!"

Holy crap was right, Richmond thought as he dialed the Sheriff's Office. Just about the time you think you have a case sewed up, all hell breaks loose. To top it off, who would have thought a notorious underworld crime figure from Seattle would be helping Jefferson County catch an escaped killer. Not even Dave's somewhat loopy writer wife could make up this shit. Barking into his phone, he instructed the duty officer at the Sheriff's Office to check Sullivan's jail cell and get out an APB.

SULLIVAN SOON LEFT the highway and kept to the back streets of Madras. He knew it wouldn't be long before his disappearance was discovered and the town would be crawling with police cars. His goal was to work his way to the west and head over the Santiam Pass. He could get lost in the Willamette Valley's crowded population fairly easily. First though, he had a score to settle.

While he had had nothing else to do but sit in his cell and wait, he had spent many hours trying to figure out how the police caught up to him out there in the woods. Other than Lumpsucker ratting him out, it would have taken more than that for the police to track him down. He went over and over the things that happened between the time Lumpsucker had been arrested and when the police found them in Skylight Cave. The only thing he could really focus on was that incident outside the Oxford Hotel when he was flattened by that crazy old bag with the walker. Could that whole scene have been a scam to identify who Sullivan was with and the car they used?

Somehow that incident vaulted the police onto his trail because the next thing that happened was the Deschutes County Sheriff's patrol car chasing them out OR 126. They managed to ditch that cop but then someone was able to quickly track them into the woods east of Sisters. By the next morning, that cave was surrounded by cops. How did that happen? Was it somehow related to the old hag with the walker? There were a number of other old coots flailing around there on the sidewalk in front of the Oxford. Were they the same fossils who were involved in the disintegration of his fund-raiser at Black Butte Ranch?

Whether anything ever made sense or not had never stopped Andre Sullivan from developing an intense grudge. Those old people were behind something somehow and he was going to make them pay. Boy, was he ever!

CHAPTER 39

BENNY MOONEY HAD shown Andre a way to get to US Highway 20 and into the Willamette Valley without traveling on any of the main highways between Madras and Sisters. He had used a comprehensive Forest Service contour map which Sullivan snatched for himself in those harried fumbling moments when Benny released Sullivan from the jail cell and ended up being locked in himself.

The plan had been to leave US 26, the main drag through Madras, and then work their way west to OR 361. That would lead them to Culver and then it was just a short hop over to Lake Billy Chinook. From there, they could make it through the woods on forest service roads to Green Ridge, Camp Sherman, and eventually not far from the Santiam Pass Summit on US 20.

Andre Sullivan had listened carefully to Benny's plan because he knew what Benny didn't, that Benny wouldn't be going with him. Sullivan now had the map on the passenger seat of the little Corolla, but following a map and driving a car without a GPS through the dark of night was indeed a challenge. Sullivan remembered Benny's instructions that right before reaching Culver, there were a couple of jogs and then a fork in the road before the highway plunged down a switch back to the lake.

The jogs in the highway were pretty easy to maneuver. The fork was a different matter. Right or left? Right or left? Sullivan hung a right and soon discovered he had taken the wrong fork as this way didn't lead to a downward switch back but along the edge of a high butte above the lake.

Finding a place to turn around on a twisting road in the black of night only added to Sullivan's angst and fueled his fury that he had to perform this escape act in the first place.

He came to a pull off where a normal individual would be compelled to get out of the car and survey the breathtaking moonlit scenery around him. Sullivan, far from normal anything, hurriedly used the space to turn the car around and, thoroughly pissed, roared back in the direction he had come. He then plunged down the left hand fork and was soon zooming through a hairpin turn to follow along beside the lake.

Lake Billy Chinook was formed by the building of the hydroelectric Round Butte Dam on the Deschutes River. It was completed in 1965 after three years of construction. The lake brings together waters of the Deschutes, Crooked, and Metolius Rivers and is a popular recreation hub for this part of Central Oregon.

Andre Sullivan didn't give a flying fig about the lake. He couldn't even see it in the dark but was aware of a huge black void to his right where even the slightest mistake at the wheel could vault him over the edge to spend the rest of his forever trying not to drown.

He crossed a bridge over the Crooked River, clambered up and over another switch-backed ridge and crossed over the Deschutes River. What lay ahead were a scant few miles of a relatively straight road before the labyrinth tangle of National Forest roads began. All of this was consistent with what Benny Mooney had explained. Sullivan, with his teeth on edge, drove into the black unknown.

Soon Andre found himself in the jumble of roads between where he now was and Green Ridge. Likening it to an upturned bowl of spaghetti would not have been too far off. The dirt roads allowed for very local access, and only the paved or improved gravel roads were the ones to follow. Although Andre questioned that the word "improved" was much of a useful description, he held some comfort in that it indicated he was going in the right direction. In areas where the gravel surface had become like a washboard, he felt his teeth were going to rattle out of his head as he pushed the wheezy Corolla to its max.

He was not able to see anything beside the road but blackness. Occasionally, he would see a light far in the distance, perhaps a camp ground or small farm. As the area flora went from sagebrush to juniper trees, the sides of the road seemed to close in on him. He passed many dirt roads heading off into the dark. Benny was right about the spaghetti analogy. Andre hoped he was continuing to head westward. He wanted to come out onto Green Ridge Road not far from the two cabins where Biceps murdered Wilbur Martin and Emil Emerson.

Sullivan knew there was one other cabin in that area he wanted to deal with. It was a large log A-frame. Brenda had had enough time to research the owners; two older people, Beth Welton and Arthur Perkins, both in their seventies. They were targets Biceps didn't get around to dealing with. Sullivan had no idea if they were involved with the other oldsters but he'd burn them out anyway.

He had a score to settle. His father had impressed upon Andre to always punish those who wronged him. Make an example of someone as a warning to others. Let it be known that one did not mess with Andre Sullivan and get away with it. So, before he had left Madras, he had stopped at an all-night convenience store and gas station to fuel up the Corolla as well as purchase a newspaper and a package of match books. With these and the dry pine debris strewn about on the ground, he would torch this cabin. Then he'd head for the west side of Green Ridge where Brenda had told him there were several cabins containing elders. He'd set ablaze as many of those cabins as he could, then be on his way over the mountains long before dawn.

The map provided by Benny Mooney showed National Forest Road 11, or NF 11, distinctly weaving its way across this area of the east side of Green Ridge. Numerous gullies had been worn into the earth by springs bubbling out of the backside of the ridge. The resulting creeks forced the road down one side of a gully and up the other side, over and over and over.

Small dirt tracks intersected the main road and Benny had made it sound like a simple task distinguishing one road from another. However, Sullivan often found himself confused, and when he would venture down the wrong way, it was not always easy in the dark to find a place to turn around. He cursed and cursed as only the entitled could curse whenever they didn't get their way. He cursed Benny, the roads, the car, and the woods, never once realizing the blame for his misfortune belonged only to himself.

As Sullivan thrashed around in the myriad of roads behind Green Ridge, a posse of assorted lawmen had hatched a plot to apprehend him. Aided by Tommy Jax's tracking system, deputies from Jefferson and Deschutes counties, an Oregon State Trooper, plus a Portland Police Bureau team of homicide detectives, were converging upon the unsuspecting Sullivan.

In case Sullivan should get through to US 20, The Black Butte Ranch Police Force stayed close to the ranch. They patrolled all entrances into Black Butte Ranch as well as US 20 between the ranch and the road into Camp Sherman.

Jefferson County Deputies were following the route Sullivan took from Madras on NF 11. Deschutes County Deputy Greg Leese, soon followed by the Oregon State Trooper, was leaving Sisters and coming in from the south, working his way around the east side of Little Akawa Butte, heading toward NF 11. Additional Deschutes County Deputies were entering the area from the southeast, heading up Fly Creek Road which intersects with NF 11. Cyril Richmond and the Portland team were headed east on NF 11, directly in the killer's path. All were in contact with Richmond who got regular updates on Sullivan's position from Tommy Jax's computer and relayed that information to the rest of the posse.

ALERT Camp Sherman, an email, phone, and Facebook network within the Camp Sherman community, notified the residents of the pending apprehension of the escaped murder suspect. All members were advised to shelter in place and open their doors to no strangers until further notice. The community rallied around the emergency and kept a watchful eye for anything peculiar transpiring in the darkness of the forest.

The Geezers had their own plan. Arthur and Adam, along with Arthur's shotgun, stood guard at Beth and Arthur's cabin. Tommy Jax stayed in the cabin's living room, monitoring his computer. Booger and Fido, unaware of the drama going on outside, were blissfully asleep on Jax's more than adequate lap.

Aunt Phil and Oliver sat in the Bentley at the intersection of US 20 and the Green Ridge Road. Old Bowels and Sophie, in O.B.'s pickup, stayed vigilant on the west side of Black Butte at the intersection of US 20 and the road into Camp Sherman. Conrad and Beth had the Volvo parked where the Green Ridge Road meets with the Allingham Cutoff Road, the only road which crosses Green Ridge next to Black Butte.

Mick and Dave, in Mick's pickup, patrolled the roads between Beth and Arthur's cabin and those of Wilbur Martin and Emil Emerson. The only thing left of Emerson's burned out dwelling was a blackened chimney which loomed forlornly against the starry night sky. Often Mick would stop the pickup, turn off the engine, and the two men would get out onto the dusty road. They would stand silently and just listen to the night. They listened for engine noises, far and near. If Sullivan made it past the posse, he would come this way. When they stepped down from the pickup, they could hear only the wind in the trees and when it swooped low to rustle the underbrush. Overhead they heard the faint feathery sounds of a hunting owl. They breathed in the sweet, cold air of a November night in the Cascade Mountains.

Mick said first what they both were thinking, "You know, Dave, you and I grew up in these woods. We hiked, fished, and camped here as kids, then life called and we had to leave, but now we're back."

"Yup."

"You know that someday we'll probably die here too."

"Suits me."

"Yeah, me too."

Dave said, "Can't imagine what it would look like here if the likes of Sullivan took away this forest and put in a theme park or some such damn thing. A glitzy resort, maybe."

"logged off the trees and left nothing but the dirt," Mick added as he looked up at the stars, tiny crystals in the icy blackness.

"Then a miner would haul that off. Pollute the Metolius with slurry and kill off the native fish."

"What would the animals do?" Mick asked. "Where would they go? The critters could hardly stop 'em, stop the humans, I mean."

"Oh, they would head up to higher ground where they'd crowd each other out until most of them starved or froze to death. If that happened with the National Forest Lands as Sullivan threatened, the earth could lose entire species."

"While a few humans got rich."

"Yeah, while a few stinkin' humans got rich."

The two men shared the silence for a moment. "Think the police will catch him?" Mick looked over to his brother-in-law but could barely see his outline against the night sky. The hood of the pickup made a ticking sound as it cooled.

"Oh, yeah! That bastard doesn't stand a chance. He's toast!"

"But there'll be others, you know, like him. If they get into positions of power they'll want to do the same thing."

"Yeah," Dave said then looked over at Mick adding, "but we'll be ready."

"Yup."

The two men could not hear any engine noises on the night wind, so they climbed back into the truck and continued their patrol. Like sentinels, the Geezer Underground watched and waited.

ANDRE SULLIVAN WAS now lost. He actually was still on NF 11 but he had taken so many wrong turns he was unsure of where he was, or which direction he was going. The road number signs alongside the roads were either missing or overgrown. The Forest Service no longer had funding to maintain the signs as in the past. Sullivan was reaching the point of panic and was starting to sweat. He knew time was running out before the police figured out where he was. If Benny Mooney ratted on him, which he surely would have, they'd catch up to him sooner or later if he wasn't able to stick to his original plan.

It was more like sooner. Like many spiders on one huge web, the lawmen were converging upon the hapless Sullivan from all the feeder roads which could be used as escape routes. There was one spot on NF 11 where all these routes converged. It was on Fly Creek not far from Thorn Spring. If their timing was correct they would all meet at the same time Sullivan reached this area and therefore cut off all avenues of escape.

Lieutenant Avery's Chevrolet Caprice rattled along NF 11 following Deputy Richmond's pickup. The plan was for Richmond to veer off onto a primitive road which would lead up and over a rise to the only other escape route which currently wasn't covered by police, NF 300. Kowalski, Banning and Avery would continue on NF 11 to the point where all the feeder roads came together at NF 11.

Richmond gave Kowalski a left turn signal and abruptly left NF 11 in a cloud of dust. He had to negotiate a network of tiny primitive tracks to work his way up a ridge. He knew these roads as though he'd been born here and he was soon at the top of the ridge. NF 300 headed almost straight downhill to NF 11 and once Richmond turned his truck onto the slope, he came down NF 300 like a falling star.

Kowalski, an expert driver himself, was doing all he could to keep the big, sloppy Caprice from spinning out of control on the washboard surface of NF 11. Banning had both hands gripped on the back of the front seat as Avery braced his feet against the transmission hump and the bottom of the door.

Deschutes County Deputy Greg Leese, with the State Trooper following his cloud of dust, knew they were getting close to the point of ambush. Were Tommy Jax's calculations going to be correct? They would all know in just the next few minutes. If the lawmen convened on NF 11 and there was not a trace of Sullivan and the Corolla, they were going to have to rely on backup from the Black Butte Ranch police. Leese suspected that also waiting in the wings was a posse of gritty old people who were furious with Sullivan. He had taken one of their own and there was no way Andre Sullivan was going to get past the Geezers.

Sullivan was lost in his own rage at all the factors which had led him to be groping his way through the darkened forest when suddenly seven sets of headlights converged upon him at the very point on NF 11 Jax's calculations had anticipated. Sullivan slammed on the brakes of the little Corolla and threw his arms across his face as he was sure he was going to be hit by at least one if not several freight trains. When all vehicles had slid to a stop and the lawmen exited their vehicles with their firearms drawn, Lieutenant Avery came casually striding out of the cloud of dust. He introduced himself to Sullivan and drawled, "Fancy meeting you here, Mr. Sullivan. You're under arrest for murder."

CHAPTER 40

THE CAMP SHERMAN Community Hall was packed. The Jefferson County Sheriff's Office had called a meeting to update the residents on the Andre Sullivan case. As with everything Camp Sherman, a party was the order of response so an impromptu pot luck lunch was organized. The community swarmed toward the hall, each individual carrying a dish to share plus the anticipation of a fun and informative time.

The Geezers loaded their plates with food and mingled among the crowd along with Jefferson and Deschutes County deputies and personnel, an Oregon State Police captain from Bend and the trooper who was involved in Sullivan's capture, the Black Butte Ranch Police Department employees, volunteers and officers. Adam and Sophie, Emily Martin, the three Portland homicide detectives, Tommy Jax and Oliver also piled their plates and settled at tables to enjoy the lunch.

Dave, Adam, and Sophie sat together at the end of a long table full of Camp Sherman residents. Adam asked Dave if his wife was still writing.

"God, yes. I just wish she was selling as much as she was writing."

"Don't have that yacht yet, huh?"

"No! Besides, she kicks me out of my own cabin because she says I talk too much and she can't concentrate."

"Well, do you?"

"Even when all I'm doing is talking to the TV, she says she can't ignore me in case I'm really talking to her."

Sophie asked, "Have you been married a long time, Dave?"

"Fifty years going on a hundred and ten."

Adam asked, "Still on probation, huh?"

"You cannot imagine!"

Emily Martin was introduced to several other women by Beth and soon found herself in the middle of a warm, friendly group all talking about the case and when the next pot luck was going to be.

After a short time, Sheriff Larken approached a podium at the head of the room. With a few people clanking spoons to glasses, he soon had everyone's attention.

"Hello, everyone. I'm glad to see so many of you here. It does a lawman's heart good to know that the community you serve is this engaged in the events your law enforcement team has recently been working." After a pause, he added, "Of course, it just could be you are all here at this potluck due to the presence of Roger White and his world famous beans." The hall erupted in laughter. Larkin continued, "It's my pleasure to inform you the killers of Wilbur Martin and Emil Emerson are now securely behind bars." This announcement was met with thunderous applause.

The Sheriff interrupted the ovation by saying, "The crimes committed by these suspects extended well beyond Green Ridge and Camp Sherman. In the process of this investigation, it was discovered that these suspects were also involved in a Portland crime scheme which may label them as the most active serial killers in Oregon's history."

In the gasps of awe which followed this announcement the Sheriff continued, "I want to introduce to you the members of the joint law enforcement team who came together to make the arrests. Please hold your applause until all members have been introduced or we'll still be here when it's time for the next pot luck. First, my Jefferson County team of Cyril Richmond..." the audience disobeyed the Sheriff's orders and applauded wildly for Richmond. "...plus Deputies Chad Anderson and Carter Chamberlain." He went on to introduce Deschutes County Deputy Greg Leese plus the other two Deschutes County deputies, the Oregon State Police Trooper, the Black Butte Ranch Police Officers, and a surprise to everyone, the three Homicide Detectives from Portland.

Once the applause died down, Larkin continued, "These criminals were more than killers. Andre Sullivan was determined to find his way into public office so that he could change the way Americans treat our natural resources. Instead of seeing the mountains, forests, and streams as precious resources to be nurtured and allowed to go on their own earth-given path, he wanted to open up the wilderness to wealthy interest groups which would ravage and exploit the land to the max; to the point of it being unable to sustain life. Why? For money, to please his industrialist donors, and because it's easier to destroy than to find a better way. We need to learn to live not on the land, but with it."

MEANWHILE, AT WARDWELL'S cabin, Fido was having great fun being a very naughty little dog. He was on the back of the couch and was working at the same window screen where he had made his escape many weeks ago. Adam's two bulldogs, too squatty to get on the couch on their own, parked on the floor to watch what Fido was doing. With his nose and tiny feet the Chihuahua worked at the screen that Dave and Mick had repaired, pushing and poking until the old screen finally stretched and gave way. With one mighty shove of his little body, Fido squeezed through the hole he had made and dropped to the ground.

The last time he had made his great escape, he had stowed away in Wardwell's Volvo and caused havoc at Andre Sullivan's gala fund raiser at Black Butte Ranch. This time the Volvo was gone, but Fido, having heard Conrad and Aunt Phil talk about "pot luck" and "Community Center" told him something was up at the Camp Sherman Community Center.

Fido also knew how to get there. He often had accompanied Aunt Phil and Conrad when they walked through the woods to take part in community breakfasts held on summer holiday weekends. Conrad would go inside and get two pancake breakfasts, his with blueberries, Aunt Phil's without, and they would sit outside at a picnic bench with other residents who also had brought their dogs. Aunt Phil would stay to help clean up the Community Center's kitchen and Conrad, with Fido on a leash, would stroll back through the woods to the cabin, as only one with a happily full belly could stroll.

Down the trail Fido ran, his fawn-colored body popping up and over clumps of grass and fallen branches as he scurried off to the Community Center, his little heart set on another exciting adventure.

"OTHERS WHO WOULD exploit the land because of greed are out there," Sheriff Larkin went on. "We have to continue to compromise with all facets of our society because protection of our natural resources will be vital in providing clean water and air for everybody." He gathered up his notes and finished with, "We cannot afford to fall asleep at this very important switch. Thank you!"

The sheriff stepped back from the podium and the room was drowned in applause. Someone from the back of the room shouted, "Larkin for Governor!" which was repeated time after time from all around the room.

Larkin walked back to the podium and when the shouting and applause calmed down he drawled, "Thank you, but no, that will never happen. I have way too much fun locking you guys up." Amidst the laughter which ensued, he said, "Now Deputy Richmond wants to say a few words."

Sheriff Larkin and Cyril Richmond exchanged places at the podium. Richmond cleared his throat and said, "It's my pleasure to acknowledge and give a big Camp Sherman thank you to a passel of characters who, with uncanny diligence and somewhat wacky ingenuity..." laughter rippled throughout the crowd, "assisted law enforcement in bringing Andre Sullivan and his accomplices to justice. Again, please hold your applause until the introductions have been made." Richmond then read the names of Aunt Phil and Conrad, Beth and Arthur, Sophie, Mick, Dave, and Old Bowels.

"I'd like to add to this group some folks who are friends of Camp Sherman from afar." He pointed to the back of the room and said, "Adam Carson from Portland and from Seattle, Tommy Jax and Oliver. Would all these individuals please stand and *now* you may applaud!"

Tommy Jax's smile was so wide his eyes disappeared in his face. Oliver, smiling shyly, stood in his odd, stick-like manner. Aunt Phil and Conrad stood, held hands and laughed as did Adam and Sophie. Beth and Arthur beamed proudly. Dave and Mick stood with Old Bowels. Dave, in the middle, held two fingers up behind both Mick's and Old Bowels' heads. Camera phones from all corners of the room recorded the moment. The thunderous ovation was enough to raise the rafters of the Community Hall and melt the snow which was now gently turning the roof white.

Once the hoopla began to fade down, a family opened the main door to leave. Through the door bounded Fido, his buggy eyes gleaming with fun. With muddy feet and snowflakes sticking to his silky fur, he used the generous lap of a resident to reach the top of the table and galloped down the long table where Aunt Phil, Conrad, Mick and Dave were sitting at the far end. In direct contrast to the snobs at Andre Sullivan's dinner, the Camp Sherman residents laughed and clapped and squealed with delight at the cute little dog and the resulting mayhem he made of the table.

Conrad jumped to his feet saying, "No, no, no, no..."

Dave looked at Mick and calmly inquired, "Isn't this where we came in?"

CHAPTER 41

BY THE TIME the hall was put back in order, the dusting of snow had stopped and the clouds opened up to reveal the clean, crisp blue sky of a winter afternoon in the Cascade Mountains. Aunt Phil and Conrad, with Fido securely confined to the crook of Conrad's arm, piled into the Volvo to return to their cabin and asked Sophie and Adam to join them.

Adam said that he and Sophie would like to walk, thank you, but would meet them at the cabin. As the Volvo putted off down the road, Adam and Sophie headed through the Ponderosa pine and Tamarack forest. When they had to clamber over a fallen tree, Adam offered his hand to Sophie although he knew she needed no help. She took his hand anyway and kept her hold on it after they were over the log. With the bright yellow needles of the Tamaracks back lit by the late afternoon sun, the two walked along, swinging their clasped hands like carefree children.

"Sophie," Adam said, suddenly somber, "I'm going to have to go back to Portland. I have some clients to see next week."

"Yes, I need to get back to my shop in Sisters. I was able to reschedule some people but with their hair continuing to grow as we speak, I'm sure they are very anxious to see their hairdresser!" Her tinkling laughter flowed through and around the trees like water.

Adam said, "I'd love to show you Portland! Maybe sometime you can take a couple days out of your shop? We could see the zoo, the Art Museum, maybe OMSI, have dinner at Jake's."

The mention of "a couple of days" was not lost on Sophie. "Sure!" she answered cheerfully, smiling at him. "How about next weekend?"

"Okay! I'll see what's going on at the Schnitzer Concert Hall and see if I can get tickets." Adam, as he and Sophie made plans for the next weekend, realized he felt alive and engaged in life. It had been a long time since he had felt this way. After an unfortunate previous experience with romance, he had put his emotions on hold, afraid to turn them loose to be crushed again. However, as he looked at Sophie's wonderful brown eyes and turned up nose dusted with the most delightful freckles, he knew he could spend the rest of his life engulfed by this woman's charms.

BUDDY SLURPED THE last of his dinner and in getting every last morsel, pushed the pan around the kitchen floor. Then, licking the sides of his mouth, he walked across the cabin to where Mick had sat in his favorite chair to watch his dog eat. The dog's toenails made clicking sounds on the old hardwood floor. Buddy plopped his fanny on the floor and put his chin on Mick's knee. Mick rubbed the old dog's ears and looked into the soft brown eyes.

"You know, Buddy, you and I are going to spend our twilight years together. That's a heck of a lot better than doing it alone, don't you think?"

Buddy's tail beat a happy staccato on the cabin floor.

"We're going to have fun roaming as much of the woods and these mountains as we can. But, I know that one day," Mick gestured towards the cabin's front door, "that door will open and Lavonne will be standing there. She'll say, 'Mick, get off your ass and come with me.' And I'll do it, Buddy. Now, it would be great if you could come with us. You'd love Lavonne! However, I can't rely on you being able to join us, at least not right away. The Geezers have all agreed that one of them will take over for me; taking care of you. Like Cyril said, 'I have a shit load of friends' and I'm grateful for every last one. The good thing is now you and I can do stuff together and I won't have to worry about you."

Buddy smiled at Mick and, with all of his heart, Mick smiled back at the old dog's sweet face. He said, "You know, the Geezers are having a meeting this afternoon and we need to show up. Are you ready to go see Conrad and Phyllis?"

Buddy huffed, stood up and wagged his tail furiously.

Mick got out of his chair and noticed that simple action wasn't as hard as it had been. His stiffness wasn't so stiff and his aches weren't quite so achy. He attached a leash to Buddy's new collar, took down a jacket from its hook on the wall and stuffed a flop hat on his head. With Buddy at his side, he walked out the door.

SERGEANT KOWALSKI WAS cold. He was up to his unmentionables in the frigid waters of the Metolius River. He had in his hand a fly fishing rod. If he had been holding a symphony conductor's baton, he wouldn't have been more confused as how to use it.

Shawn Avery had brought along on this trip fly fishing rods and reels. Cyril Richmond had equipped the Portland detectives with waders. Starting with Kowalski and not far downstream from the Camp Sherman store, Richmond found a spot in the river where there was a good hole which might contain a fish eager to rise to a fly. He had given Kowalski a lesson on how to flip the rod back and over the water in a figure eight pattern.

Cyril made it look like the rhythm of a dance, back and forth, back and forth, the line flowed in graceful curves as the water carried the fly downstream. He did this with such apparent ease one would think anybody could do it. Sure.

Kowalski practiced what he'd been shown. The big Sergeant held the rod with his thumb on top of the grip. He pulled several yards of line from the reel, running the line between the reel and his index finger so he could control the slack. He pointed the tip of the rod at the river, then raised it until it pointed straight up, his hand between his ear and shoulder, and brought his arm down as though he was hitting a hammer. Over and over.

The plan had been to give the Portland men a taste of the sport during the late afternoon following the pot luck. Then, first thing the next morning, they'd fish again for a few hours before Avery, Banning, and Kowalski had to return to Portland.

After leaving Kowalski, Richmond travelled downstream with Avery and Banning. He knew of two more good holes which might be fish hideouts. He positioned each man where they could fish without getting tangled with each other's lines yet where they could see each other.

Things were going smoothly. Avery and Banning joked back and forth, giving each other silly advice. Avery cast toward the hole and let the current carry the fly past the hole just to the point of running out of line but not quite dragging the fly. The next time, a bit closer to the hole, he placed a cast that no self-respecting fish could resist and nailed a very handsome Kokanee. All of the Metolius River is catch and release fishing, so Richmond showed him how to remove the fly while keeping the fish in the water and pointed upstream so that it had adequate water flow through its gills. Avery felt ecstatic that he had actually caught one and that the fish lived to carry out its life cycle in the waters where its life began.

Banning hadn't heard much from Kowalski, so he looked upstream to see him standing in the water, holding his fly rod somewhat stupidly with both hands. Banning looked at him curiously and asked, "Hey, Trevor, did you catch something?"

Kowalski looked over his shoulder at the hopeless tangle of fishing line and Serviceberry branches, the fly dangling harmlessly several feet over his head.

"You could sorta say that."

THE DOGS LOVED when the Geezers got together and it didn't take long after the potluck for the Geezers to convene at Aunt Phil and Conrad's cabin. Mick and Dave, along with Buddy, arrived first. The men would work yet again on Fido's hole in the window screen. Beth and Arthur with Max, Old Bowels, Tommy Jax and Oliver also arrived. Accompanying Old Bowels was a happy observer of this unique band of oldsters, Emily Martin. Aunt Phil had a huge carafe of coffee on the breakfast bar and everyone helped themselves and then gathered around the fireplace, stepping over the dogs and parking their fannies wherever they could find space. Adam and Sophie soon came through the door, their faces fresh and flushed with their walk in the cold November air. The cabin was so crowded, they left the front door open to let in some cool air.

"Needless to say," Conrad began once everyone had settled, "Richmond is on to us."

"Boy, is he ever!" Dave added.

"So much for being clandestine," Mick said, "Do you think revealing who we are at the pot luck was intentional?"

Arthur turned to Mick, "You mean to make us quit?"

"Well, yeah."

"I think we're reading too much into it," Aunt Phil said. "By letting everyone know we helped was his way of demonstrating he was grateful. I don't think it was anything more than that."

"Yeah, maybe," Conrad added, "but it might put a crimp in our activities."

Old Bowels asked, "You mean we'll have to get into costume just to get out of Camp Sherman without a whole flock of folks following us to see what we're up to?"

"Right. Our target might suspect something if they spy us coming towards him with the entire Camp Sherman community following," Mick replied.

"You think?" Dave said, laughing.

"Well, if that happens and the target gets scared off, we'll just have another Camp Sherman party right there on the spot!" Sophie was getting into this nonsense. Emily smiled and chuckled.

"If they're going to follow us, they better bring enough food along for a party," Beth added.

"Did somebody say party?"

The Geezers all turned around at the sound of a voice at the open door. Cyril Richmond was standing there, casually leaning on the door jam, his hands in his pockets, his blue eyes flashing with fun.

Aunt Phil recovered first. "Come on in, Cyril! Can I get a cup of coffee for you?"

"Nah, thanks, Phyllis. I just thought I'd stop by and say a personal thank you for your help. I felt I had sufficiently let you know to stay out of the investigation. I didn't expect you to listen to me, but since none of you got hurt or worse, I have to say I'm glad what you did or we may never have caught that bastard.

"However," Richmond went on, "I just thought I'd drop a not so subtle hint that under no uncertain terms are you to *ever* do it again." He raised one eyebrow and looked around the room at the Geezers, all looking like school kids caught playing some naughty game.

"Who, us?

"Yeah, us?

"Nope. Never again, Cyril."

"You can count on us, Cyril."

"You betcha, Cyril!"

Mick and Dave pointed at one another and said, "Him?"

Richmond raised his hands in the "I give up" position, turned and tossing a smile over his shoulder, walked away, shaking his head.

TOMMY JAX AND Oliver were staying at Black Butte Ranch one more day before pointing the Bentley in the direction of Seattle. They were living up to their promise to equip all of the Geezer's cabins with alarm systems. They had only two cabins left.

Adam packed up his gear. Along with his dogs, he walked Sophie to her cabin to say a final goodbye before he returned to Portland.

Old Bowels needed to leave in order to take Emily Martin to the airport.

The rest of the Geezers fanned out to return to their own cabins, leaving Aunt Phil and Conrad alone.

Conrad closed the door when the last Geezer left and said to Aunt Phil, "What would you think about staying here for the winter and not going back to Portland, at least until after Christmas?"

She put her arms around him and said, "Anywhere with you is where I'd like to be. Besides, it would really be fun to see what Christmas is like in Camp Sherman!"

"Beth's daughter Nancy always has us for Christmas."

"Well, we'll give her a break this year, bless her heart."

"Think the Trail Blazers will miss us?"

"They're struggling so hard in the league, they may not even notice that we haven't been there."

"They might think they are failing *because* we haven't been there."

"In that case, we better stay away. I wouldn't want an entire basketball team of seven-foot tall guys chasing us down the street."

"You got that right."

"We just talked ourselves into staying, didn't we?"

"It do look like it, darlin'"

DEPUTY CYRIL RICHMOND stood at the edge of the meadow. The sun had gone down behind the craggy volcano Three Fingered Jack and he could feel the chill of the coming winter seeping into his heavy coat. He often came to this spot to sense the enormity of nature in all its glory. Sometimes it was when he felt overwhelmed or, as now, after a successful case when he needed to settle his mind and put things into perspective.

This wilderness had been home to indigenous people for thousands of years. Sometimes when he stood on this spot, he could sense their presence, as though they were standing nearby but just out of sight. He felt them especially tonight after he and the Geezers and his fellow law enforcement members had driven to ground an evil force which would have ruined these sacred lands forever.

Long ago he vowed to the spirits of those long disappeared souls that he would maintain to his last breath a vigil to protect this pristine forest; the animals, plants, and birds which had shared these mountains with native people for eons.

Something caught his eye, over there in the dark, at the edge of the forest. A buck stepped daintily into the meadow and stood looking at him. As though it recognized him and accepted his quiet presence, the animal flicked its tail and ears, lowered its majestic head, and began nibbling at the sweet green meadow grass.

With a smile, Richmond turned down the trail to home.

Emily Martin looked out the window of the Alaska Airlines jet as it took off from Redmond. At Portland she would connect with a flight to New York. As the plane lifted her away, she could pick out the east sides of Black Butte and Green Ridge. Through the haze, she could barely see an area approximately where her dad's cabin waited. Emily whispered, "I'll be back, Dad. I'll be back."

THE END